A LOST TALE
DALE ESTEY

SF
ace books
A Division of Charter Communications Inc.
A GROSSET & DUNLAP COMPANY
51 Madison Avenue
New York, New York 10010

A LOST TALE

Copyright © 1980 by Dale Estey

All rights reserved. No part of this book may be reproduced in any form or by any means, except for the inclusion of brief quotations in a review, without permission in writing from the publisher.

All characters in this book are fictitious. Any resemblance to actual persons, living or dead, is purely coincidental.

An ACE Book

Published by arrangement with
St. Martin's Press

First Ace printing: June 1982

Published simultaneously in Canada

2 4 6 8 0 9 7 5 3 1
Manufactured in the United States of America

This novel is for my mother, who thought of the title; my father, who kept pulling on wishbones until it got published; and to those numerous people, from Agnes to Ralph-Pierre, who may indeed have passed like ships in the night, but did so with all lights blazing.

Author's Note

IN THE dark ago, bands of people now known as Celts came from north central Europe and spread across the continent. They had no one king, and no one government; yet they were all joined by their belief in the immortal soul and their love of the magic and truth of nature.

Although ruled by different kings, the Celts possessed a unifying class of leader known as the Druids. A Druid was both priest and judge, connecting men to those nebulous gods who surrounded them and interceding in daily affairs when justice was elusive. The Druids held the poems, the history, and the religion of the Celts; made sacrifices; kept order; and told of things yet to come. Roman emperor and Norse chieftain, who both feared the savagery of the Celt, feared the knowledge of the Druid even more.

Centuries do not pass without change, however, and the fierce independence of the Celts eventually led to their downfall. Because they had no fear of death, they were frenzied fighters and terrorized the enemies they encountered with their wildly painted bodies and vicious yells. Yet they met their match in the methodical plans and numberless legions of Julius Caesar's army, against which abandoned ferocity could do only so much. Caesar brought roads, baths, and order, and although he too would die by the sword, he began the rout of the Celts. Their territory shrank, eventually receding to the British Isles and finally coming to an end at the hands of the Norsemen, in the sixth century A.D. on the Isle of Man.

The Isle of Man, thirty-two miles long by eleven miles wide, is situated in the Irish Sea between Ireland and England. The Isle is named after Manannan, the Celtic god of the sea who, it is said, still protects his island with a mantle of fog whenever there is danger. Celtic traditions have lingered on Man, for though it was conquered by the Vikings, the island did not succumb to an alien way of life but instead incorporated the new ideas into the old beliefs. Manx government and laws are Norse, yet traditions and ways of personal life come from the Celts.

Today the Isle of Man is as modern a place as one could want to find. It has airports, hotels, motorcycle races, and an industry that produces ejection seats for jet planes. Man is a tourist haven, and a tax refuge for many rich celebrities. It has retained its individuality by being an autonomous part of the United Kingdom, making its own laws, and referring to Queen Elizabeth as the Lord of Man. Yet all new edicts from its parliament at Tynwald must be pronounced in Manx Gaelic before they can become law, and hats are still raised at the Fairy Bridge out of respect for the wee folk. And yes, more likely than not, the cats one might see there will have long back legs and no tails.

But if one leaves the port of Douglas, or the larger towns of Ramsey and Castletown, and abandons the modern roads for the narrower ones that lead to the coast and countryside, time folds over itself and takes a snooze. There will be old folk with stories to tell, and younger people who do not want the past to disappear. There will be mugs of Manx ale known as *jough*, and voices on the breeze that are never quite heard. There will be ancient cottages, and tiny churches that have seen centuries of use. There will be an occasional stand of oak, wells of deep water, and the strewn rocks of long-past holy places. There will be graveyards, where the weary rest, having seen times of joy and times of peril.

One such time of peril—a most dangerous time—was caused by the actions of Adolf Hitler. In 1940 a war raged and threatened the whole earth with more than it knew. Strong force was needed to confront the madness, and not just the force of arms. Like people

A LOST TALE

elsewhere in the world, the inhabitants of the Isle of Man prepared to fight the evil, to stop the destruction of their way of life. In the wood, and by the streams, they were not alone in their endeavours.

Some of the following events are pure fiction.

PRAISE FOR DALE ESTEY'S
MAGICAL TALE...

"A strangely charming tale with more than a whisper of fable."

—*Booklist*

"The premise that Druidic powers are not only still alive but can face down modern evil in the form of Hitler's forces works well in this fanciful tale ... The image of the sturdy Manx trailing their preternatural heritage into the atomic age is an intriguing one."

—*Publishers Weekly*

"The novel explores territories where dreams and insight melt the borders of lifeless convention and positivistic superstition. Nice magic."

—Richard Monaco

"Dale Estey has the altogether too rare talent of blending magic and modernity and making it plausible."

—Patricia C. Wrede

"I read Dale Estey's A LOST TALE in one swift sitting on an island in the Carribean, where the wind blew, the rain fell torrentially, and the lights kept going out. But that is not the only reason I kept turning the pages. This book is not only a real spellbinder but it has things to say, too. So many people think that what they do does not matter in the world, and A LOST TALE makes it clear that the smallest of us can have a profound affect ... I look forward to the next work by this very talented young writer."

—Madeleine L'Engle

I

IT WAS a bomber's moon. At least that is what her father called it, pointing his stick into the sky with a thrust and a curse. Yet he dreaded it far more because it was full. He still felt the troubled tossings of his wife as she had twisted in her sleep, while it filled her mind with forebodings and sullied dreams. "A bomber's moon, Brigid," he said, touching his daughter's shoulder. "You'd best be careful tonight."

"I can't be harmed when I'm with him."

"Aye." He drawled the word out, for he was trying to explain something he did not understand himself.

"That's the way it has always been," she said.

"I know, girl, I know." The man slid down to the door sill, grasping her arm until she was sitting beside him. His massive hand stroked her long dark hair, remembering that it had been blonde twenty years ago when she was born. "These things, Brigid, the way they are now," he began.

"I really should go." She touched his rough beard, but her eyes were looking into the woods, out toward the sea they could both hear in the distance.

"Aye, but—" he was about to let her go, wait and say something another night, when he would have thought it out better. But as she turned to look at him, the moon gleamed from her eyes, and he gripped her arm tighter than ever. He was afraid of the moon. It was no longer a friend.

"Brigid, it is not the same now."

"I can't be harmed, father."

"We don't know that." He tried to talk slowly, for when he got excited his voice growled, making him sound angry even when he was not. "Your mother and I . . ." he looked away from her, could not take her penetrating glance. "Your mother is not sure anymore."

"I am sure." She kept staring at him.

"But your mother, Brigid. You get your power from her, and if she doesn't feel that it is safe anymore . . ."

"What has she said to you; that I'm not to go?" Brigid put her hands in her lap and stared at them. "Has she said I can't go?"

"Your mother is worried, Brigid." The slowness of his voice drew out the *r* sound, made a low rumble in his throat. "Sometimes they fly over us, Brigid, if they haven't got where they're going; or they're coming back and haven't got rid of their damn bombs."

"That doesn't happen very often."

"It happens often enough, girl." He took both her hands in his. "It's happened before, when they got off course and don't want to go home with their load. Sometimes they hit the sea and sometimes they hit the rocks, but sometimes they hit something else, like old Patrick's place, and him with the new well just dug. There wasn't enough left to put into one of his own cigar boxes."

"He's the only one, father."

"Aye, the only one so far. But, my girl, you can bet that Herr Hitler has one or two more Stükas to send against Mr. Churchill."

"But there's nothing they want here."

"No? Them with Jersey, Guernsey, and Alderney. Neutral Ireland on one side of us, and enough Nazi subs circling to make a fence. And you know about the ships and guns in Castletown."

"There's nothing here worth their while."

"Brigid." He placed his hands on his knees. "Your mother is scared."

She looked sharply into his eyes, wondering whether she had really heard right. He did not look away though, did not say any more.

"Mother is never scared of anything," her voice was low.

"She is now, Brigid. There is something she doesn't—"

"Are you scared?"

"These things, Brigid, the way they are . . . Na, na, let me finish. I know, we're old and we get cautious. But don't forget your mother was once like you, had the power until we were married. And when the time comes, you'll pass it on to your daughter. Like it's always gone on in the past, and it should go on in the future . . ."

"What do you mean, it 'should'? Why is mother scared?"

"She had a dream about the Oaks."

"And what?" Brigid jumped up, her hands made into fists. "That never happens, we are not supposed to be able to do that." She stared down at her father. "What does it mean?"

"We don't know, Brigid." Her father stood slowly, his stick helping to support his bad leg. "Your mother doesn't know, the Druids don't know, the Head Druid doesn't know. There's been some talk, but all—"

"Talk about what?" She stepped closer to him. "What talk, what have they been saying, the Head Druid, what—"

"He says that our ties with the past are to be strengthened. The traditions sometimes have hinted that a circle started centuries ago, began its curve here on Man, and must eventually come back upon itself."

"But what does it mean?" Her voice was loud.

"It's never been stated, Brigid. That's the trouble, girl, that's the trouble. There's only one thing they're sure about, and they didn't even—"

"And what's that?" She started to walk toward the woods, but turned quickly and came back to him. No, he was not afraid; she should have seen that. She took his hand again, grasped it hard. "What won't you tell me?"

He stared into her brown eyes, traced a finger over her long cheekbones. She would find out anyway; she should know for her own good. He took his hand away.

"It's a warning," he said.

"You're talking daft, man." The words were out of her mouth before she realized. She turned away, confused; she had never spoken that way to him, not even in jest. She reached behind her and touched one of his arms. "You know that I didn't mean that.

It's all the . . . " her voice stopped. "These things you're telling me sound so absurd, you must see that."

"None of this has been easy for any of us, girl." Had it been anyone else, he would have been angry. She probably did not mean it, that was true enough. He could never be like her, or like her mother. He had not the ability to summon the creatures, had never seen any of them, in fact. He was a strong man who was there when strength was needed. At other times someone else would have been chosen. He was sure, for instance, that Brigid would need someone much like herself, someone who had the inner vision to see what most others could not. He swung his daughter around to face him, combed her fine hair with his rough fingers.

"I don't know why we wasted our time and worry. Your mother said you would go anyway, that Morrighan herself, with her flashing sword and bloody head, wouldn't have stopped you. We've just wasted our breath."

"You know as well as I that mother would go out tonight, and not take notice of Adolf's wee bombers."

"Aye. But it isn't just the bomber's moon. It's the dream as well —the dream more than anything. When a circle returns to its beginning, Brigid, it does two things. It meets up with itself, and completes its work—its reason for being. But also . . . " He paused a moment, remembering his wife's worried voice as she had described her fears. "But also, when the ends of a circle finally join, they trap everything inside."

"But if the Head Druid doesn't know what . . . "

"Girl, nobody knows everything." He gave a tug on her hair, which made her squeak. "And that goes for you too. I'm sure when I was your age I wasn't such the smart one."

"Oh aye?" She stepped away from him and whirled around a couple of times, her long skirt flying. "And wasn't it just last week that Sam Rutter was telling us about you and the night on the town? And he even said it that way, like it was in capital letters: 'The Night on the Town.' " She winked at him.

"Aye." He was smiling his slow smile. "Well maybe Sam doesn't quite remember the way things really happened, he certainly seems to have forgot his own part in it."

"And wasn't it Mr. Sam Rutter who told us—not mentioning any names, he says—that if we ever find the poor tavern in Douglas overlooking the bay, the holes can probably be seen in the bar, plaster or no plaster."

"Sam's getting old," he smiled, touching his head. "And a bit forgetful."

"You mean he's left something out?"

"Now you're a sly one, aren't you? Answer yes or no and I'm a Christmas goose. Well, you can just be left wondering, for I'll not be a goose, or the Chicken Rock, for you and your shining eyes. Go practice your wiles on the nice young men, and leave your father to his sedate old age."

"There's none of the young men that hold any interest for me, William Crovan, and well you know it."

"Aye." He stroked his nose as he watched her carefully. "And there's not one young man on the Island, from the Calf to the Ayres, that doesn't feel like a good howl at the moon whenever he sets eyes upon you."

"Well, they can be keeping such thoughts to themselves. There's no man on the Island, or betwixt Belfast and Solway Firth, that has what I want."

"There's many that'd love to tell you different, my girl." Her father chuckled deep in his throat, remembering what it had been like to be young.

"And what dirty-old-man thoughts are causing you to grin like Lugh about to have do with Rosmerta? A shame it is when a graybeard starts on his foul reverie."

"When you get to be an old, enfeebled crock like me," he walked slowly, pausing for breath and exaggerating his limp. "Well then, my girl, all you have are your memories."

"As the talk goes about you—tired old father—it sounds as if your memories alone should be enough for any man."

They looked at each other and smiled, humor having displaced the tension between them. Her father knocked a stone away from him with his stick, then turned and glanced into the woods. The leaves gleamed with a gray glow in the moonlight. He spoke to her over his shoulder.

"In my day children knew their place, and were trained to hold their tongue out of respect."

"Forgive me, father dear," she cooed. "It must be my wretched upbringing that makes me such a winsome girl."

"Winsome girl. You're as winsome as a sea gale."

"I go my own way, right enough," she said. "But could it be, in some small way, the influence of my parents, who seem to take no notice of time or convention."

"Now you're not going to blame your old . . ."

"Particularly of time," she added.

He glanced up at the moon and sighed. It had already moved slightly across the sky, and she was impatient to get away. He was still worried, but the chances of something happening were very small. When even the Head Druid was not sure of the signs, it was silly of him to take such fears upon himself. The bombings were accidental; there was nothing on the Island of any importance. They wanted such places as Blackpool, Leeds, Manchester even. And as for the dream, well, there was no sense of his thinking about that. That was apparently beyond them all. She would go anyway.

"Aye. Well, I'll walk you part way." He started toward her. "Someone has to see you're safe from all the young men here until you reach the shelter of the trees."

"Oh? And I'd like to see one of your hot ones try a trick or two with me. It's them that will need protecting." She waited until he came beside her, and then turned to the tree line.

He took her hand and walked away from the house. "One of these days, Brigid, your own hot blood will start to boil, and then it will take a lot more than me to keep you in hand and housebound. Oh, and I pity him."

"Yes, father," she gripped his hand fiercely. "It will happen, and I'll know when it happens."

They came to the edge of the trees, and he bent down to kiss her cheek. "Take care," he said. He watched her go, his eyes following her movements as she slipped between the trees and was as quickly lost from view. He stood staring a minute longer, then turned from the woods and slowly went back to his home. When he reached the door, he gazed once again at the moon.

"She's gone then?"

He looked away from the sky and toward the house, where he saw his wife standing in the doorway.

"Yes, Fenella, as you said she would."

"You didn't expect anything less, did you, William?" His wife stepped from the house and came toward him. "Afterall, the girl has got almost as much stubbornness as you."

"And the touch of your madness," he said. They stood staring at each other for long moments, until William reached his hand toward her, and she held it. "So we're both to blame," he said.

"She'll need all that the two of us have given her," said Fenella, her grip tightening on him. "Her time of childhood is over."

"What do you mean?"

"There's something in the night," she looked toward the darkened woods. "Something on the land which puzzles me, and something in the air which makes me fear. I don't know what's to happen, but Brigid will need all our gifts to succeed."

"She's smart," said William. "And she's hard."

"Is that enough for her to find her way through the mists of time?" Fenella lowered her eyes and looked directly into his face. "Whatever it is, from centuries ago, is coming back to us. That's a lot to ask of anyone."

"She has the power," answered William. "She has her training. We all know our places, and do our best."

"My sensible man," said Fenella.

"My enchanting woman," answered William.

And they kissed beneath the bomber's moon.

It was not a thick forest, easy enough for her in the dark, and in the moonlight she almost ran. Once she was out and away to see him, she nearly forgot about the war and the planes and—though not as easily—her mother's dream. She would, of course, have stayed home if the Head Druid had told her to do so. The fact that he had not made her certain there was nothing wrong. He had not restricted her visits after she had begun to flow and became a true woman. Before then, it had been the Druid council that decided when she would visit, and when she would not.

The first time she could remember was with her mother. She must have been very young, because her mother was carrying her. She was not scared, had wanted, in fact, to reach out and touch him, for he was so beautiful.

"No, Brigid," her mother had said. She started to cry, and at that, he had turned and disappeared back into the trees. She learned quickly, and the next time her mother took her, she did not move and made no sound. He stood with them for a while and gazed at her a long time. Brigid stared back, but finally she had to look away from the powerful eyes. He even walked around them once and then, quietly as before, was gone. She did not cry.

Brigid stopped at a sound. One of the night birds probably, gliding through the leaves. An owl perhaps, even a hawk. Or a forest animal, rustling over the grass and roots, in pursuit of some scurrying meal. Moon madness, her mother called it, the way animals all acted strange in the full light of the moon, just like the waves, and some people. She kept standing for a few moments, but the sounds were gone. All she could hear was the sea breeze moving through the trees, and the waves themselves, much closer now, breaking against the coast. She gave a last look around and continued along the rough path.

The next clear memory Brigid had of seeing him was when she was three or four. She was running through the trees, stumbling quite often on roots and stones but never letting her mother help her. It was a windy, cloudy day, and she came to the beach, where large waves dissolved into rolls of green-white surf. She had never seen such big waves, and she turned around for her mother, because she was afraid. Her mother was nowhere to be seen. Brigid was getting ready to cry when, above the sound of the waves, she heard a noise to the other side of her. She turned so quickly, hoping for her mother, that she stumbled on the pebbles and fell. When she got to her feet, he was standing about five yards away, looking down at her. She was startled—so much so that she did not hear the waves or feel the spray, did not wonder where her mother was. But she was not afraid. He would never scare her now.

It seemed a long time she stood, rooted like one of the trees behind her. Her eyes never left his face, and Brigid was sure she could have stood there forever, just looking at him. Then he moved. Very slowly he came toward her, and she was tempted to step back, even to turn and run, find her mother, for she sensed that things would never be the same. He stood beside her and looked down into her small face, his wild eyes never leaving her own. It was time; no matter what her mother said, it was time.

She reached out and touched him. He lifted his head, slowly turned, and moved down the beach. When Brigid looked around, her mother was watching. She ran into waiting arms and let her mother carry her all the way home.

She was not far from here, Brigid thought, that first time when she touched him. She had never met him any farther than six or seven miles from where she lived, though her mother said that he moved over the whole island. Brigid left the path and walked down into a small clearing where he sometimes waited. She did not expect to find him there; when the moon was large he usually liked to be on the beach. Something, however—she did not really know what—drew her to the little glen, and it was with a sense of disappointment that she found it empty. Empty when she got there, at any rate, but she felt that something had been there, not long before. It was not he, she knew, nor anyone from the houses in the area; they never came near at all. It might have been one of the Druids; they did come once in a while. She would tell her mother as soon as she got home. Her father might have to come and look, to make sure.

Brigid went back to the path and continued, a bit more quickly, toward the beach. The trees were thicker, the darkness deeper. It was in the dark that she had met him alone for the first time. She was twelve; the moon was having its monthly way with her; and her mother decided it was time for her to see him by herself. Brigid had known something was wrong when they last saw him together. Her mother did not stay in the background as usual but stood beside Brigid, even holding her hand. She then asked Brigid to leave first, something she had never done. Brigid slowly walked up the beach toward the woods, but as she turned around to look, she saw her mother standing with her arms around his neck. Brigid had never dared to do that, and she quickly looked away and ran to the shelter of the trees. Her mother had never come to see him again.

A few weeks later, Brigid had gone out by herself, through the moonstruck trees. She was unsure; her mother had said nothing, had given her a kiss at the edge of the woods. Her father had stood in the doorway, waved his large hand, and she had seen his teeth smiling in the moonlight. Yes, she was unsure, but she was also excited, thrilled that she was to see him alone for the first time. It would be like her first touch, the shock when her fingers had met his body and almost burned. In her hurry, she had lost her way in the woods, the sea sounding closer at times and then farther away. Brigid had wandered around, her young girl's panic becoming overwhelmed by frustration and the worry that she was going in circles, when she stopped abruptly and peered in front of her. She had seen a flash of white. She started running then, and in a minute she was on the beach, sliding on the pebbles and sand. He had his back to her, looking out over the sea. She ran toward him, her arms outstretched, ready to hug him around his neck, as she had seen her mother do that last day. But he walked away before she could reach him, shaking his head. She would soon learn that years must pass before her time came to do that. The young girl was hurt, but her mother's daughter accepted it without question. They had spent that night walking along the beach, getting damp from the spray.

Brigid was now a minute away from that beach when she felt, rather than heard, someone following her. Animals had their own movements, their own sounds close to the ground. She slowly turned toward her right until at last she was parallel to the beach and moving away from the place where she usually met him. She went swiftly in this direction for a time and then stopped abruptly. There was movement behind her, and although it quickly halted, it did not stop fast enough for her not to hear. Someone was following, not chasing after to catch her, but following to see where she went. Brigid pretended to be fixing her shoe, in case the person behind was close enough to be watching. Then she started again.

She had to get away from the beach, turn around and try to reach her parents. She could not lead anyone to him; she could not let anyone see him. She was his one great weakness; through her he could be caught, could be killed. Her father—she had to get to her father.

Who could it be; who was out there, following so swiftly through the woods? The Druids had forbidden everyone access to this area, except for her own family. It could not be anyone from around here. Or else it was a madman. Who else but a madman would dare to come here, to stumble upon something that the Druids allowed no one to see? To risk the certain death that the Druids would demand? The moon—did the moon bring out some crazed being to wander through the forest?

Brigid stopped once again, and the noises behind her ceased. She realized that the person was closer than before. Could someone who was crazed move so carefully and quickly through the trees? She had not heard a stumble, or so much as a branch snapping. As she paused, panting slightly for breath, she noticed that all the night sounds had ceased. There were no animals rustling through the brush, no flutters or calls from birds moving through the trees. She was taking too long circling back to her parents' house, but she did not want to appear obvious. Yet she was still too close to the beach; he would be walking up and down in his impatient manner. And if he felt that she was in trouble, he would come to help.

"Silly shoe," she said aloud, hoping the person who followed would hear. Then she quickly moved through the woods, indirectly heading back in the direction of her home. The sea sound was a bit more distant, and she hoped to have a few minutes more to lead her pursuer. She did not think she could risk to stop anymore; whoever was there was much closer than she had suspected. She could try to hide; there were many nooks and hollows in which to lie and be quite invisible. But if he came looking for her, he would be even closer to the danger that followed. No, if anything, she must start moving more quickly, get to her home.

Brigid paused a second and could hear that the sounds were moving up, between her and her parents' house. If the person came closer to her, she would be forced nearer the beach. She started to feel fear. This should not be happening; her mother had said no one ever came here, that there would never be any danger. But also she had been warned that she must never, never, lead anyone to him. Brigid started moving more quickly, dodging off the path and into the rougher part of the wood. She wondered whether she should yell, try to get her father's attention, although he was probably too far away to hear. If she did call out, however, he might come up from the beach. If he heard her over the surf, he would certainly come.

Brigid stopped beside a large tree, and between gasps she listened in terror. There was no pretence left now, for the footsteps did not halt but kept on in a hurry. They were much closer, too, and were almost alongside, ready to force her down toward the beach. If she stood right where she was, it would probably take some time to find her, and in that time she might yet get away; whoever was there might make a mistake and give her a chance. But she was not far enough away from the beach.

Brigid started to run. Her fast movement gave her a slight head start, and she took advantage of it to get as close to her home as possible. She swept around the trees and over the rough ground, keeping her head down so the branches would not slap her face. She could hear the smashing footfalls behind her, heavy boots breaking up the woods almost at her heels. She gave an extra spurt of effort, but it was no good; her pursuer was right behind. She dove headlong for a big stick and twisted around to strike out, only to see a pistol pointed at her chest.

"Bitte, Fräulein, halten Sie."

It was the tone of the voice that made her lie still. Even then, with a gun aimed at her, Brigid was quite prepared to jump and swing with her stick, for she knew that a shot would bring her father. And if she were killed, he would not come from the beach but would know immediately and would stay away. She did not mind her own death; she was willing to give that. She did not leap up, however, hoping for a lucky hit, because of the voice. It did not command or intimidate with rough authority. Instead, it was almost pleading, as if she were the one holding the gun. It was a voice without threat.

"*Bitte, Fräulein.* Please."

Brigid looked past the pistol and saw a gray uniform. Over the right breast was a small swastika and eagle emblem. As she looked higher, she found the moon-drenched face of a young man staring down at her. The face was clean-shaven, and the stranger did not seem to be much older than herself. Brigid gripped her stick and started to stand.

"*Nein.*" The pistol indicated that she stay seated.

Brigid hesitated, and then, staring into the man's eyes, she very slowly stood. The gun did not cease pointing at the vicinity of her heart, and the man stayed exactly where he was. Brigid held her stick firmly in her right hand, and with her left she brushed twigs and leaves off her skirt and awkwardly swept hair from her eyes. Finally she let both hands drop by her side and stared at him.

"What do you want?" she said.

He continued to stare at her, the pistol not moving.

"What do you want?" she asked more sharply. "You're one of Hitler's boys, aren't you?" She shifted the stick slightly in her hand, trying to get a better grip so she could hit the gun away. His voice startled her.

"Ja. Ich komme aus Deutsch—"

"I don't understand your stupid language. Try to speak something civilized, or has Herr Hitler gotten rid of all the civilized—"

"The board." He moved his pistol.

"What?" She was suddenly scared again.

"Please," his voice was sharp. "The board. Please put away the board, miss. I do not desire to shoot you."

Brigid looked at him questioningly and then glanced down at the stick in her hand. She gave a small smile. "I'll get rid of my 'board,' if you'll put that gun away." She held the stick out by her side and relaxed her grip on it until it was slightly swaying between her thumb and forefinger. When he saw her do this, he slowly lowered his pistol, and when she dropped the stick to the ground, he placed the pistol back into its holster.

"Danke schön," said Brigid.

"Bitte schön," he replied.

He saw that the stick was in easy reach near her feet, and Brigid realized he had not secured the flap of his holster.

"Do you speak German?" he asked.

"What?" She was surprised. "No, no I don't." She looked at him and shrugged. "Everyone knows *Danke schön* means thank you."

"Why would you foreign people want to know a language that has no civilization—did you not say that?"

"Any language that has Hitler for a spokesman can't—"

"If I may point out, miss, Herr Hitler is an Austrian."

"And it's the same thing; you're all really German."

"Ach." Brigid did not notice the slight gleam in his eye. "We have been instructed that you English all think alike."

She moved a step closer, shaking a finger at his face. "I'll have you know, Herr Nazi soldier, that I am not English, but a Manx, and very proud to be from the Island, and that my ancestors go back for over—"

"And you," he came up to her, glaring into her eyes. "You must be made to know, I will tell to you, *und vergessen Sie nicht*, I will have you not forget." He struck his open palm with his other fist. *"Ich bin Offizier in der Wehrmacht. Ich bin kein Nationalsozialist."* He kept staring at her, but now his fist relaxed. "I am Hauptleutnant Rolf Scholl, a soldier, and not a Nazi. I do my duty."

"What do you want here?" She was surprised by his passion. He was a soldier, but not a Nazi. Was that so important to him? Brigid wondered what he would be like if she could meet him some other way. "We're in the middle of nowhere. What could you possibly do for the Third Reich around here?"

"I cannot tell you," he replied. "It is a job to do." He looked toward the sound of the sea. "A job for a German soldier," he added.

Brigid wanted to get him farther away from the beach, somehow lead him inland.

"Tell me, Rolf Scholl." He looked startled when he heard his name. "I've forgotten that lieutenant part." She tried to smile, tried to sound friendly, and was puzzled to find that it was not difficult to do. "How were you able to follow me so easily through the woods? I could hardly hear you til near the end."

"Well, miss . . . " He paused.

"Brigid"—should she tell him—"Brigid Crovan."

"Charmed." He actually touched his hand to his cap. "Well, Fräulein Crovan, the German army teaches its men very well."

"And quite a bit of luck," she said. She liked him, and it was not right.

"Yes, perhaps the luck, miss . . . "

"I'm called Brigid."

"Brigit. Yes, a good name." He smiled at her and stepped closer. "Perhaps some little luck, some of the good luck, yes, perhaps it was with me. Or it was not with you, *verstehen Sie*, do you understand? The luck was perhaps against you, yes, for you are now my captive."

"And what do you think you'll be doing with me?"

"I must have you." He looked over her shoulder. "I must keep you away from your people, Brigit, until my work is over."

"I'm going to be your prisoner?" Brigid's mind was racing. She had never thought of that; she had assumed everything would be over quickly, that she might still get to see him tonight, that she would soon be back home and talking to her parents.

"I will not hurt you," the soldier looked at the ground near her feet. "And you do not have to worry about other things. I am not going to touch you. I am a German officer." He looked back to her face. "It is . . . it is O.K." He smiled at her, happy to use a bit of the slang he learned. "If you follow me when I speak, there will be no trouble. It will be O.K."

"I'm not an American; you don't have to use those terrible expressions with me." Brigid almost laughed when she saw the puzzled look on his face, and without thinking she reached over and touched his shoulder. "Don't let it bother you, Rolf; you probably think we all speak the same." He did not back away from her.

"You people are insane," he said, pointing a finger to his head. "First it is English, next you must be the Manx—is that right, like the little cat that . . . *was ist, ohne* . . . that has not a tail, yes?"

"Yes." She was almost laughing.

"And now I must not use the terrible ex—esprec—"

"Expressions."

"I cannot use the speech that is of the Americans." He was smiling now, looking into her eyes. "In Deutschland, where I come from, yes?" Brigid nodded at him. "When Hitler—Hitler the Austrian, yes—when Hitler talks, he is often using the terrible German, his language is very bad, but Brigit," he paused slightly, "but Brigit, we all admit that he is speaking German."

Brigid could not stop herself; she started laughing. She stared at the young man, who looked so proud because he had made her laugh, and she had to hug herself to keep from touching him.

"But you are so close together over there." She made the shape of a ball with her hands. "All close together. You see, Rolf, the Americans are way across the ocean, though if they ever get into the war you'll see enough of them. But they're so far away that they've mixed the language all up, and then being down south does something to their minds. It's not quite as bad with the Canadians; we can talk to them very well."

"You have seen the Canadians?"

"Why, yes."

"Where?" He tried not to sound too interested.

"In Castletown, of course. They've had ships there and some of the . . ."

"The what?"

"Rolf." She sounded angry. "You're acting like a German soldier. I shouldn't have told you what I did. What would the governor call them—military secrets. Don't ask me any more such things, Rolf; don't make me your enemy again."

"I am not your enemy now?" he asked.

"No." She looked straight into his eyes.

"No." He sounded troubled; his hand went down to his holster, secured the snap. "You are right, I feel of it also." Rolf lowered his eyes from her face, absently plucked a piece of grass off her skirt. "Brigit, what am I going to do with you? I cannot now do you any harm, yet you must try to stop me from my job."

"Why don't you surrender?"

"Surrender?" He stepped back abruptly. "How can you say that? I am a German officer; it is . . . *unmöglich* . . . that I surrender. Why do *you* not surrender? Why do you not take me to your people, so I can capture them? Why do you not tell me of the Canadians?"

She grinned at him. *"Touché,"* she said.

"Was?" Then he smiled too. *"Ja. Touché.* That is good, Brigit. *Touché.* You understand me. You do understand me, do you not?"

"Yes, Rolf." She took both his hands in her own. "In spite of your very remarkable English, I understand you perfectly."

"What about it of my English?" He sounded slightly offended. "I have learned the good English in school, and at university in München, and in the army. I was put with this job because I talk English."

"I didn't mean anything." She squeezed his hand, thinking that men are all alike, you must never hurt their pride. "It's just that once in a while you don't speak like a native."

"I will get better, Brigit. With practice I will improve."

"How old are you, Rolf?"

"My age? *Vierundzwanzig.* I mean, I am, what is it, four and . . . yes, twenty-four. Why do you ask the question?"

"Because," said Brigid, stepping close, "I wanted to figure out how many years I'm going to have to teach you the language." Then she kissed him.

When he finally stood back, he looked down at her in surprise. "Do you foreign ladies always act so quickly?"

"Only when we are certain. Now come, we must go down to the beach." She started to walk away.

"Go to the water? But why?" He began to follow.

"It is time for a meeting," she replied.

IV

BRIGID DID not even wonder whether she was doing the wrong thing. She had never doubted her feelings, had never hesitated when a special glow came over her senses. Her mother had told her that that was part of her power, and that if there was even the hint of some suspicion, she would know it was the wrong thing to do.

She had been tested once, although she did not know it at the time. It was when she was sixteen, and the Head Druid had told her to go to Cashtal yn Ard, one of the most sacred Celtic places on the Island, and break off part of the porthole for him. It was through the rock porthole that one had to go to reach the burial chambers. The Head Druid said that he needed a piece of this passageway for a ritual he was supposed to perform, and it had to be obtained by a virgin.

She had not felt right about it, going to this sacred place for such a reason. Time and mercenaries had done enough damage over the centuries, so what remained was all the more important. Brigid asked her mother what she should do, but her mother's only answer was a shrug of the shoulders and the comment that it was not her decision to make. Brigid spent the night before with him on the beach, and although she did not dare to say anything about it, the wrong that she felt intensified when he was close. It had been the worst night of her life.

Early next morning—the Head Druid had instructed that the stone must be chipped away at sunrise—she got her father alone outside the house and asked him whether it was right. He had sounded more gruff than usual and would say only that that sort of thing was none of his business but was for her and her mother, and that it was her decision, Head Druid or no. So she took the hammer and chisel the Head Druid gave her and rode her horse quickly through the dawning light to Cashtal yn Ard. She jumped off her horse as soon as she arrived, took the tools from her saddlebag, and started walking toward the stones.

She thought that if she did not hesitate, did not take time to think, it would be easily done. But as the sun's rays touched the jagged rocks in the gallery of cists beyond, she could hear the ancient monolith roar in many strange and dusty voices, words and sounds from the great distance of time. She sweated so that the tools almost slipped from her hands, and her whole body shook uncontrollably.

Brigid walked quickly across the foreground, while the sun's rays touched stone after stone, stroking them with fingers of gold. As she came closer to the smaller rocks of the porthole, the old voices joined in a shrill, chanting shriek. Brigid was crying, the tears running unchecked down her face, and she reached the porthole as the sun struck her in the eyes, making the scene before her shimmer in a haze of liquid light. The noise was deafening, and her last hope gone, for she had prayed that he would come, would cross the rock-strewn ground and take her away, show her that she was doing wrong. But he was not there; no one was to help her at all. Almost blinded by tears and light, Brigid stopped before the porthole, the screaming voices swelling to a hysterical pitch. Her hands shaking violently, she placed the chisel on the smaller of two stones, and at that instant the voices stopped.

There was not a sound, of wind or bird or sea, as she raised the hammer above the chisel—not a sound but her own ragged breath as she cried. She was to obey the Head Druid at all times, but this was not right. Why was there no one to help her? Why had he not come? They would punish her for disobeying, the Head Druid had spoken—but this was not right. She had never felt so terrible; what was she to do? The sun now gleamed off the hammer in her hand, cast its shadow across her breast. The feeling, the terrible feeling —yes, she might just as well put the chisel through her own heart. The pain would be the same. She dropped the hammer to the ground and rubbed her hand across her eyes to get rid of the tears. It was a beautiful morning; the sun rose into a cloudless sky. Brigid reached out and touched the larger rock of the porthole, splayed her fingers and drew them across its rough surface. She looked at all the stones now bathed in the risen sun, then turned and threw the chisel as far as she could make it go.

She looked back to the porthole to find the Head Druid standing on the other side. He spoke, only to say that it was a waste of a good chisel. She had learned—learned a lesson that they knew she must learn by herself—to trust her own feelings. To realize that if there was the slightest doubt, the slightest hesitation at all, then it was wrong, no matter who said differently. She could now always trust herself.

Brigid stopped abruptly and grabbed Rolf's hand.

"Yes, Brigit?" He was surprised. "What do you want?"

"What is it about you, Rolf? You can't be that deceptive."

"Deceptive?" His voice questioned as he squeezed her hand. "You mean to tell the lies. Why no, Brigit, I cannot speak any lies to you. Only if I am to be possessed by the British. You know, if they hunt me out and I must surrender, then I would not tell them things, you understand; I would keep the mouth closed. But you have not interest in my job, or in secrets about the German army. These are the only things I could not tell the truth to you. Everything else is very correct, but you feel that, you know that, yes."

"But there must be more." She started to pull him along with her again. "It isn't just because you are honest; most of the people I know are honest, and yet I've never shown anyone what I am going to show you. I had the feeling, Rolf, when I first heard your voice, that you are very special."

"Maybe it is because you are so special," he answered. "I am just a soldier, and before that I studied the history at university. I have done nothing grand, and I have done nothing terrible in my life. I am—what is the word—I am the same as everyone else, nothing special."

"Oh no, Herr Scholl." Brigid stopped him by a fallen tree and yanked him down beside her. "There is certainly something about you, and although it isn't necessary to know, I have the feeling I'm going to find out. And as for doing nothing 'grand,' as you call it, after what I'm going to show you tonight, you won't be saying that ever again." She looked toward the beach. "Ever again."

"What is it, Brigit? Where are we going, what is to see?"

"Don't you hear anything?" She squeezed his hand hard. "Feel anything?"

"I can feel you when you break my hand, yes." Rolf put his other hand over both theirs. "And of what I can hear, there are not many of the sounds in the trees; the animals must all have the fear and are still silent. Our chase will probably keep them in their shelters for the end of the night. There is, of course, the sound of the sea. We must not be too far from it."

"You haven't listened closely enough to the night. There's something else beyond those trees besides the waves. Between the sounds of the sea, Rolf, almost a part of it, aye, there's another sound there, a lovely sound. Try to hear."

"But I am listening, Brigit. I cannot—"

"Shh," she placed a finger over his lips. "Shh, don't be talking about it, but listen. He's there, waiting, and I'm going to take you to him. I feel as if I must. What is there about you that makes this wild thing right? Shh. Listen, listen."

Rolf sat forward, his elbows on his knees, his chin resting on his hands. What was she doing to him? He was an army officer, highly trained, a killing machine if necessary. She was his enemy, her country at war with his. He was here to help win that war. Yet now, he was completely at her mercy, sitting in the dark with his eyes closed, trying to hear some strange noise from the beach. And why, when he was with her, did all thoughts of the war leave his mind, to be replaced with memories of his birthplace, the joining rivers, the forests, the ruins? He had not thought of these for a long time. And what was he supposed to hear? There were waves and . . .

"Brigit. What is it, that noise?" He grabbed her arm.

"Shh. Shh. That is it. Listen."

His eyes were open now, peering into the moonlight, trying to see through the trees. For a second there would be something over the wind, an instant later part of the surf, and then nothing. When he was certain it was only imagination, the sound would come again, a soft yet sharp touch on the stones, quickly splashed away by the crashing waves. On the wind it drifted, like tiny pebbles falling. Then the gust of wind that brought it to his ear took it on past him and threw the sound into the trees behind.

"Ah," she pressed her knee against him. "You do hear it, don't you? I can tell by the way you look. You don't believe it."

"It is like to be asleep—like a dream."

"A dream?" She squeezed his hand until he felt pain, was surprised at the strength of her. "A dream to most people, Rolf, a dream that they would not believe—would not be willing to believe."

Brigid did not loosen her grip as they both watched through the trees. They did not know it, but their eyes followed the sounds they could not see, glanced to and fro when the crashing water and the roaring wind allowed the sound to reach their ears, stroke their minds with wild visions.

"We must go to see," said Rolf.

"Now you're the anxious one," she laughed. "Oh yes, we'll go and see, there's no doubt about that. You're starting to feel it, the look in your eyes."

"This is where you were going tonight," said Rolf. "When I came across you in the woods. You moved with such a purpose that I was sure you went for the help, that you had seen me. That is why I came to stop you. But it was not that at all."

"No," said Brigid, standing with her back to him. "And soldiers and war were the furthest things from my mind. As you shall see." She turned around and pulled him to his feet. "And you will see, that what there is about you, you're going to understand. Somehow, the power is in you. I can feel that I am going to be able to share this with you. My mother had no one but me—so few of us ever do. Oh, father is a lovely—is a beautiful—man; we both love him so much, but he is still not a part, he cannot be one with us. But you, Rolf," she put her arms around him and held him close. "You are going to be able to do these things with me. Together we are going to have great strength."

"If you say it is so, Brigit. How are we to have so much strength that you talk about?" He placed his hands on her shoulders and brushed back her hair. "I do not know what it is you talk about, but I can feel that you are right."

"Oh yes, I'm right, I'm so very right." She closed her eyes as his fingers brushed her neck. "I also know that you are a German officer, but what is your opinion about another kiss in the dark?"

"Brigit, even an officer—and a gentleman, yes, is that not what the English say—even such a one as that would find it . . . " Here Rolf smiled broadly, "Would find it O.K. to take the kiss." His lips touched hers, and almost as quickly his tongue was probing into her mouth, feeling the quick response of her own. One of his hands stroked her long hair, while the other held her more tightly. He was becoming conscious of the outline of her breasts against him when something else, something distant, intruded into his mind, and he broke away suddenly, startling her.

"Rolf, what is it?"

"Quiet." His voice was hard, the tone threatening. He stood back from her and gazed at the sky, turning toward the sea.

"Rolf?"

"Do you not hear that, Brigit?"

"You mean what we heard before? I told you we were going to meet . . . " Her sentence trailed off. That was not what he meant; she could hear it now. Something was dreadfully wrong. "Rolf?"

"It is a bomber." His voice was flat.

"Are you sure?" She turned to the beach, tried to hear the other sound.

"*Ja*. It is one of ours. Heavy. Coming back with its bombs. Maybe lost. I know these sounds very well, Brigit."

"Come then. We must get there quickly." She grabbed his hand and started to pull him along, but he held back and spun her around until she was facing him. "What are you doing, Rolf?" Her eyes glared.

"Where are you leaving to, Brigit? We are completely safe here; we cannot be seen through the tree leaves."

"Rolf." She pulled at him harder. "We've got to get to the beach."

"The beach?" He gripped her hand even more tightly. "Brigit, that would be insane, to go on to the beach, in this moon. We would be seen for many miles. From the airplane we would be a great target."

"There's no time to talk about it." She broke away and started to run, but he was quickly behind her and put his arm around her waist, hauling her back. She spun around, but he held on to her hands.

"Brigit, they will just go on by, they want to get home, and there is nothing here. But if they see people moving, especially on a beach, they will think of boats, and they will drop the bombs, maybe shoot the guns. A plane alone can do such things and say later that it has sunk a boat, yes, or blown up a tank, and no one will know any better. If you go out on the beach, you will give this plane a reason to drop the bombs. We will stand on this spot, here, and there will be no trouble."

"But he's on the beach." She wriggled violently in an attempt to get away. "They'll see him."

"Who is there?" Rolf freed one of her hands.

"Who we are supposed to meet." She was yelling, and she struck him on the chest. "Don't be so dense. Help me."

"But he will surely hear the bomber, Brigit, and get into the trees. No one would be stupid enough to stay in the light."

"He will." She tried to break away again. "He will. He'll stay and wait for me, he won't leave until I come. Rolf, you just don't understand. There's no time to waste, we've got to get there. Come and help me." She turned to look into the sky over the beach. The sound was much louder now, much closer. She swung back to face him. "Will you help me?"

"Of course I will help, Brigit." He let go of her hand. "If someone is on the beach, we must get him away, but ... " He too looked up as the trees started to throb from the bomber's engines. "It does not have any sense to it, no one would stand out and ... "

"When there's time, Rolf," she almost pulled him off his feet. "I'll tell you when there is time."

They started running the short distance through the trees. Branches hit them in the face, and once Rolf got his foot caught under a root and sprawled face-down, hauling Brigid to the ground beside him. As they scrambled to their feet, the shadow of wings crossed over their faces, and the roar of the engines made them cover their ears and instinctively duck their heads.

"He is very low," yelled Rolf. "He has seen something."

"What do you mean?" Brigit gripped his jacket.

"He should not be that low." It was Rolf who started first for the beach. "They do not usually fly like that. He has come down because he has seen something moving." Brigid started running beside him, and he kept talking. "From the plane, even in this moon, you cannot really see what is below you, only movement. You can see if something moves, then make to decide if it is worth the bombs. We will make more movement, Brigid; they will have more reason to bomb."

"But he's still on the beach."

"Yes," Rolf sprinted through the last trees. "Yes, then we must make the fast movement, must get him into the woods." He skidded slightly on the sand, dropped to one knee so he would not fall, and looked as far up the shore as he could, sweeping with his eyes between the trees and the pounding surf. The sound of the plane's engines, which had begun to fade slightly, was once again increasing, and he looked up to see the bomber passing over the edge of the trees.

"Brigit," he reached out as she started to pass him and hauled her to the sand beside him. "It is starting to circle; it is coming back. Get down. Do not make the target."

"We've got to get him," she screamed.

"Where, Brigit? I do not see anyone."

"Down there. Down there in the other direction. He's coming toward us." She pointed past Rolf along the beach. "Help us."

Rolf turned around as she broke away and started running. The terrible roar of the bomber, as it started to circle back, filled his ears as he frantically looked past the running girl to see who was there. The sand and stone of the beach shimmered in the moonlight, and at first he saw nothing. Then a white form started coming toward the girl, and although he did not believe his eyes, he finally saw and understood.

"Mein lieber Gott, das Ein—" but before the words were out of his mouth, a gigantic explosion tore into the water behind him, and he was thrown into the sand under a shower of mud and rock. The plane roared over the trees as he crawled to his knees, wet and dazed.

"Brigit!" he yelled, clearing the dirt out of his eyes. "Brigit!" He looked frantically along the beach and saw them both running toward him, as the bomber made yet another circle. "The woods, Brigit. Go into the trees. Get him into the trees." He saw them both turn and head toward the woods, and he managed to get to his feet and haul his pistol from his holster. He was no longer a German soldier, on the same side as the plane overhead. He was fully aware that shooting his pistol at the bomber was not only completely futile, but also a signature on a death warrant. He knew only one thing—get them into the woods. Maybe his actions would make the bomb fall a little sooner, hit the water again and not go into the trees. He backed slowly toward the waves, raising his pistol into the sky as he searched frantically for Brigid. He could still see them, they were too close, they could probably be seen from the sky. The scream of the engine once again filled his head, and he turned to face the rapidly approaching bomber, which was low over the water and coming directly at him.

Rolf pointed his pistol in the direction of the rushing aircraft and started shooting wildly, not caring whether he hit it, hoping only to make it drop its bomb before it reached the woods. His six shots were quickly gone, but they had some effect. The pilot started firing his own guns and at the same time, not knowing how many weapons were below him, yanked back on his stick and started pulling up into the sky. Rolf could hear the bullets rip through the air, and as he finally dove into the crashing waves, he felt one tear into his left shoulder.

He rolled over on his back in the water, and as he looked up, he saw the bomb fall from the belly of the plane, directly over his head. A large wave swamped him and rolled him like a corkscrew toward the beach. Rolf found himself in about a foot of water and tried to scramble to his feet against the waves. He could see the plane pulling up high over the trees and saw the flash of the bomb striking onto the beach close to the tree line. Then he was knocked headlong into the water again, hitting his wounded shoulder against the rocks as the roar of the explosion reached his ears.

Rolf was caught between the power of the waves and the shock of the explosion, and he tumbled among the rocks and pebbles, swallowing water and getting hit by flying earth and pieces of tree. He finally felt ground beneath him and painfully crawled out of the water. The left sleeve of his uniform was drenched red; he could hardly see through the haze of smoke and sand, and he could not hear a thing. He tried to shake the effects of the bomb's explosion from his head, and he thought he was yelling for Brigid, but he was not sure. As he attempted to stand, he noticed that he was still clutching his pistol. Once on his feet, he started walking drunkenly up the beach, hoping that the smoke would soon clear. He could dimly see something moving, and as he got closer, each step a painful effort, he saw Brigid coming from the trees, pointing in his direction. She seemed to be shouting, and he vaguely wondered what she was saying to him, when he looked to where she pointed and saw a man walking toward him, aiming a rifle at his head.

Brigid's father had grabbed his weapon and started running to the beach as soon as he heard the airplane. His bad leg made movement difficult, but he could still go quickly when he had to and was near the shore when he heard the first bomb hit. He knew by the sound of the engines that it was a small dive bomber and thus had no more than a couple of bombs. He released the safety and moved nimbly through the trees in the direction of the fire and smoke. His weapon was a powerful hunting rifle that he had obtained shortly after the war started. He had some reasonable hopes that if the plane was low enough, and if he could hit it in the engine or gas tank, he would be able to do some real damage. He looked up through the trees as the plane began to circle, and although it was still too high, he thought he might hit it when it returned.

He paused to catch his breath, then started running through the trees again. He was close enough to see the moon reflecting off the water when he heard the aircraft make another diving run. Then he heard gunfire and knew that someone had been spotted on the beach.

Thinking it could only be Brigid, he broke through the trees and fell to his knees to aim the rifle more accurately. He managed to squeeze off a few shots before the bomb landed farther up the beach and threw him sideways in a shower of sand. He rolled with the explosion and came to rest in a clump of bushes. Because the bomb had fallen into the soft sand, much of the force of the explosion was absorbed. After a few seconds he got to his feet and started to walk back along the shore. He noticed that the plane was not returning.

When the sand and smoke started to settle, Brigid's father could hardly credit his senses. What he saw was Brigid emerging from the trees, heading toward the water. When he looked in the direction in which she was going, he saw a wounded German soldier coming out of the surf, waving a pistol at her. Dazed himself, he could not understand what had happened. Had the plane really crashed and was this a survivor? Was this the start of some type of invasion? He raised his rifle to kill the German.

What was Brigid doing? Why did she not run away, go back into the woods? She was yelling something, but he could not hear her clearly. She was pointing at him; maybe she was asking for help. The soldier had seen him now, but he kept on coming, pointing his pistol toward Brigid. His arms trembling from shock, her father aimed the rifle at the soldier's head. Brigid was starting to run between them; he must shoot quickly. She threw herself in front of the soldier just as a white-maned head touched her father's arm, and a long, spiral horn gently nudged the rifle aside.

V

BRIGID'S MOTHER went from one bed to the other, and placed a folded blanket under her husband's bad leg. Her husband gave a grunt and opened his eyes, looking at her hazy shape against the candlelight.

"What will you be doing with me then, finishing off what the Germans started?" He touched her arm.

"Shh," she took his hand and held it.

"And why are you wanting me to be quiet?" he asked.

"Because, one of your nasty Germans is over there in the bed next to you, and if he wakes up, I don't want him feeling worse than he is."

"And how is he?"

"Bad."

"Have you sent for young Alice?"

"Yes. As soon as we got you both back here. But young Alice is just starting out in taking her grandmother's place, and I don't think even her grandmother could help this time. Yon lad's shoulder is shot to pieces as far as I can tell. What he needs is a doctor."

"You'd best send someone to Castletown, then."

"William Crovan." She placed one of her large hands on his own.

"We have a doctor take one look at that wound, and he'll have the military here in a spit. And then our Jerry boy is off to the king's country and locked away tighter than Hitler's moustache."

"But he needs the doctor?"

"Oh aye." As she looked over to the other bed, her hazel eyes shifted color. "I've sent Brigid off to get the Head Druid; it will have to be his decision. I've never seen the likes of it."

"What do you mean?" He bunched the pillows behind his back and pushed himself into a sitting position.

"Do you remember what Brigid told you on the beach?"

"Every wild word of it." He reached up and took one of her long braids between his fingers, giving it a slight tug. "It's my leg that's got banged around, not my head. I remember it all, including the touch of his ivory horn on my rifle, and if that doesn't shock everything out of me, nothing will. You know I've never seen him before, not all these years with her, and none of the time I was courting you. And there I am, putting my arm around him when my leg gives out, and he kneels to ease me onto the sand. It must have been a sight when you got there, my love."

"It was the dream, William," she stared into his face, seeing something else. "The dream about the Oaks. When I reached the beach, it suddenly made sense. You, leaning against his flank, and Brigid kneeling over the boy down by the water. All these things that could never happen, just like the dream."

"Is everything she said," he looked away from his wife's face and over to the other bed, "is it all true?"

"All of it, William. He's come for a reason, and I don't know what it is. And he is special, just as Brigid says; he is very special, and I don't know why that is, either. But I can feel it."

"Has he said anything?"

"Nothing that I can understand; he mumbles to himself in German."

"Well, he must be something to make Brigid jump in front of him like that. If I hadn't been stopped, the shot would have gone right through her." He started to put his good leg over the side of the bed and felt her hand on his shoulder.

"Now, where will you be off to, William Crovan?"

"I may as well see what all the fuss is about," he said. "All I saw was a lump of gray lying on the beach." She helped him ease himself off the bed and supported him as he hobbled across the room. "Not a bad-looking sort, is he?"

"Almost too pretty. He won't pass for a Manx."

"Aye." He looked at the face, and then at the blood-soaked cloth wrapped around the shoulder. "Put some dark color on him and get some Island clothes. Maybe . . . " he peered closer, touched the face gently with his rough fingers. "If he doesn't mutter that damn language of his, we might get him past the doctor. Make him operate here, tell him the lad is too sick to move—that's true enough, anyway." He looked up into his wife's eyes. "After all, we've got to save Brigid's young man, don't we?"

"You think he's the one, then?" She looked down at the white face.

"After the way she was talking about him? Oh, that one's a goner all right; he doesn't have a chance."

"Now William." She playfully struck his arm.

"No more chance than I did when you put your designs on me and set out to make sure . . . "

"My designs?" She snorted in laughter. "Why, you old liar, as if it wasn't you who chased me half over this island, with the Druid council against it and my father threatening to have you sent away. Everywhere I went, there you were on that horrid old mare of yours, that should have been glue years before."

"And there was nothing wrong with old Bess," he put in.

"Nothing that the knacker couldn't cure."

"And I'm not so sure that you didn't know when I'd be out on the land; I never had to search that hard."

"I'll not be admitting anything," she smiled at him.

"As for old Bess," he continued, "if my old liar's memory does me true, it was on her back I got my first kiss from you."

"Stole," she corrected.

"Aye, I may have stolen the first one. But when you turned around, ready to slap my face, the others came free enough."

"Maybe it's true," she said.

"And," he put his arm around her. "You didn't mind old Bess taking it into her mind to stop for a while under the trees." He gave her a slow kiss on the mouth. "Old Bess had some good points about her when the occasion called."

"Come then, William Crovan, enough of your memories. Back to bed with you." She helped him walk across the small room and was just settling him on the blankets when the outside door opened. There was a slight draft of late summer air before the door was quietly shut, and quick footsteps crossed the front room and came toward the bedroom. Brigid's mother started toward the door, but it was quickly opened, and a small woman hurried in. She carried a basket over one arm and had a small knapsack on her back. Ignoring Brigid's mother and father, she walked swiftly to the other bed, removing the kerchief that tied back her short blonde hair. Although only twenty-seven, she had a face that had seen much pain and suffering. She put her basket on a small table by the bed, slipped off her knapsack, and then bent over to peer at the wounded man.

"Well, my people," she turned toward the other bed. "What will you be having me do then? We'll need the healing powers of both Christ and Teutates to get this bugger up and around."

"You can't do anything?"

"What would you be liking, William Crovan?" She bent over her knapsack and undid the flap. "Would a simple resurrection suit you?" She took out some bottles and a pair of scissors, placing them on the table.

"We need none of your mouth, young Alice." He pushed the pillows into various positions beneath him. "You're as bad as your grandmum, a few strokes worse if such a thing is possible."

"Is that so?" She took out two knives, a large spoon-shaped object, and numerous bandages. "Your trouble, my man, is that you don't like all these years of gran and me seeing you with your pants down. Who else keeps you going on that leg of yours, which you took out on one too many fishing voyages, even after gran warned you?"

He was about to say something more, when his wife touched his shoulder and spoke. "How is your grandmother, Alice?"

"Tired." Alice looked up from her work. "She's very tired today. When she heard it was a shooting, she wanted to come, but she's just unable to. She hasn't had to deal with many gunshots, and I've only seen one—you know, the one a couple of years ago, that man out near Santon Head. But that wasn't bad, only through the flesh of the leg. This one's a mess." The last thing she took from her pack was a large magnifying glass. "Speaking of legs, old Billy, what have you done to yours?"

His wife came across the room. "He's gone and wrenched it again, and the knee too, when he was thrown by the bomb." She stood beside the bed. "Is there anything I can do for you?"

"Yes, please." Alice took a large handful of leaves, roots, and berries out of her basket and tied them loosely in some gauze. "Put these in a small pot of water, and put it over the heat. And then bring in a nice big basin of hot water. I may as well clean this up and do what I can for the doctor." The older woman took the things from her and left the room. Alice took another jar from her knapsack, and a wad of cloth. "Get your breeches down, old Billy; I may as well fix you while we're waiting."

"Aye," he grumbled from the other bed. "I suppose we have to go through this again," he said, undoing a button.

"And as many times as you bang up that leg." She went across the room toward him. "And be quick about it, man, or I'll have to start helping you myself."

"Nay mind that, I can do it." He slipped his good leg out but had trouble getting the other one free of the cloth. "And don't you go digging in as much as you did last time."

"It's the digging in, as you call it, that does most of the good. Now while I'm having the pleasure of your wrinkled old flesh, why don't you tell me all that's happened, and what it is all about." She took the top off the large jar and spread green ointment on his upper thigh, from the hip almost to the knee. As he described what had happened—between grunts of pain—she dug her powerful, stubby fingers into his leg and moved up and down, pulling at the muscles and kneading the flesh. He could not tell her everything, but there was more than enough even with what he left out. She asked a question now and then but knew when not to ask too much. All the while he told her the story, she massaged and dug at his leg, getting him to roll over part way through, so she could do the same to the back of his wrenched limb. He called her a butcher once in a while, and she knew that she was hurting him a great deal. Her fingers were aching by the time he rolled over on his back, and she was glad to stop. Alice noticed the boiling water waiting by the other bed but paused for a rest anyway.

"I hate to admit it, young Alice, but it does feel better. Now what about the knee?" He smiled at her, wiping away sweat.

"Now William, the poor girl needs a rest." His wife picked up the pair of scissors. "Sit down a while, Alice; I'll cut off these old bandages for you." She started to snip through the bloody cloth.

"Thank you." Alice sat down on the edge of the bed. "And as for your knee, we'll just have to let nature take care. If I start prodding and twisting on that, it will undo some of my grand work on the rest of your leg." Alice replaced the lid on the jar of green ointment. "Is he ready for a going-to, then?"

"Yes, Alice, I've got the bandages off."

"Is the pot boiling yet?" She got off the bed, crossed the room, and started soaking some cloth in the hot water.

"Yes, it should be good and ready in a short time." The older woman started to move away, but Alice stopped her.

"You'd best stay here. If this one starts thrashing, I'll need you to hold on to him. He's going to wake up sometime."

"All right, Alice." She went to the other side of the bed.

Alice took the wet cloth and started to wash away the caked blood and grit. The wound started to bleed again when she did this, but she had things ready to put on and stop it. She had Brigid's mother help her move Rolf over on his right side, and then she cleaned his back. There was a ragged hole seeping red—almost black—blood. Alice had seen where two bullets had gone in the front of his shoulder, one just below the collarbone and the other right at the top of the armpit. But this single wound at the back indicated that only one of the bullets had come out. There were no protruding pieces of bone, and she wondered whether some miracle of the gods had spared him that much, anyway. Alice thoroughly cleaned the wounds and then applied various salves to kill germs, lessen the pain, and stop the bleeding. She then loosely bound the wounds in dressing and helped ease Rolf onto his back once more, pulling the sheet up to cover him.

"I think there's one still in him," she said.

"Can you get it out?" Brigid's father asked.

"Who, me?" She looked across the room as she washed her hands. "Listen, my man, I'll not go fishing around inside there," she pointed to the shoulder. "The most I've done is take out a fishhook or two from some poor fisher. That over there is a job for a doctor."

"Aye. That's what I thought. I was . . ." He stopped speaking when he heard the outside door open. There were running feet, and then Brigid raced into the room, closely followed by a massive man in coarse white pants and a belted blue tunic. It was the Head Druid.

The Head Druid was exceptionally tall, a good head and shoulders above nearly every other man on the Island. He was strong and quick, and when he moved across the room, the light gleamed from his rich green eyes. His usually clean-shaven face showed thick stubble that was as black as his long hair. He was a powerful man of forty-five, as strong now as when he became Head Druid ten years ago. He gazed down at the face and touched the pale forehead.

"Yes, Alice."

She looked around at the others, then went and stood beside him. She looked up into his face, leaning backward because he towered over her. "Two gunshots. One of the bullets is still in him. The shoulder might not be as bad as I thought it was, but it's still a sad mess, and he's lost a lot of blood. The bullet will have to come out; we'll be needing a doctor."

"No." He moved the sheet down to take a better look. "No doctor. Go and meet your grandmother, Alice. I've already sent for her." He pulled the sheet back into place. "We cannot take the time to deal with the outsiders effectively. The army is already swarming over the beach. Brigid has had to take him elsewhere." He turned to look at Brigid and her mother. "You are sure about him?"

They both nodded.

"You're right to be." He touched Alice on the head. "Get going, girl, your grandmother."

"Oh yes, of course." Alice started to hurry from the room but turned at the door. "The drink will be ready to give to him now; he'd best have it." Brigid's mother followed her out of the room and went to the kitchen. The Head Druid walked over to her husband's bed, closely followed by Brigid. He touched the other man's shoulder.

"How is the leg, William?" he asked.

"Young Alice has twisted me around into some sort of shape again, but I'm not going to be moving much for a while."

"You are not meant to be a match for a bomber."

"I might have, you know. If I'd had a little more time, I might have brought that bastard down."

"Oh aye. Let father have his go at them and Mr. Churchill could retire in a month and spend his days rolling cigars."

Brigid turned as her mother came back into the room and went to help her give the hot liquid to the wounded man. She eased him up against the headboard as her mother placed the cup against his mouth. The hot fumes alone began to revive him, and as he groaned and moved his head back and forth, she managed to pour some of the fluid into his mouth. He coughed and tried to avoid the potent mixture, but Brigid gripped his head firmly, and he was forced to drink. He stopped resisting when he opened his eyes and saw Brigid standing beside him. He made a face at her and pointed to the drink, but he finished a final cup before her mother took it away to put back over the heat. He winced when he tried to move, and Brigid put a hand on him to keep him in place. When he finally spoke he was looking directly at the tall man who was staring down at him.

"It is obvious that you are the leader, yes." When the man nodded his large head, Rolf continued. "Then I must inform you that I am Hauptleutnant Rolf Scholl of the—"

"No, no, Rolf." Brigid leaned closer to him. "You don't have to say that; he's not that kind of leader."

"No?" Rolf turned back to look at the tall man. "You are then with the government, if you are not military." He turned questioningly to Brigid when she started to speak.

"You will come to understand, after you've been here for a while. You just have to learn about him, about us, with the passage of time. There are centuries of knowledge, of legends, of the traditions that make us what we are. Your old life is distant, Rolf. A new world started when you saw him on the beach."

"Das Einhorn."

"Yes, the unicorn. You helped us; you made it possible for him to remain, and he in turn saved your life."

"It saved my life," Rolf looked from one face to the other. "But I do not remember, how was—" He gave a start when another voice broke into his question.

"That was on account of me, lad. I was ready to blow more holes in you than you've already got, when he pushed my rifle aside. I thought you were going to shoot Brigid."

Rolf tried to sit up and look across the room. It was the first time he knew that anyone else was present. Brigid helped to hold him up, and he peered over to the darkened corner.

"That's my father, Rolf. When he heard the airplane he came down to see if I was all right, and he brought along his rifle. You were the only one walking around that made a good target." Brigid looked over as the door opened. "And that's my mother. She's the one that knew you were coming, though she didn't really know it. Her dreams only told her that something was going to happen."

Rolf looked at the other woman. "You knew I was coming?"

"Yes, in a way. It was a disturbing dream."

"I have a—what do you say for the sister of your parent?"

"An aunt."

"Yes, is so. I have an aunt, who is the sister of my mother. It is said she looks much like her. My mother is dead, yes, when I was very young. A train crash near Leverkusen. My aunt has dreams, she tells people things. In the future, you know. And she also has powers; many seek at her house for help."

The tall man stepped closer as Rolf was talking, and he ignored everyone else as he stared at the soldier. Brigid moved aside as the Head Druid came closer still.

"Your family, Rolf," the green eyes bore into him. "Where do they come from? Where were you born?"

"Regensburg."

"Regensburg?" Brigid gave a little laugh. "Why, I've never even heard of it. Where in earth is it?"

"Well, Brigit," he looked over to her. "It is down south from—"

"It is southeast of Nuremberg, and northeast of Munich, on the right bank of the Danube where it joins the river Regen."

Rolf turned quickly to the Head Druid, looking at him closely. "You have been there then, to my town."

"Upon occasion," the tall man stroked his chin. "Regensburg, as you call it, used to be known as Ratisbon. But Brigid and her mother will recognize it by its original name of centuries ago—Radasbona."

"Radasbona?" Brigid looked quickly at the Head Druid, and then over to her mother. "But that's one of the oldest Celtic settlements on the continent." Then she gazed at Rolf. "Some Irish Celts settled there before the birth of Christ. That's how old it is."

"Not only Irish, Brigid." Her mother looked at the Head Druid, who nodded his head. "There were a couple of Manx who went too, a Druid and his woman. Of course the names of countries didn't mean much then; there were people from many places who formed a small settlement."

"But what does this—" but before Rolf could finish his question, the bedroom door opened and a short, fat woman entered slowly, her scraggly white hair in disarray about her head. She was quickly followed by Alice, who closed the door behind them.

"You'll have all your questions answered in time, Rolf." The Head Druid motioned the newcomers over to the bed. "But now we had better do what we can to heal you."

The old woman went over to the bed and peered at the wounded shoulder. "Get those wrappings off him. Give him something to put him to sleep. And get me a chair."

Alice bent over and started to cut off the new bandages, while Brigid brought the old woman a chair. The Head Druid moved out of the way and went to stand by the other bed. He spoke once in a while to Brigid's father, but his eyes rarely left the activity around the wounded man. Alice, after the bandages were cut away, rummaged around in her basket and came up with a small brown packet. She motioned to Brigid's mother to move away from the bed and whispered in her ear.

"Take a small spoon of this and put it into a nice large mug of your old man's best whisky. Stir it good and bring it in. It'll put the Jerry out in less than five minutes." Brigid's mother left the room and Alice went back to the bed. The old woman was leaning over Rolf, inspecting the wounds. She had made Rolf lay on his side and was going over him front and back. She prodded none too gently and made him wince.

"Two in and one out. See this. One went in just above the armpit and came out down on the back, missing the ribs. Other hit here, at the base of the neck. Went through the bones without hitting any. Gods were with this one, right enough. Scapula seems to have stopped it. Got to dig. Alice, wash this mess off." The old woman sat heavily in the chair and took a leather case out of one of the large pockets on her dress. She handed the case to Brigid with a grunt. "Take these, girl, and boil them good. Put them on a plate or something, and boil that, too."

As Brigid left the room, she met her mother coming back with the mug of whisky. Rolf took a drink and coughed, which made Brigid's father smile and call across the room, "Strong stuff, eh lad? This war tries to stop you from getting anything, but there's a boat from Dublin once in a while that nobody knows about. Comes in to Dalby Point it does, and gets brought across the Island. You'll be getting the real stuff there, Rolf."

"Strong enough to knock him out, it'll be." The old woman gave a dry cackle, which puzzled Rolf. He then thought she was laughing at his reaction to the strength of it, just as Brigid's father had. He found it very strong, that was true, but he did not want them to think he could not drink it. He did not mind getting drunk if this old woman was going to cut into him. The less he knew, the less he would worry about her abilities. He smiled in the direction of the two men, and took a last drink of the whisky. The old woman took the mug from him and placed it on the table. Then she took a thick magnifying glass out of another of her voluminous pockets, and after making Rolf lay very straight on his back, she started to inspect his shoulder carefully and thoroughly. He was starting to yawn and was feeling drowsy when Brigid came back with the sterilized instruments. Because the small table was already cluttered, Brigid's mother brought another from the front room and placed it near the old woman's chair, covering it with a damp cloth.

"Get us more light." The old woman settled back into her chair. "Here Alice, you take a good look at all this," she handed the magnifying glass over, and Alice took her place looking at the shoulder.

Brigid's mother came over with a large lamp, and the old woman took it from her and held it on her lap. Rolf's head fell to one side of the pillow and stayed there.

"He's under then." The old woman hefted herself to her feet and bent over his face as far as her bulk would allow, lifting up one eyelid, and then the other. "Well, what d'you think, girl?"

Alice looked startled. "Why, the bullet has to come out."

"Of course the fucking bullet has to come out." The old woman gave Alice a rap on the knuckles and sank into her chair, holding the lamp once again. "Can you slice Jerry open and get it?"

"Me?" Alice went white.

"It isn't the lamp I'm talking to, my lass."

"But I've never done anything like this."

"Time to learn." The old woman took the cloth off the plate of knives. "I know you've been rushed into things since your mum died. Can't be helped. Go wash your hands."

"But gran, that's why you're here."

"Me?" The old woman snorted. "These old hands can't cut anymore; they're not steady, got the shakes." She nodded in the direction of the Head Druid. "Himself knows that. I'm here to tell you what to do, but you're the one that's got the hands. Now get and wash." She watched Alice leave, then reached over and took a white jar from the basket, which she handed up to Brigid's mother. "Spread this all over the shoulder, keep out infection. Then you and the young one get on the other side of Jerry, and be good and ready to grab on to him if he feels something he shouldn't." The old woman turned up the lamp. Brigid's mother did as she was told, then she and her daughter took their positions on the other side of the bed, Brigid looking drawn and worried.

Alice came back, drying her hands on a small towel. She looked down at her grandmother and started to say something. The old woman just shook her head and pointed to the largest knife.

"Nothing to be said, girl. Waste time. Pick that up and do as I say. If you get doubts, stop and ask me. Once you get in him, don't have doubts." The old woman pulled her chair as close to the bed as possible and held the lamp on the edge of the mattress. "Where do you think it is, then?"

Alice glared at her grandmother, then pointed with the knife to a point a quarter of an inch below the clavicle.

"I think it's down there, resting on the middle part of the scapula."

"Good, that's what I think, too. Now you slice a nice line from his collarbone to a point a little below where the bullet is. Don't make it too deep, and don't hunt around inside. Keep it steady."

The room was silent as Alice made the first incision, following her grandmother's directions with a firm stroke. Blood started to ooze from the cut, which the old woman staunched with small wads of cotton. When Alice had finished, her grandmother pointed to another knife with a long, slender blade, and Alice picked it up.

"Now, my girl, this part is just as simple, as long as you don't stab anything of Jerry's that wants to be left alone. Take that one with the blunt end, and start probing around for the hunk of metal what's causing all the trouble. Be real careful, because the lung's not very far away. Don't go too far afield; if it's not right around there, I'll try to think of something else. When you feel anything, give a yell."

Alice took the tool and inserted it into the base of the incision. She was terrified of hitting his lung, or even puncturing an artery or vein. She was not even sure whether her grandmother had ever done anything like this; certainly she had not since Alice had started helping with the cases. This was a far cry from a fish hook. Alice paused to wipe the sweat from her forehead and looked over at the two women on the other side of the bed. Brigid's mother looked back at her and smiled, but Brigid stared at the wounded man's face, then at the operation, then back to his face. She was biting her lower lip and twisting her hair in her left hand. She occasionally touched the pale face with her other hand.

Alice moved the instrument back and forth, hoping to feel the resistance of the bullet, but after carefully probing for a couple of minutes, she came across nothing. She stopped and looked down at her grandmother, shaking her head.

"Go deeper."

Alice pushed the blade in further and again prodded from side to side. This was almost as bad as a nightmare, and to make matters worse she thought she saw a look of doubt on the old woman's face. If they did not find it here, things were going to be a lot worse for the wounded man. Her grandmother was clearing away some of the blood when Alice finally felt the piece of metal, and at that instant the soldier started to jerk around.

"Fuck." The old woman jumped from her chair, dropping the bloody wad of cotton and moving the lantern to one side. "Hang on to him there, hold him down." As Brigid and her mother put their arms across Rolf to keep him in place, the old woman put her hand over Alice's so the knife would not move. "Don't lose it now, keep it nice and steady. We can't dig all night."

"I'm sorry, gran."

"Not your fault. It happens sometimes." She kept clutching Alice's hand, moving ever so slightly when Rolf twitched. "I could tell the way you stopped that you'd found it. This bastard calms down and we'll get it out." Brigid's mother had one hand on Rolf's head and held him firmly on the chest with the other. Brigid secured his good arm and put a lot of her weight across his stomach, looking in fascination at the two hands—one wrinkled and old, the other young and strong—that held the long instrument inside Rolf's shoulder. She wanted to pull the old woman away and do something herself, or at least yell out for them to take care.

"You still feel it?"

"Yes, gran."

"Good." The old woman moved her hand and flexed her fingers.

"Now, my girl. I'm going to hold that knife while you get a couple more tools. When I tell you, you let go very, very slowly. Hold it with your other hand just above where you have it now, then let go and slide that hand out of the way." She made sure that Alice had a good grip on the tool with her other hand, then touched her head. "Move that hand away now." Alice slowly moved her hand across the sheet, and her grandmother took her place, gripping the damp metal Alice had just left. "All right, now let go with the other hand." Alice relaxed her grip, and the old woman was left to hold it alone. Sweat trickled down her lined face. "Get that one with the long handle, that looks like a little scoop. Ease it down in here till it's on the other side of the bullet. Be quick at it."

Alice's fingers left streaks of blood as she wiped her hands on the towel. She carefully did as she was told and soon was probing for the lump of metal.

"Mind. Don't push it any farther away." The old woman looked at Alice with tired eyes. "For God's sake hurry, my hand is bad."

Brigid looked over to her mother, who kept stroking the wounded man's forehead and pretended not to have heard the old woman's plea. It was not the time to say anything. Brigid's gaze returned to the slowly moving hand hunting for the piece of metal and watched in amazement as it stopped searching.

"Gran."

"You have it, girl?"

"Yes."

"Are you sure?"

"Yes, I can feel it in the scoop."

"Do as I say." The old woman grunted and took a deep breath. "Give it a little shove to see if I can feel it." Alice moved her hand ever so slightly, and her grandmother grunted again. "You're there, I felt you. Now, my girl, this is it. Once we start moving, you keep moving. We can't lose it, Jerry here won't take much more. When I say, we'll press together and haul it out. Quick and smooth. Keep it tight. You ready?"

"You all right, gran?"

"Never mind me. You ready?"

"Yes."

"Smooth and quick then." The old woman pressed her blade against the bullet, wedging the lump of metal against the instrument Alice held. "On three, girl, and don't stop." She looked at

Alice and then counted. "One, two, three." Together their hands moved up, drawing the bullet out of Rolf's shoulder. The old woman stared intently as the two instruments came closer to the surface of the skin and gave an exhausted smile as the bullet popped out and rolled down the white flesh to come to rest on the mattress.

Alice put an arm around her grandmother and gave her a hard hug. The old woman looked pleased but gently pushed her away. "None of that, girl. It's a job, but I'm too old for it." She settled into her chair with a sigh and looked at Brigid's mother. "What I could do with, missus, is a good mug of your old man's Irish." Brigid's mother smiled, and started to leave the room. "And one for the girl here, too." She grabbed Alice by the hand. "You did good, lass. Next time I won't be there, you'll have it all to do alone." She stretched over and picked up the bloody bit of metal. "And you'll be able." She handed the bullet to Alice. "Here, keep this. My mother used to say, 'The first is the worst.' You look at that, and you'll remember what you've done. Now clean yon lad, and stitch him up; it's bed for me, and soon is best."

Alice dropped the bullet onto the plate with the instruments and then soaked a clean towel in the basin of warm water. She noticed Brigid standing on the other side of the bed, still holding on to Rolf's arm. She handed the wet cloth over the bed, and Brigid hurried to stand beside Alice, feeling grateful to be allowed to do something.

"Is it over?" Brigid's voice was low.

"Oh yes." Alice put all the instruments together, and picked up two jars of ointment. "We'll clean him, put this on him to stop infection and help the healing, stitch him together, and let the rest take care of itself. He's a strong one; there shouldn't be any trouble."

"How long before he's better?" Brigid finished washing his shoulder. "I mean before he can start getting around."

Alice looked down at her grandmother, who was carefully holding the mug of whisky she had just received. "Getting around, girl." The old woman looked up at Brigid with tired eyes. "As for getting around, he'll probably do that before your father. But he won't be good for much in short of a month. Lost blood. The wounds'll take time. Probably have a weak arm the rest of his life." She paused to take a drink and gave a satisfied look. "Nothing terrible, though; Jerry's lucky considering."

Alice had finished putting the ointment on his shoulder and was now stitching up the incision. When she had finished that, she put fresh dressings on the wounds and then made a sling for the wounded arm. "Now when he comes 'round, he's not to move the arm. I'll be leaving some things for the pain, and I'll be back later to change the dressings." She finished her work and sat down on the edge of the bed, taking a drink from the mug Brigid's mother had been holding. Brigid was about to ask something when the Head Druid came across the room and spoke to the old woman.

"How soon can he be moved?"

"Shouldn't be for a week."

"Can he move tomorrow?"

"If he's real careful, and not moved too far, yes."

Brigid looked at him in shock. "Why can't he stay here?"

"Your father and I agree that he has to disappear. If anyone starts searching, they must find nothing. First we must destroy that uniform and then hide him. We believe we have found the right place, and the right man. As soon as he wakes tomorrow, he's away." He looked down at Rolf a moment, then turned and touched the old woman. "You still have the gift of healing; it was a good job." Then he turned to Alice. "And you're learning very well; we'll be fortunate with you around." Without another word he strode out of the room.

They left Rolf to sleep, but in the night a white figure came to his bed, and an ivory touch gave benediction to his wound.

VI

THE SMALL stone church was dominated by two Celtic crosses, one in the graveyard, and one atop the roof. Graves surrounded the church, and the stone shaped like a Celtic cross stood nine feet tall above an ancient plot. It was close to the church, almost under the east window, and thus did not stand out. The other Celtic cross was made of wood and was in need of repair and paint. The church itself was weathered, the stone pitted by storm and cold.

A stone fence surrounded three sides of the churchyard, but the fourth was allowed to face toward the sea unhindered. The newer graves were on this hill, the ground between fence and church already filled. Although the ancient church, or *keeill*, was no larger than most of the other ones on the Island, centuries of death had filled the land around it, so a new section of graveyard was necessary. There were still few graves, and the land was almost clear to the rough grass and stony beach that marked the water's beginning. A wide slice of the land was left for the whims of high tide, so there would always be a long stretch between the last graves and the living sea.

Manannan's Mist hung on the sea and settled over the graveyard in the dim light of the early morning. From a distance, it was difficult to see anything through the white haze. Except for a fleeting glimpse of the nearest tombstones, the landscape appeared deserted. Upon moving closer, however, one could hear a sound over the sloshing of the waves. If one passed through the gate and rounded a corner of the church, the harsh, scraping sound became pronounced. With a tempo that did not vary, one rasping noise followed another with mechanical regularity. After a minute it was as if the noise had always been there, and existence was difficult to conceive of without it.

The Head Druid stepped closer to the sound and stopped to observe the man who was making it. The man in the grave, throwing shovel after shovel of dirt onto the pile behind him, was small and dark, with a balding head and graying hair. He had not seen youth for many years yet was surprisingly strong, with powerful muscles cording his neck and shoulders. The dirt kept flying with precision, and the man seemed to get neither tired nor bored. He did not slacken his pace or look behind him as he spoke.

"And what would the Head Druid be doing with the likes of my humble person? Watch out for the dirt while you're at it."

"We want your help, Ogma."

"The dirt, you know." He kept on digging, bent over his work. "It's a wonderful thing. It feeds us when we're alive, and then it covers us when we're dead. Might be the one time most of us do any good—when we rot. Go back into the ground, fertilize the land. You ever noticed . . . " The gray man straightened with a grunt and turned slightly. "Ever noticed how good the crops are near a boneyard? Ask any farmer; aye, it's choice land, the best." He thrust the shovel into the pile of dirt behind him and jumped from the hole. "In the old days, they used to fight over the land that was near a *keeill*, or if the time came to build a new one, the richest would tempt the bishop, or whoever had the last say. You ever seen the spuds or the corn from around a graveyard? Especially the root vegetables; my, but they're large and juicy. Best land for growing anywhere, and you can believe that or not."

"If you say it is so, Ogma, then I will reserve judgment."

"And well it would be for you to do so, Taggart. There are times when I think that working with the dead may cloud my judgment just a bit. 'Tis often a bone of contention with me, at any rate."

The Head Druid started to walk toward the water. "There is someone I want you to hide for us, Ogma."

"Is he dead or alive?"

"Does it make a difference?"

"Oh no. Just professional curiosity."

"We don't want you planting this one. He is in a bad way and has got to have the chance to get better."

"Ah, 'twill be the German lad."

"You hear things quickly."

"I know where to listen, Taggart. I can hear the worms a-chewin' if I put my mind to it."

"Can you help us, Ogma?" They came to the beach grass and stopped walking. The fog was still thick, although they could see a few meters out across the water. Manannan's Mist was slowly dispersing; in an hour or so the coast of England would be seen.

"When's he to be here?"

"As soon as he wakes and has something to eat."

"And what's he to do, Taggart? It's far from inconspicuous to be sitting around in a graveyard, unless you're dead and mouldering."

"The best will be to keep him out of sight as much as possible. When his arm gets workable, he can help you dig or do other chores. Maybe he can help fix things in the *keeill,* or any jobs that might take him into the woods and keep him there. I'm sure there are plenty of things to be thought of with your fertile imagination, Ogma."

"And who's to be looking for our Jerry friend?"

"It could be no one." He turned his back to the sea and looked up the slope toward the *keeill,* noticing how the sun turned the cross on the roof a shimmering yellow. "Or it could be everyone, from His Majesty's Forces to the Gestapo." He moved his head slowly and stared into the eyes of the small man beside him "Or it could be the Otherworld that will want him the most."

Ogma spun around on his heel, and his voice was harsh. "The Otherworld? Why would something from there want him?"

"For one thing, he has seen the unicorn."

"That's right, Taggart, tell it all at once. Don't mind my old heart."

"He saved the life of the unicorn, and his life was saved in return. We believe he is the one who will help check this sweep of fire that threatens the world, if the war is not stopped. It will not be a flood, this time."

"Let me get back to my pit, Taggart. The dead don't give me a tenth of the fears that you do. What makes you think that any of this is true, anyway?" They started walking toward the *keeill*. "No, let's go sit by the church in the sun, and I'll have a pipe. They say Jesus turned the water into wine, so He won't begrudge me a smoke." They stopped beside the new grave, and Ogma picked his shovel from the pile of dirt. "Always keep your tools close, you never know when they'll be needed." He placed the shovel on his shoulder and continued toward the church. "How do you know this is true?"

"Brigid felt it about him right away."

"Ta, that silly little thing. She's barely a woman yet, why do you expect her to know about . . . "

"There is also her mother. As soon as she saw—"

"That flighty goose, why she's worse by half than the child. She was always a witless girl and has only got worse since she married that lunk of a William Crovan."

"Now, now Ogma. Contain your rantings so near the holy house."

"It's the truth I'm saying." He stopped by a tombstone and placed the point of his shovel on the toe of his boot. "Why it was ever allowed that she should marry that ox-brained man is beyond reason. I know it was before your time as Head Druid, and there wasn't much you could do about it. But the fact is that he was way below her, he had none of the—"

"The fact is, Ogma, that you wanted her yourself, and when she went for someone else—what was the title of that unpleasant song you wrote and made a part of the south Island's lore—oh yes, 'Ball-less Billy,' seems to come back to my mind. Aye, you can chuckle, it is still popular in the less couth sections of the Island."

"Ah-hah," Ogma drew out the laughter, slapping his hand against the top of a tombstone. "Oh aye, that was a good one, six verses plus a beautiful refrain, and I made it all up while digging the Quiggin brothers' grave, you can believe that or not. And any of it I forget myself, I can go into any pub and get someone to tell me. I wonder how our grand William felt when he first heard it."

"I doubt that he ever has."

"And what do you mean by that?"

"Well, Ogma, drunk or sober, who would be man enough to tell William Crovan to his face. Bad leg and all, he was willing to take on a whole invasion last night by himself, if that is what it had been."

"I've never said anything against his bravery, Taggart. I'd much rather have him by my side than against me. But I still don't know why someone like her would even look . . . "

"It's a long time to be bitter, Ogma."

"Oh, it's the waste." He hit his shovel against the heel of his boot. "It's the terrible waste of what could have been. If she had only married me." He looked up imploringly at the tall man beside him. "Do you know what my life might have been like, with her there to talk to, having her there to love? Sometimes I still think of her when I'm lying in bed; even when there's a woman with me, I think back to those days when I wanted her so much. I can even tell you the first time I saw her, how I thought even then that she was the one I wanted."

"Ogma, there were so many who wanted her, just like all the young ones today want to catch Brigid. It is part of the power that they have, part of what they are. So many wanted her."

"Knowing that doesn't help much, Taggart."

"Storms and years, Ogma."

"Aye, they both pass. And they both leave change." He replaced the shovel over his shoulder, and they slowly walked the rest of the way to the stone-walled *keeill*. Although summer still had a few days by the calendar, the weather was turning chilly, and it felt good to get out of the morning breeze by the shelter of the church. When they reached the tall Celtic cross, Ogma leaned his shovel against it and went around the corner of the church. He returned carrying a weathered stump of wood, which he placed at the base of the cross and tilted slightly to the right. He looked up with a smile.

"Since I don't get many visitors Taggart, you can have the comfy seat. You can lean back and rest in style. I've had that stump for about six years, and it's getting nicely broken in. Piece of driftwood it once was, tossed way in by a storm down near Little Ness, and when I saw it, I said to myself: 'Ogma, that's just made for your arse,' you can believe that or not. Brought it back here and, after trying it around, found this is the best place for it. Nice and smooth, won't have to worry about any splinters in your britches."

"And where do you plan to sit?"

"On my coat. My coat will keep me from getting wet. I left it in my wheelbarrow, won't take a minute to get it." He called over his shoulder as he walked around the corner of the church. "I would have needed it this morning if I hadn't been in the pits." He gave a snort of laughter as he returned with a stained brown coat over his arm. "Just like a miner you know, only a miner in reverse." He folded the coat and placed it at the base of the Celtic cross, then slid down and sat on it, not far from the Head Druid's feet. "Ungh, that's more like it." He took a pipe from his shirt pocket. "I feel close to miners, you know. And moles if it comes to that. I always do a bit of a special job when I plant a miner, not that there's many would notice—or care, I suppose." He wriggled a bit, getting matches and tobacco from his pants' pocket. "I put them a bit deeper, you see, than I do most ordinary folk, about half the length of my shovel more. I figure they're used to being deep and will be more secure when I put 'em that way. And I always put a piece of what they were digging in with them, you know, a piece of lead or a bit of silver. Had a couple of miners come back from Newcastle and put in a lump of coal with them. I even had one poor fellow—he got drunk in Douglas and fell into the bay and drowned—well, he had once done a bit of mining in South Africa. Had the devil of a time to get a wee piece of gold for him before the burying." He tapped the tobacco in the bowl and lit one match, and then another, continually drawing until smoke came in a steady stream. "Me and the miner, Taggart, we got a lot in common. They take out and I put back in. Both work in the earth, both shovel and dig, but I always get the last word, eh. They can all say and do as they like, but I make the final decision for them. You can believe that or not, but I sometimes think of myself as the Final Miner." He stopped puffing on his pipe and looked up into the face of the other man. "You get my meaning, Taggart?"

"Yes."

"Aye, you always do. Probably the only one who really understands. You're a smart one, and there's no two ways about it." He paused a few moments, enjoying his pipe, then took it out of his mouth in a slow movement. "You got any ideas about the Jerry, then?"

"He'll need new clothes for a start."

"That won't be hard to arrange in my business. I can't guarantee a perfect fit, just approximate, you understand."

"I'm sure you'll come across something, Ogma. I don't know

how long he'll need a quiet place, and a job to keep him out of the way. Probably a few months at least, until the whole affair can be forgotten. Give him a chance to grow a beard and speak the language better. Fix him up with a background, and if things work out as they appear, perhaps have him join the Circle."

"He'll be ready for that?"

"Yes, I am quite certain. I did not tell you that he comes from Regensburg. I believe there is much more to him than meets the eye; the potential is certainly there."

"All right, Taggart, I'll be waiting for him."

"Good. He'll come around as soon as he's able."

VII

WILLIAM REACHED to grab one of the blankets that had slipped down on him in the night and gave a grunt as he moved his sore leg. He would have to be careful for a good month, if not longer, and also put up with the women's fussing over him. He had trouble deciding which was worse—not being able to do his work, or having them hover all the time.

He pushed himself up on his elbows and looked across to the other bed. The figure in it was still asleep and appeared not to have moved once during the night. William turned and glanced out the small window. The light was still faint, so it must be early morning. He knew the Head Druid wanted to move the soldier as soon as possible, and that it was probably time to wake him. The boy could only have slept six or seven hours; that was hardly enough. William was wondering whether to wait another hour or so, when there were footsteps in the hall, and the bedroom door opened. He turned his head as his wife walked in and started to cross the room.

"Fenella."

She turned at her name and came over to his bed.

"I thought you'd still be asleep. How does the leg feel this morning? Did it cause you any trouble?"

"It's as good as it should be, I suppose. Isn't that what woke me, anyway. Still worrying about what's to happen to Rolf."

"Yes. He's got enough trouble with those wounds, let alone having to hide out as well. What did you and Taggart plan last night, where is he going to be put?"

"It's supposed to be a secret."

"And who am I going to tell, the governor and the military?" Her eyes flashed in anger.

"It's really the Head Druid who says this; he's the one who thought it up." He saw the impatience in her eyes and hurried on. "We really think it's best if we keep Brigid away from him for a while, maybe not too long, but enough . . ."

"Brigid?" Fenella pulled her hand away and got up from the bed. "Did something hit you on the head from that bomb, William Crovan? That poor girl is almost mad from worry about the lad. She didn't get to sleep until long after—"

"It isn't Brigid we're worried about."

"What do you mean?"

"It's him—Rolf. We don't know enough about him."

"But William." She sat on the bed beside her husband. "He saved her life. She feels right about him, and so do I. Even the Head Druid admits that he is . . ."

"Rolf could be a threat to her world."

"But surely not."

"I know we all feel that way, Fenella. But there's too much at stake. You knew yourself, when it was your turn, that it was unwise to take any chances. If Brigid led the wrong person to the things she knows, it would complete the disaster that is already happening. The creatures of her world, the powers that she can contact, they have been the final force since the ancients—from first to last the unseen guides."

"But he won't do any harm," she insisted.

"Maybe he won't mean to do any harm, Fenella. But if he has power and doesn't know it, he could be dangerous for just that reason. Taggart is having a meeting of the full Druid council to talk it over, but until then he wants Rolf out of the way."

"You know that Brigid won't have to be asking anyone where he's got to. She has her own devices to find things out, and if that doesn't work she's got a host of others to do the searching for her. How long do you really think you'll be able to keep him hidden?"

"About a week, maybe more."

"A week? On this island? Why, that won't be possible. You'd have to ferry him to the Otherworld to keep him hidden for that length of time."

"You're almost close enough to be right."

"What do you mean?"

"We're sending him to stay with Ogma."

"With Ogma?" Her eyes widened with an incredulous stare. "But the man reeks of corpses."

"Exactly. Can you think of a better place? Who or what is going to go around him? It's as good as the devil himself."

"That horrid little man. Do you know he wanted to marry me once? No wonder you looked good to me then."

"You have a nice way of putting things, Fenella."

"Well, if you're seriously thinking of sending that poor wounded boy into the care of that . . . that gray dwarf, you don't deserve anything nice said about you. What's he supposed to do with him, anyway?"

"I don't know, my love. From the looks of him he'd make a very good mourner."

"Any more smart thoughts, William Crovan, and you'll get a whack on that sore leg that you're not like to forget."

"That's right. I imagine you're just waiting to do me in so you can run into the arms of your old love, Ogma, and settle down to the comfortable life of stitching up the clothes he steals from the dear departed."

They stopped speaking and looked at each other, then she bent over and kissed him on the forehead. She stood slowly. "All right, William, I won't say any more. Maybe there is some sense to it, but it's unpleasant all the same. I'd better go over and wake him, so he'll be ready for young Alice when she comes."

"Nay, spare us that. Is Mona's Murderer coming here so early?" Because he was speaking, he did not hear the footsteps, or the opening door. "Get young Alice and that old witch of her grandmother together, and you have the most gruesome set of ghouls that Manannan ever allowed to—"

"William—shh." His wife was staring at the door, looking troubled and amused at the same time.

"Don't shush me, woman." He got up on one elbow to find out what she was staring at. "You know as well as I that those foul-mouthed . . . " He saw the objects of his description glowering at him from the doorway. "Oh no," he said, as he slouched back on the pillows.

"Oh yes, old Billy." Alice and her grandmother came in and closed the door. "Your sisters of mercy have come once more, swift as the one-eyed stallion, to give you succour in your time of need."

"Oh no," he groaned again.

"Let me get my hands on that black-hearted bastard, Alice. You go and tend the Jerry." Her grandmother went to the bed and peered down at the face on the pillow. "And how is the leg today?" Her smile was unpleasant.

"Do you need any help, Alice?" Fenella turned away from her husband's bed before she laughed outright and walked to the other side of the room where the young woman was bent over the soldier.

"I'd just as soon let him sleep, but they did want him up and moving this morning, didn't they?"

"Yes, they've got a place for him already." Subdued swearing came from the other bed, and Fenella moved close to Alice so she could whisper in her ear. "I thought your grandmum would be done all in. I'm surprised to see her here at all, let alone so early."

"So's your old man, eh?" Alice smiled as another grunted curse came across the room. "Grandma will be given' him a goin'-to, you can bet right on that one." Alice lowered her voice. "She wanted to come and check on Jerry. She felt so grand about what we did last night. I think she was really worrying about not being so good at healing anymore. If she takes to old Billy with a vengeance, that may be more the reason."

"I hope she'll leave a piece of my man for me."

"He's going to have to put up with our digging for a while, missus."

"But he'll be all right?" Fenella tried to hide the concern in her voice.

"Yes. Yes, I think so. Took a bad turn this time, up near the hip. Lots of digging to get that straightened out." Alice turned to look at the sleeping man on the bed. "He's better off than Jerry here, anyway. Where are they going to take him?"

"I don't think I can tell you, Alice. The Head Druid wants it kept a grand secret."

"Well, me and gran will have to know, missus. We're going to have to be looking at him every day for quite a while yet."

"I hadn't thought of that." She looked past Alice to the figure on the bed. "They're going to have him stay with Ogma."

"Now that's not a pleasing choice," said Alice. "The lad is far from death's door. It will be quite a shock." Alice was about to say more when her grandmother called to her.

"Come finish old Billy off, my hands are tired." The old woman came across the room. "And try to ignore his foul language," her wrinkled face showed the trace of a smile. "You'd think he'd be a bit more civilized around ladies." Alice suppressed a giggle as she passed her grandmother and went to the other bed.

"Don't take that 'finish off old Billy' too serious, lass," he said as she placed her hands on his legs. And then, in a voice that could be heard in the whole room: "It's a bloody piece of business when they get the butchers working in relays."

The old woman bent over the soldier and felt his head, then placed her ear over his mouth and then his heart. She straightened and looked at the woman beside her. "That lot's normal; he hasn't taken any peculiar turns. We may as well wake him. Where's your girl?"

"Brigid?"

"Aye. It'd be better to have something nice for him to see when he wakes up."

"Brigid sat up with him most of the night, she won't have had much sleep."

"No matter. She's a young thing and can get it back. It'll be good for Jerry—go and get her."

As Brigid's mother left the room, the old woman went and stood beside Alice. William looked up at them both and then placed his hand over his eyes.

"Great Lug preserve me. The Buggane of St. Trinian's would leave the roof alone if you two flew past."

"And how does the leg feel now, you complaining old bastard?"

"Nay mind the insults. When will I be able to get moving around, and I mean more than a hobble."

"Well, old Billy," Alice looked at her grandmother, who gave the slightest of nods. "You've gone and done a bit more to it this time. It's going to take a while."

"How long, Alice?"

"You're going to have to be in bed for two or three weeks, and be careful after that for another couple of months."

"Is it that bad then? Is that why it hurts so much when you two take to me?"

"Yes, I'm afraid so." Alice paused before she went on. "That's one of the reasons grandma came along this time. She knows your leg a lot better than I do . . . "

"Aye, she's had more years of torture."

" . . . and you need the best job that can be done on you."

"Girl's right, Crovan." The old woman tapped his knee none too gently. "You've buggered yourself good this time. Old men should leave such things to the young ones."

"Aye," he pointed past the women toward the other bed. "There's your young one. You'll be seeing where it's got him."

"More fool both of you." The old woman muttered something beneath her breath, then decided to say it out loud. "I've been pickin' up the pieces of men's stupidity for over fifty years, and we'd be no better or worse if none of it had happened. The only one who benefits is Ogma. Undertakers never starve."

"Now even a senile old bitch like you can't be going to blame Hitler and his thugs on me. That aren't fair."

"Shh, shh," Alice looked from one to the other. "You'll be waking the Jerry boy with all your commotion."

"Well," the old woman kept staring at William. "It's time he was awoke anyway; they want him moved as soon as possible, don't they?" She glanced at Alice and then slowly walked to the other bed. "Where is the lass, anyway? We'll have to wake him without her."

"I'll go see," said Alice and left the room.

While she was waiting, the old woman pulled the blankets partially off the soldier and started to check Rolf once again. With mild proddings she went over his chest and torso, making sure that nothing was wrong. She checked his heart and breathing and had just started feeling the contours of his mouth and face, her own head almost touching his, when he opened his eyes.

"Mein Gott!" His voice had a tone of disbelief, and he tried to burrow back deeper into his pillow, while he brought up his arm to shove the figure away. The pain stabbed him immediately, and he gave a deep groan, his arm falling back to the bed.

"Are you mad, boy?" The old woman took a package out of her

skirt pocket and selected a pill from one of the containers. "You'll be damned lucky if it doesn't start the bleedin' again." She reached for a glass of water and held the pill near his mouth. "Well, take it, it isn't for staring at." Rolf looked at it dubiously and started to speak, but she interrupted him. "It's one of those new things, called the morphine. It'll help with the pain. Now don't make me shove it down your throat." Because she looked as if she would do it, he quickly swallowed the pill.

"At least you cause less trouble than . . . " Her sentence was interrupted by a commotion at the outside door of banging and yelling. At the same moment Brigid burst into the bedroom, followed by her mother and Alice.

"Rolf, are you all right?" Brigid ran to the bed.

"T'lad's all right, never mind him. What's wrong?"

"Someone's coming, that's all I know." Brigid was almost incoherent and grabbed at Rolf's hand.

"It sounds as if they're near ready to knock the door in."

"Nay, nay. It's a solid door." William spoke as he painfully swung out of bed.

"And where are you going?" Fenella ran over to stop him.

"I'm the master of the house, aren't I? Who else should answer?"

"What will we do about him?" asked Alice.

"Get him into the kitchen," he started to hobble from the room. "If it's necessary, Brigid, you try to get him hidden somewhere in the woods."

"You at least can let me help you to the door," said Fenella.

He leaned against her as they went into the hallway. The pounding on the door continued as Alice and Brigid helped Rolf get out of bed. They went with him as he walked unsteadily to the kitchen, while the old woman hurriedly gathered medicines and bandages. She threw the bed together so that it looked made and had just picked up Rolf's army jacket when William painfully returned.

"It was one of the Druids. He came to tell us that there was a British lorry coming along. They're hunting for the lad; they found his pistol on the beach. Someone told them about hearing my rifle last night, so they're coming here."

"How could anyone know it was your rifle?"

"Ah, the boys in these parts, they know their guns. It's no good getting him out into the woods; if they've got a truckload of Tommies they'll find him sure. I've sent the Druid on to get hold of Taggart, and Fenella's gone to tell the rest in the kitchen."

"There's nowhere in the house to hide him?" The old woman put down the things she was carrying, then sat on the bed.

"Here?" William lay back on his own bed. "Nay, there's nothing here. Our house is a bit larger than a lot of Manx cottages, but there's really nowhere to hide someone that wouldn't be found out right away. The loft is dark, but they'll have torches."

Rolf came back to the bedroom, followed by the three women. He looked at the injured man rubbing his leg.

"I must go, Herr Crovan. It is not right to be a trouble to your people, when you have helped me. Brigid says there is to be no hiding here."

"You can't run, lad, they'd be on you in no time."

"But the British are coming, yes?"

"Yes, you're right. But if they've got a lorry load of troops, they can search those woods well, and we don't have time to get you to some of the safer parts of the forest."

"Then I will get as far as I can and surrender."

"No." Brigid put her hand on Rolf's good arm and turned to her father. "We can't let him get captured; they'll put him away for the rest of the war."

"Brigit." He looked away from her and spoke to William. "I cannot be found with this family, in this house. It will cause trouble with all of you; they may make everyone here prisoners."

"Daddy," Brigid was near tears. "We've got to do something."

"Lass, I don't know what. There's no time anyway; they can't be far away. He'd best make a run for it."

"*Ja, ja*. This is the only thing to do. Get me my jacket, and I will go. The war will end sometime."

"Hush tha mouth, Jerry." They all turned and looked at the old woman sitting on the other bed. She shoved her bulk off the mattress and came over to the group. "With your shoulder you can't run any faster than this old cripple." She touched the other man on the foot. "You trip once and they'll hear you from here to Ramsey." She looked up and squinted into the young soldier's face. "You're a bother, lad, there's no two ways about it, but we might just save you."

"What do you mean, gran?"

"Well, my girl, it's a story my mam told me once—your grandmother. Funny story too, something she saw, but there's no time for the telling of it. About a man with a woman in his bed who wasn't his wife." She turned away from Alice and spoke to Brigid's mother. "Missus, you got any big quilts or blankets in the house, nice wide ones?"

"Yes, there's a special quilt for our double bed. And some blankets put away."

"Good. Go get them." Fenella started out the door, but the old woman called after her. "Where'd the lass sleep last night?"

"Why, with me." She looked at her husband. "In our bed."

"Good, good. There won't be an extra bed to explain. And bring any spare pillows you got. Hurry about it." The old woman turned toward Alice. "Get old Billy into bed, and when the British get here, start working on his leg again." Alice started to say something, but the old woman cut her off. "Never mind questions, just do it. And you," she hit William on his foot. "When those soldiers are here, I want you to moan and yell all you can. You do it enough anyway." She went over to the window and pulled the blind, making it very dim in the room. "You two, get over to the bed." Brigid and Rolf followed her directions, and she hurriedly started fixing the bedclothes. "Now here's what we're going to try. Jerry, you get in there and curl up on your good side, nice and comfortable, 'cause you might not be moving for a while. You, girl, get under the covers and pretend you're sick. We'll wait till your ma is back with . . ." She turned as Fenella came in carrying the extra bedclothes. "Good, let's be quick; they won't be too far away."

The old woman took the clothes already on the bed and pulled them down to the bottom. She pointed to the side next to the wall. "Lay as flat as you can, Jerry. We'll try to give you a little space to breathe." As he slid across the bed and settled beside the wall, a motor was heard roaring into the yard. While Rolf made himself as small as possible, the old woman reached over and snatched the pillow from under his head. "You won't be needing that. Now missus, you go let them in, and keep them talking as long as you can. The rest of you say as little as possible so we don't get caught out. Alice, start going at that quarrelsome old bastard there, and if he don't yell, give him something to yell about."

Fenella went to answer the hammering on the door, and the old woman hurried with her plan. "Lass, put those extra pillows where you're going to lay—that's right, they'll lift you up some. Start groaning, old Billy, make them hear you. That's good, they'll think there's a murder." As the old woman talked she placed the sheets and blankets over Brigid and then bunched the extra blankets and the large quilt over the now hidden figure of Rolf. "Close your eyes, lass, we're going to pretend you've gone queer. If I give you a poke start ranting about something."

"What, for God's sake?"

"I don't know—sunshine, food . . . " The voices in the outside hall became louder, and footsteps approached the bedroom. "Shush now. Jerry, can you breath?" She took the muffled grunt for a yes. "Don't move a muscle, you hear?"

"Gran." Alice's voice was urgent.

"What?" The old woman turned abruptly. "Don't scare me."

"His boots."

"Boots?" The old woman looked down by the bed leg. "Fucking hell." She grunted as she picked them up.

"I'll take them," William whispered harshly through his moaning. There was a hand on the doorknob as the old woman used all her strength to toss the boots across the room. Alice dodged as William reached and grabbed them in his hands. He stuffed them under his pillow and gave a loud grunt as the door opened.

Fenella was talking loudly to the two soldiers who followed her into the room. "I had no idea there were any Germans on the Island, major. Do you think we're safe by ourselves?"

"Certainly, Mrs. Crovan, certainly. My men are searching around your house right now. If there's any trace of them, we'll spot it."

Fenella stopped near her husband's bed. "William, this is Major Ross and Sergeant Baker. They heard it was you who shot at the plane last night, and they want to ask you some questions."

"Glad to help if I can, Major Ross. Sergeant. Young Alice, leave off my leg while I talk to the gentlemen."

"I really should keep at my work, Mr. Crovan. The best job is done right away, while I have your muscles loose."

"I'll only talk to him a minute or two, miss," said the Major.

"All right, sir," Alice smiled at him. "I guess that won't matter."

"Thank you." He turned toward William. "Did this happen to you last night, when the bombs fell on the beach?"

"That it did, Major. I'd banged it up before, but this made it worse."

"Did you see anything strange there last night?"

"The Nazis were dropping bombs on me."

"Yes, yes, of course. But I mean, was there anything else?"

"That was enough, Major; it don't happen all that often."

"Did you see anyone, Mr. Crovan?" The major sounded exasperated.

"When—last night?"

"Yes, on the beach, last night, when you shot at the bomber."

"Why, no sir. No one was there. Except my daughter."

"Your daughter?"

"Yes, Major. Brigid was with my husband last night." Fenella gave a short nod toward the other bed. "That's her."

"Did she get hurt, too?" Major Ross peered across the room. "It's so dark here that I hardly saw her."

"Well," Fenella groped for words. "I . . . "

"She's gone daft." The old woman got out of her chair by the other bed, which made the sergeant standing near the door give a slight jump. "That's why I got the room so dark." She left Brigid and came over to the other bed. "When she sees light, she thinks it's the bombs again and starts carrying on. You see, her mind's a bit funny, 'cause she thinks her old man here was killed when the bomb hit. We'll probably get her better, but she's always been a bit weak in the head."

"That's right, Major," William cut in. "Takes after her grandmother."

"Yes, I see." Major Ross looked uncertainly around him. "And you, er, you saw nothing else while you were on the beach?"

"The bomber was enough."

"The reason I ask," the major glanced around the room once again, "is that we found a German pistol near the water, not to mention some peculiar tracks in the sand. And, you know, the people around here act strange when we ask about this area. It's as if it were haunted or something."

"Well, Major Ross," Fenella looked into his eyes, "the Manx are a superstitious lot, and the war has put them on edge. They probably don't want much more than to be left alone."

"Yes, Mrs. Crovan, you may be right." Major Ross glanced over to the sergeant. "At any rate, we believe there might be some German soldiers around, so we have to search everywhere. I hope you don't mind if we look through the house."

"Of course not, Major. But do you really think someone could have entered the house without our knowing?"

Major Ross nodded to the sergeant, who picked up his rifle and left the room. "There's always the chance, Mrs. Crovan. They're very sneaky fellows, and sometime in the night he could have broken into the house, sneaked up into the loft. He might have even hidden under a bed. How many of us check under our beds, after all?"

There was a clunk from the other room as the sergeant bumped into something. "I wish your man could be a bit more quiet. Some unexpected noise might startle the girl. I'd better go back to her." The old woman went to the other bed and stood by Brigid. Brigid opened one eye, but the old woman put a hand on her forehead and pressed it shut. "The poor dear still has a bit of a fever," she called over her shoulder.

The Major stared at the other bed for a few moments, then spoke to Fenella. "I hope your daughter gets better soon."

"Thank you, Major Ross. The whole affair has been a shock to her."

"Yes," added William. "Thinking I was dead and all." He gave a loud grunt, which made the major look at him. "Sorry. I guess I turned when I shouldn't have." The boots dug into his neck.

They all turned as the sergeant came back into the room. "Nothing anywhere, sir," he said to the major. "Not a trace of anything out of place."

"What's left, Sergeant Baker?" asked the major.

"Nothing but this room."

"All right, get it done so we can leave these people alone. And Sergeant, please be as quiet as possible, so you don't wake the girl."

"Yes, sir." Sergeant Baker went over to the closet and poked in among the few clothes with his rifle. He went over to the bed where William lay and got on his hands and knees, first peering under the bed, and then sweeping across the space with his rifle. He inched back out and walked to the other bed. The old woman stood aside as he once again got on his knees and searched. His job finished, he grunted as he stood by the old woman.

"That's a pretty lass," he said, looking at Brigid.

"Yes. Yes, she is, poor dear," answered the old woman. She tried to move between the sergeant and Brigid, but he stood where he was.

"There seems to be a lot of blankets on the bed," he pointed with his rifle barrel.

"It's the fever, Sergeant." The old woman managed to squeeze her fat body between him and the bed and pretended to touch the girl's forehead. "Sometimes she's burning up and kicks all the clothes off her, and the next minute she's freezing and shaking so much that all the blankets in the house don't do much good. It's from the shock of last night."

The sergeant lowered his voice. "Is she really crazy?"

"Aye, as a coot."

"I had an uncle who was starkers," said the sergeant. "He was a market farmer, and one day he started saying that all the vegetables were out to get him."

"What happened to him?" The old woman was curious.

"Oh, they had to lock him away. He died there a few years later —choked to death while eating a carrot."

In spite of herself, Brigid started to giggle. She managed to keep her mouth shut, but her body was shaking. Sergeant Baker noticed this and looked down with concern.

"You were right, the poor lass is starting to shiver again. Here, I'll help you pull the covers on her." He started to reach across the bed for the large quilt.

The old woman, her squat body between her hand and the sergeant, reached over and pulled Brigid's ear as hard as she could. The girl opened her eyes and gave a loud shriek, which made the sergeant jump back in fright. The old woman gave another tug, and Brigid started ranting and screaming.

"Oh, my poor father, poor old father. Blown up into food for the fishes. Bang, bang, he blew apart, pieces of father going to the fishes. I hope they choke. Fishes throwing up my poor old father all over the ocean. We can bury him and sing little songs. I'll sing real good. Here's old dad, laid away, we buried him on the Island, a piece a day. The bomb blew him up, all over the place, we haven't yet found any of his face." Brigid gave a shudder, then started humming and moaning in tune.

"Sergeant." Major Ross called across the room. "I think we had better leave now."

"Yes, sir, thank you, sir." Sergeant Baker crossed the room and stood by the major. "There's nothing here, sir."

"Obviously." The major spoke loudly to drown out the girl's

humming. "I'm sorry for any trouble we've caused you, Mr. Crovan. I hope you understand it's a job we have to do."

"Of course, Major."

"We have to look everywhere."

"Certainly, Major Ross. And I hope you find who you're looking for."

Major Ross and the sergeant crossed to the door. Fenella quickly went past them and into the hall.

"I'll see you out," she said.

"Thank you, Mrs. Crovan," answered the Major. As she went along the hall, the two soldiers paused in the doorway and looked back into the bedroom.

"That girl's really a nut case, Major," whispered the sergeant.

"I wouldn't invite any of them to my home," answered the major, and they both hurried along the hall to the open door.

As soon as she heard the outside door close and her mother shove the bolt, Brigid jumped from the bed and hauled the covers off Rolf. He opened his eyes and blinked.

"Are you all right?" asked the old woman.

"Bitte," gasped Rolf, who was still entangled in the sheets. "Hit me on the nose, *schnell.*"

"Hit you?" The old woman looked puzzled. "I don't understand."

Brigid reached over to him. "Scratched, he wants his nose scratched." She moved her fingernails across the tip of his nose.

"Ja. Ach, ist gut." He stopped struggling, and the old woman reached as far as she could to loosen the sheets. Brigid's mother hurried into the room and crossed to the bed, while her father, with a great sound of satisfaction, pulled the boots from under his pillow and threw them to the floor.

"Bloody hobnails, almost broke my neck," he said, as he settled back on the bed. "How's the lad, Fenella?"

"He's all right, just an itchy nose."

"Good. Now would you get a couple of bottles of my best whisky, and give them to Alice's grandma. If anyone earned the best Irish there is, 'tis she."

The old woman was slumped in a chair by the bed, with her eyes closed. "Thanks to you, mister. But I wouldn't be minding a wee drop or two right now."

"Are you all right, gran?"

"Yes, child. Yes, I am. Just too old for all this, is all."

"You were wonderful," said Brigid, and she bent down and kissed the old woman on the cheek.

The old woman opened her eyes. "And you make a grand looney."

"That she does," called William. "I was just about to cry over my demise, what with all those fish spitting me up everywhere. That's quite a revenge the herring would get."

"I tried to imagine what a crazy person would be thinking. I thought that I would keep seeing you get blown up."

"Heh, heh, heh," the old woman's wheezing laughter came from deep inside her. "You near scared that sergeant to death when you first yelled. He jumped like a hare."

"I couldn't do much else when you pulled my ear."

"Served you right, starting to giggle like that."

"You shouldn't have asked about his uncle—choking on a carrot."

"A carrot, heh, heh," she wiped her eyes. "I had to know."

Fenella came back with two bottles under her arm and a large glass in her hand. The old woman took the two bottles and put one each into the large pockets on her skirt. She then took the glass and took a deep drink. She wiped her mouth and held up the glass.

"That's to the bloody British army, may they win the war and get off the Island."

The Head Druid arrived in time to meet the troops leaving down the road. As soon as he found everything was all right, he told Rolf to be ready to leave within the hour. He arranged to have Alice or her grandmother visit the wounded man every day and cautioned Brigid to be patient. He then hurried away again, intent on other business.

VIII

MANANNAN'S MIST was a memory by the time Taggart reached his destination. His long strides had taken him unheeding through fields and glens as he moved steadily inland. These last days of summer were beautiful, and he usually enjoyed the warmth and pleasant smells. He had a dull feeling, however, that there might be little time left for the pleasures of life.

The Head Druid paused by a small stone gate. It had been a long walk and he felt tired. He wanted to get counsel from all the other Druids and would do so eventually. But first he needed reassurance that his feelings were correct, that his vision was not being misunderstood. Events would happen too quickly to allow any time for mistakes.

He went through the gate and walked up the sloping track between the towering trees. The path narrowed even more as it wound up the side of the hill, and the large trees blocked most of the sunlight, making Taggart's walk cool and dim. At the final turning the path abruptly stopped at two large dark oaks. Taggart had to squeeze through the narrow opening between the trees and came out the other side in the midst of a small clearing. At the center was a circular stone well, beside which sat the woman he had come to see. The only female Druid on the Island, she tended this sacred well. She sat with her back to Taggart, her long black hair falling over the white shift she wore. As he watched, she picked a fallen hazelnut by her feet and tossed it into the water. It bobbed on the surface for a moment, then a large red fish leaped, took the hazelnut in its mouth, and disappeared back into the inky gloom.

"Hello, Katherine."

She rose and turned to meet him, the sleeve of her gown trailing through the water. Her wide brown eyes mirrored the healthy glow of her face as she smiled. She stepped forward, the leaves casting shadows across her slender face. Tall for a woman, she did not have to look up as far as most people to see into his eyes.

"Taggart. You leave things late."

"I can do nothing until it is time."

"Your time is like the summer days. It gets shorter, the leaves start to fall." She came toward him, holding out her hands. "Your visits are too widely spaced."

"I am rarely the master of my hours, Katherine." He took both her hands and then kissed her. He was aware, as always, of her scent and her strength. He released one of her hands and led her to a small bench near the well. "There is the chance, you know, that if I came as often as I wished, I would have time to do little else."

"Are you waiting for me to get old and gray?"

"A woman of thirty has no worry of that happening for a long time yet to come."

"Perhaps, Taggart. But do you choose to ignore that we may not be allowed our allotted time?"

"Yes, Katherine. I sometimes choose to ignore that possibility."

"But no longer?"

"No. In fact, our chances seem to disperse with the mist."

"And you come to me," she stared into his eyes. "For what?"

"When all is said, I suppose I want to be told that what I already know is true."

"Everything is red, Taggart."

"Red, yes." He paused to stare at her. "The color of death."

"The clouds are red when the sun rises," her eyes did not leave his face. "And red again when it goes down. Red doe begats red fawn, the birds fly red feather and wing. The flowers confuse the bees with their same color. And it is always red fish, Taggart, jumping in the well and splashing in the stream. There are no silver fish, no flashes in the depth."

"You point a steady finger."

"All else is illusion, Taggart. A mirror reflects a lie; beware of what is backward."

"It is to start here?"

"Yes," she let go of his hand. "Somewhere on the Island."

"And soon?"

"Yes, Taggart. Seven settings of the sun at most, two daybreaks at the least."

"That is less than . . . "

"Red, Taggart."

"What?"

"Red is the color of fire."

"Fire here on the Island?"

"In time, it will return. Start and finish will be on the Island. Islands of fire, seas of flame, cities and people will scream and turn black. Die and turn black."

"Can it be stopped?"

"Yes." Her eyes were closed now, her head swaying to and fro with each word. "All things can be stopped. Every movement breeds its own destruction. That is the way of the Order. No man or beast, no thought or force, are independent."

"How can you be sure, Katherine?"

"There is no permanence, so all can be changed."

"Will this be stopped?"

"All things can be changed," her voice was a child's voice, almost singing when she replied.

"Will . . . this . . . be . . . stopped?" Taggart leaned toward her.

"All things can change."

"Katherine?"

"All things can change, all things can change." The words were hurried, tripping over each other as they raced from her mouth. Her whole body rocked with the tempo of the words. "All things can change."

"Katherine." He took hold of both her hands. "Come back to me now, you've told enough."

Her hands were slack, her head tossing from side to side. She started to slip from the bench, and Taggart had to put his arm around her to keep her from falling. He had rarely seen her this bad and wondered whether the vision was taking her too far. He knew that the things she saw were sometimes unspeakable.

"Katherine," he spoke directly into her ear. "Don't try to do too much. There is time; you've told me that there is still time; don't do it all at once."

"Can change can change can change." She was getting breathless, the words were becoming softer. Her body was slumping, the frantic motions became more subdued.

"Katherine," he had to put both arms around her and hold her next to him. "It is all right, try to come back."

"Change." Her head lay against his shoulder, the words now spaced by deep breaths. "Change." Her body stopped its intense shaking, and she moved gently against him.

"That's right. That is good. It will be like waking up, just open your eyes." He wiped sweat from her face. "Just . . ."

"It will take you." Her voice was low.

"What?"

"To stop the fire." She leaned against him now, not moving. "It will take all of you."

"Who, Katherine?" He raised her head so he could look into her face. "What can be done?"

"The Druids, the stranger, the virgin, and . . ." Katherine was breathing regularly now, as if slowly waking from sleep.

"And who?" Taggart almost shook her but thought better of it. "How can it be stopped?"

"The beasts," she slowly opened her eyes. "Especially the one-horned, the power of ivory. The purity." She blinked her eyes, sat upright. "The stranger and the ivory will help you most. But you, Taggart, you must join them at the right moment or the flood's work will be repeated by flame." She closed her eyes again.

"Katherine."

"I am all right, Taggart. The power has passed. I must rest now." She leaned against the smooth tree bark, picked a leaf off the bench. "Would you get me a drink of water?"

"Of course," said Taggart. He made certain that she could sit by herself, then walked to the well and filled the silver cup, plunging deeply beneath the surface of the water. A one-eyed fish leaped over his arm, snapped a colorful insect into its mouth with a wink, and slid back into the water without a ripple. Taggart carried the dripping cup to the bench and handed it carefully to the woman. She raised it to her lips, then hesitated, and finally held it away from her.

"Oh, Taggart," her voice was nearly a whisper. "You must hurry."

"What is it, Katherine?" His voice held concern.

"You must act quickly," she said and turned over the cup. A stream of blood poured to the ground, poured and poured as if it would never end.

IX

"Spades is trump, lad, there's no need to ever be asking that. Around here spades is always trump." Ogma slapped down a card on the fallen gravestone. "And there's the ace, that takes everything in the end." Ogma gathered the worn cards together and slipped them into one shirt pocket, taking his pipe out of the other. "Have a smoke before I go back to cutting away those bushes." He lit the pipe, striking a couple of matches to do so, and puffed a ball of smoke around his head before he spoke again. "That shoulder bothering you?"

"*Ja.* It has the pain. Coming here in the wagon—I know you attempted the most easy way over the road, but I still was shaken."

"That back road's a bitch for sure, especially when you had to be under the burlap. All for the better, though. Those Tommies took one look at the pine box sticking out the back and didn't come near us. Nothing soldiers hate more than to be reminded of death." Ogma pointed to Rolf's shoulder. "One of the women will come to look at that soon's the dark is here. Pray it's the girl and not the old witch—that mistake of God should have been in the ground years ago. Would give me great pleasure, that would."

"Brigit has said she saved my life."

"Aye, the old terror knows her job." Ogma moved closer to Rolf and lowered his voice. "But if you stop to think of it, lad, has she really done you a favour?"

Rolf was puzzled. "What do you mean?"

"Well, look at it this way." Ogma stopped a moment to keep his pipe going. Once the smoke was streaming from it, he started speaking again. "Alice or her fat old grandma fix you up, get you running around doing your work or poking it into Brigid, and where . . ."

"What is that with Brigit?" Rolf was having a difficult time understanding this strange man. He was helping him hide, and the tall leader said he was all right. But he seemed to dislike everything, and just by the way he smiled, Rolf felt it was something unpleasant about Brigid. He could guess what the smile meant.

"You know what I mean, lad." Ogma sucked on his pipe and winked. "I'm not so old as to forget what young men think of with their women; I can still . . ."

"Brigit is not a woman who belongs to me."

"Ah, lad, women, women—that's all they're for. And each time you do it, it's like a death, all that grunting and moving as you dig into a little hole. Groaning away and gasping for breath as if it all really meant anything. Fooling yourself, lad, if you think any of them love you, because it's only their way of having power. And when it's all over, you couldn't be any quieter than if I laid you out in a casket myself. That's all it really is, people just fool themselves if they think any different."

Rolf did not like the conversation. "It is time we went to work the bushes, yes?" He moved his leg as if to stand.

"I'm trying to tell you something, lad." Ogma's voice was rough with the beginnings of anger, and his face remained tense until he saw Rolf settle back. "The bushes can wait, there's nothing worth rushing about around here."

"If you say." Rolf was now keeping a cautious watch on the other man.

"There's no one who knows it better, lad." Ogma scratched the side of his head. "I've seen it all, seen them all acting out their lives." The sweep of his hand could have indicated the graveyard or the world. "And they've all ended up here, no matter what they did or where they did it. Just like when you're with a woman, you grind away and then it's all over, it doesn't mean anything." His pipe had gone out, but he paid no attention to it. "Just like when that fat old woman dug out your arm, what's she really done for you? It will all end sometime; it's the same shuffle to the grave if you get there tomorrow or the year after or sixty years from now. I can't be cheated, lad." Ogma pointed from one grave to another to another. "I got them all, whether they scratched and clawed trying to get away, or they just sat there, that final revelation on them. If they were rich they got planted lying on satin; if they was poor they bumped around in pine. They could stink from the sea or waste away to a shadow, go at childbirth or get mangled in machinery." The small man gripped Rolf's knee. "But do you know what, lad?"

"*Was?*" Rolf felt a bit of fear.

"Do you know what they're doing now?" He let go of Rolf's knee and patted the ground by his foot. "They're all down there, waiting for us to come and join them. They're all the same now, white bone and grinnin' teeth, all mixed together in a jumble. All they were proud about, that they patted and perfumed, strong muscle or rich fat, fine flowing hair or work-hard back, deep blue eyes or sweet-tasting lips—do you know what it all is now, lad, do you know where it all went? It's turned, lad, gone into worms and turned to shit." He pounded his fist on the ground. "Worm shit, that's what's waiting for us, and nothing more. So that old woman saved you, eh? Patched you up, and they want me to keep you safe, thinking you'll marry Brigid and everything will go on as usual." Ogma stared into Rolf's eyes and then slowly looked away. "You only live a second, lad, when that cold air hits you in the face for the first time, and then it's just a slow death. And everything you do, everyone you love, all the grand ideas that you have, they're nothing more than ways to forget what you got waiting for you." Ogma turned back to Rolf and glared at him, making him tense his muscles. "You think you're in love with Brigid, don't you?"

"*Mit* Brigit?" Rolf wished desperately that she could be here now. This old man made him feel worse than when he was shot. "*Ja*, I think of Brigit as . . ."

"Well, you don't." Ogma pointed his empty pipe at Rolf's chest. "It's all a lie, there's no love anywhere. It's all attempts to forget the grave, is all. You start feeling alone, so you hunt for someone else and call it love. Do you think there'd be such a fuss made of it, ballads and stories and ceremony, if people didn't really doubt? If love were such a real thing, there wouldn't be any need of all this convincing. Clinging together, spurting out seed to make yet another desperate life, because the more miserable people there are, the less miserable we feel." Ogma's gray face was now flushed to a peculiar mottled color, and he settled back as if exhausted, putting his pipe into his pocket. He had just closed his eyes when a noise from the brush made him jump to his feet, with Rolf close behind. They turned to see the Head Druid come into view, followed by Brigid. In the distance they caught a glimpse of white from the corner of their eyes and heard sounds on the falling leaves.

"The sad thing, Rolf," said Taggart as he stepped closer, "is that Ogma really believes most of that foolishness."

"What's she doing here?" yelled Ogma as he rushed forward. "You said that she wasn't supposed to see him. It's dangerous enough without any silly girl mooning around in heat." He had to dodge aside as Brigid rushed past to be with Rolf. "All this will come to no good, Taggart. You shouldn't have brought her."

"Calm down, Ogma." The Head Druid placed a hand on the small man's shoulder. "If it makes you feel better, you can pretend that she just wants to forget death for a while and so came here to share her misery." He looked over Ogma's head at the two young people, holding hands and gazing at each other. "They hide their suffering well, don't they?" He glanced back to Ogma. "I had nothing to do with her being here; I met her a short distance back just a moment ago."

"But how did she know?" Ogma's voice was shrill.

"She wasn't alone."

"What do you mean, Taggart?" He spun around to look at Brigid. "Has she got the whole Island farting around out there?"

"It wasn't a person with her, Ogma. She's not meant to be away from him."

"Not a person," he slowly turned to Taggart. " 'Twas the unicorn that brought her here, then, showed her where to go."

"Yes."

"I understand not hearin' you, Taggart, now I know how she got through the brush without any sound. You gave us a start, I thought maybe my time had come, you can believe that or not."

"I have doubts, Ogma, that your time is ever going to arrive." He stood closer to the short man and lowered his voice. "Have you learned anything about the lad?"

"He seems to be what he seems to be. He doesn't want to talk about why he's on the Island, but I think 'tis just he doesn't want to break his honor. He has strong feelings about his damned military code—giving away secrets and things like that."

"Don't be harsh, Ogma; you wouldn't trust him at all if he acted differently."

"I don't trust him now." Ogma glanced back at Brigid and Rolf. "Yon lass can grow till she reaches the heavens and smite the Island in half, and all the beasts can join together to sing Jerry's praises, and King Orry himself can lead me to heaven along Raad Mooar Ree Gorry, and I'll still not shake the feeling that there's something wrong with the boy."

"Ogma, you've said yourself that you can't find anything the matter with what he does—or says."

"I'll tell you what it is." He grabbed Taggart's sleeve, his strong fingers pulling the tall man after him. "I'll show you what it is." Ogma led the Head Druid across the yard to the newly dug grave. "I've worked with them all my life; I've planted more people than you know. I've picked them up, scraped them up, cleaned them up, and hunted for the pieces. I've cut them out of machines and been to my elbows in pus from bloated fishers. They've come old and brittle, and fresh from their mother's belly. Some so old you'd swear there was nothing in their clothes, or so beautiful in youth you'd think a touch would wake them. I've sat with the children and waited for them to get up and play. Some of the women have been so beautiful that I've been tempted to lay beside them. I've had to bury ashes—whole families of ashes, looking like you've left bacon too long in the pan. Yes, and the lover who murdered, with the widdy still around his neck after the hangman was done. They've all come to me, and I've put them all away. For years I've cleaned up the mess." His eyes glittered and his voice shook. "And Taggart, I've found something out, something about them, something they all have in common. No matter who they are, or how they go, they all have the smell. They all have the stink of death on them, as plain as any perfume. Washing the body don't get rid of it—nothing can. It's in the hair and on the clothes." Ogma turned from the Head Druid to point at the couple near the water. "And it's on him. It gets worse, and it is stronger than ever. I can smell death on him, Taggart, like I've never done on anyone." Ogma reached down and picked up a clod of dirt. He crushed it in his hand and threw the pieces into the open grave by his feet.

They scattered across the bottom of the pit, and a small cloud of dust came from the dry earth. "If I took my pick at him right now, we'd be the better off."

"There'll be none of that, Ogma."

"Aye, I thought not."

"If what you think is true—and I can't deny that I feel unsure about the lad myself—we still have to find out why he is here. No matter what he appears, I'm certain that if destruction is around him, he does not really know it. At worst he's some sort of instrument that is going to be used."

"Maybe, Taggart. But used how?"

"That's what we're to find." Taggart stared down toward Brigid until she looked up, then inclined his head to show he wanted them to come back. As she took Rolf's hand and started up the slope, the Head Druid lowered his voice. "If the time comes to do something drastic, I don't want you acting on your own, Ogma. Decisions will be left to the Druid council, or, if there is no time, then I will make them. For the moment, there does not seem to be any danger." Taggart started to cross the field to meet Brigid and Rolf. "It would also be nice, Ogma, to keep your depressing ideas to yourself. The lad is in enough pain."

Brigid and Rolf slowly came up the hill, talking and laughing. Rolf could not keep his eyes from her face, and occasionally he forgot and reached to touch her with the hand in the sling. Regardless of the coarse gray suit that Ogma had found for him, he still walked like a soldier, and the Head Druid felt it was a thin disguise.

"Rolf," Taggart called to him.

"*Ja.*" He looked away from Brigid, startled.

"You're going to have to learn to slouch, lad. Don't move about as if you were on a parade ground." Taggart went toward them. "Come with me, I want to talk to you."

"May I come?" Brigid's voice was anxious.

"Yes, it's all right." Taggart pointed to the small church. "We may as well go into the *keeill.*" He herded them toward it. "The three of us together are too noticeable out here." As they walked around the corner of the church, Ogma returned to clearing away brush, keeping a careful watch for anyone who might come.

The Head Druid opened the door and followed Brigid and Rolf into the small building. Although larger than many of the ancient churches on Man, it was still only nine yards long by five yards wide. The first foot of the walls consisted of field stone, while the final foot was made of mud and clay. The peaked roof was held in place by narrow timbers and thatched with straw. Even in the full sun, not much light came through the small windows, making most of the interior appear lost in gloom. Taggart led them to one of the rough pews, and they sat with Rolf in the middle and the Head Druid on the aisle. They let their eyes adjust to the dim light, and then Rolf nervously cleared his throat and spoke to the Head Druid.

"May I ask you something that is a problem to me?"

"Of course, Rolf, any question at all."

"Danke—I mean, thank you, Herr Taggart." He was plainly nervous, so Taggart did not rush him. "What I do not understand, is that we are in this church. This is a Christian church, yes, like the one my parents and I went to, for Jesus Christ and God and the Holy Mary. Am I not right about that?"

"Yes, Rolf, this is a Christian church."

"Excuse me, Herr Taggart, I do not want to cause offense, but this is not of your religion, or that of Brigit. You tell me that your beliefs are of long ago, even before Jesus. Is it not wrong that we should be in this place? What are you doing here?"

"This is my church, Rolf."

Rolf was more confused than ever and felt embarrassed by his confusion. He stared at the Head Druid, glanced over to Brigid, and then returned to look at Taggart. "I do not understand. What do you mean that it is your church?"

"I am the minister here, Rolf—the parson."

"But," the young soldier's mouth fell open. "But you are also the chief of the Druids."

"Yes."

"But how can you be both?"

"It all depends on to whom I'm talking."

Rolf closed his mouth, but he was still perplexed. "I do not understand, Herr Taggart."

"It makes things much easier, Rolf, that's all." Taggart touched the soldier's knee. "You see, there is not much difference between our old religion and the new one of the Christians. We both have one major god and believe in an immortal soul. We both prefer honesty and truth and have strong ties to knowledge. We believe all people have rights and should be treated justly. When the early Christians and their fervent zeal—such as all young religions possess—confronted the old Celtic order, instead of excessive conflict, most of the ancients decided to incorporate themselves into the church. Many Druids became priests, while Archdruids became bishops. There were, of course, those who wanted the old ways, and some fighting and bloodshed occurred. But today, Rolf, for the most part, we are content to come to church, follow the rituals, and keep our own secrets."

"Such as the unicorn."

"Yes, Rolf, and other things as well. Strictness and age have made Christianity far more rigid than it used to be. For instance, in the Holy Bible, the unicorn is mentioned seven different times, from Numbers to Isaiah. Some of Brigid's favorite phrases come from these sources."

"The one I like best," said Brigid, "is in Numbers 23:22: 'God brought them out of Egypt; he hath as it were the strength of the unicorn.' But I'm also fond of Job 29:9: 'Will the unicorn be willing to serve thee, or abide in thy crib.'" Brigid smiled and stroked Rolf's cheek with her fingers. "Try not to think that all this is very strange. Our people are more interested in truth than in whom to worship."

"I find it difficult to believe." Rolf turned from Brigid back to the Head Druid. "The Druids and their teachings have just been stories—talk from the past. And now, here you and your people are, and the unicorn, yes, I have to believe in what I see. I cannot ignore my eyes."

"It should not be that hard, Rolf." Taggart shifted slightly on the hard pew, attempted to get more comfortable. "We are not detracting from the church; if anything, we help retain much of the mystery that the modern age has taken from religion. Our powers, and the forces we control, are all part of the unseen supernatural that is the basis of any religion. It is the trend of taking supernatural God from the churches to replace Him with a system of morality that is ruining religion—not us. Obviously, in a 'rational' age, we keep most of our secrets among ourselves. They have no less the power because of that." Taggart stopped speaking, and the small church was quiet as Rolf thought over what he had just heard.

"What is strange, Herr Taggart, is that I do not think of these things you tell me, and what I have seen, as a surprise. I do not understand this; my training is to make me one who is sensible, yes? And yet, here I am feeling the strong desires for Brigit and working for a gravedigger."

"Then it's time I asked some questions about your past. You may know more about our ways than you realize."

"Anything you wish, Herr Taggart; I will tell you all that I can. But there is nothing like any of this, which I have seen in the last couple of days."

"I'm most concerned with the place where you were born, Rolf, and the things you think about and like or dislike."

"You want to know about Regensburg?"

"Yes. What it means to you."

"Regensburg? Well, Herr Taggart, Regensburg is the most beautiful place in the world." Rolf stopped a moment and stared in front of him. "I miss *die Rettich*—the radishes, the huge white radishes." He turned excitedly to Brigid. "They are as big as your hand, sometimes much larger. And they taste so wonderful . . . " He turned quickly back to the Head Druid. "When you were in Regensburg, Herr Taggart, did you not have some of the radishes?"

"Radi und Bier? Of course I did, Rolf; there is nothing like your white radishes washed down with beer."

"Ja, ja. You have had them. And you are right, it is a taste of itself." He grabbed Brigid's hand and looked at her. "You will come sometime, Brigit, when all this is done. I will show you my city, and we can have the radishes together. Yes, that is what I want, the two of us to go through Regensburg." He stopped speaking, still clutching her hand and looking in her eyes.

"I'd like that, Rolf, very much."

"Then we will. We will." Rolf turned slowly to the Head Druid. "Regensburg is more than just a place to live for me. I feel that I am a part of it; yes, the buildings and the rivers are to me as old friends. When I would feel bad about something, or lonely, even when I was a small boy, a child, I would go and walk through the city and it would make me feel better. I am not close to people, or my family, so I go walking. The most friends I have been was when I was *ein Domspatz,* in the choir of the cathedral. We were called the Cathedral Sparrows and had a lot of the fame in that part of Germany. But I was quite young then; my voice has not such a good sound now." Rolf paused and smiled to himself. "I was dressed more nicer then." He touched the coarse sleeve of his old jacket and frowned. "I would always go across *die Steinerne Brücke*—the Old Stone Bridge—on my walks. Summer or winter, it was always part of my walk to go across the bridge. Sometimes I would stand in the middle for half an hour or more, crossing from side to side and watching the lights in the city. That is one of the last things I did before I left for the army." Rolf stopped for a long moment, his mouth slightly open. "I am so afraid that it will be destroyed by the bombs." He looked down, his voice shaking. "What would I do then?"

"You'd stay here, Rolf," Brigid's voice was low.

"I would try." Rolf raised his head. "Yes, where else would I go now?" He gave her hand a quick squeeze.

"Where else would you walk, Rolf?"

"Oh, yes, Herr Taggart," Rolf smiled at the Head Druid, "I was thinking elsewhere, yes?" He released Brigid's hand and continued talking. "I would do different things, so the walk would not get to repeat itself. Most often, my favorite way was to go along Thundorferstrasse, and under the trees. Then through the Alter Kornmarkt, past the Old Chapel, back along Schwarze Bären Strasse, Pfauengasse, Residenzstrasse, and Kamgasse to the Baumburger Tower. There I would sit on the steps of the Rathaus for some time before I went home. I live about fifteen minutes away, not far from the river. The old part of the city is lovely. I had a room at the top of our house, with a tiny window and its own tiled gable. And, when I became older, I would stop in at some of the taverns, yes, and have some glasses of beer. *Weiss,* yes, a beautiful beer made from the wheat, and with a slice of lemon. Those were good nights."

"You would do this often?"

"Yes, Herr Taggart. I would walk through the city two or three nights a week. It was always a—to make me easy—a relaxation, yes, it was more easy to go to bed."

"I can imagine you did a fair share of sleeping with all that beer you had in you," said Brigid. "I'll be hoping that beer is all you took home with you from those taverns."

"What does she mean, Herr Taggart?" asked Rolf with a wink.

"Why, I'm not sure, Rolf. It could have something to do with country matters, but that would not concern someone from the city now, would it?"

"Men," Brigid snorted. "Age and homeland mean nothing; they all have the same ideas."

"That's enough talking for today, Rolf." The Head Druid stood and stretched his legs. "It is time Brigid and I . . . "

"Herr Taggart," Rolf jumped to his feet. "I almost forgot the ruins, the old Roman ruins at the Niedermünster Kirche. You could see so much history at once."

"Yes, Rolf," Taggart waited for the other two to go ahead of him. "History is very important." He followed them out of the *keeill* and made certain Rolf was in the safe care of Ogma, before he and Brigid went their own ways. There was much work waiting for him tomorrow.

X

IT WAS a cold morning, unusual for an early autumn day that saw the sun shining from a nearly cloudless sky. Taggart walked briskly up the mountain road, the sharp wind stinging his clean-shaven face. He had on his thick white tunic, which went below his knees, and his woven black pants. He carried his carved oak staff in his right hand, and he occasionally tapped the road when some thought bothered him. Anyone who met the Head Druid quickly stepped aside without a second's thought, and watched him pass sensing of menace in him. Taggart was not a man to stop or question today.

Halfway up the mountain Taggart left the road and continued along a rutted track. It passed through some scraggly brush for half a mile, until it entered the open fields of a small farm. The smell of harvest was in the air as Taggart walked along the edge of the large market garden. He heard noises from the back of the barn, so he went around the building. He found a thick-set man attempting to fix the spokes of a broken wagon wheel. The man moved with some difficulty, the years having lessened his physical abilities. His long beard, although almost white, still had traces of its original dark color. Taggart walked up beside him and helped to steady the wheel.

"I've been expecting you, I have." The older man barely looked in the Head Druid's direction. "And you won't be here to talk about preparations for the rites of Samhin."

"Surely, Jeremy, you mean the feast of All Hallow's."

"Some of us still like the old terms," he said with a wink.

"Old ways, new ways," Taggart turned the wheel. "They may be all gone soon, equal in oblivion."

"You know, Taggart," the other man tapped a spoke into its hole. "You'll not be pleasing company with that kind of talk."

Taggart gave a rough chuckle and propped the wheel against the wagon. "Why aren't your sons doing this for you, Jeremy? You are supposed to rest these—"

"Because I won't let them, is why." He placed his hammer near the wheel and slowly straightened his back. "A man's got to be doing something, or he's just eating food and making shit."

"You've done enough in your life."

"And there's no need of stopping now, Taggart, is there? The white hairs don't call for that."

"We'll be needing you for far more than fixing wheels, Jeremy. You'd best take care of yourself for a while yet. You said that you knew I would be coming."

"Aye, Taggart. You can feel it all around."

"With all this trouble, why do you spend time fixing a wheel?"

"Oh, I've got faith in you, lad. Besides, one may as well go with a fixed wheel as with a broken one." As he spoke he took a battered pipe from a pocket and began filling it with tobacco from a small drawstring bag. "You'll be wanting to call the Druid council, won't you?" As Jeremy spoke he glanced behind him. "Let's sit and be comfortable, Taggart." Jeremy led him to the turf pile, and they both sat on a stack of the drying fuel. "When do you want the meeting?"

"Tonight."

"Have you spoken to the others yet?"

"Not yet, Jeremy. I thought that I'd start with you."

"You'll be wanting a full council, I suppose."

"Yes. This is as sacred as any meeting we have ever had. Our worship at the festivals can be no more important than our joining tonight. The power that we shall need will start to flow, from us to all the other forms of existence. The ancient times surround us in every idea, every particle of earth. We need the past and the present to make our future, and we need their help more than ever now."

"And what is to happen?"

"There will be no more birth and only death. The German soldier . . . "

"Was that all that shootin' t'other night?"

"Yes. This soldier has come to us for a reason. He seems to be the one intended for Brigid, yet he is more than that. I believe he's a part of our distant power, in line from some past Druids who left the Island centuries ago. Our actions can muster enough force to combat almost anything, but the puzzle is where we are to aim it." Taggart paused in his speech and stared at the moss on the back of the barn. He seemed to be listening to something from far away.

"What is it, Taggart?" asked Jeremy, taking the pipe from his mouth.

"Whenever I think of Rolf, the German boy, I hear the laughter of the fairies, far away and high on the air, mocking me. It's as if they were saying, 'If only you knew, if only you knew.'"

"Knew what?"

"They never tell. Yet I feel the same way about him. Somehow, in spite of himself, he is not only the key to the solution, but also the core of the problem."

"Can one man be both?"

"A man who passionately loves a woman is the one most likely to kill her. There are no worse enemies to any cause than people who have turned against it. I think he has the power of midnight, the joining of two days. He will choose his destiny at the second it is offered." Taggart rubbed his large hands against his legs. "Whether that will be Brigid and her life, or the something other that must inevitably oppose it, I cannot say. I can only listen to the laughter on the wind."

"Taggart, if you do not trust him, the man is not safe to have around, no matter who or what feels otherwise."

"You doubt the unicorn, Jeremy?"

"Oh, that it's magical, I don't deny. I cannot be a Druid this long and ignore the power of magic. 'Tis the beasts have helped us as much as we have them, I suppose." Jeremy shifted his rump on the slab of turf beneath him. "But to me, Taggart, for all their powers, they still don't know how to reason like a man. It's all instinct— a powerful instinct, I'll grant you, that can do marvelous things—

but just instinct none the less. I'll trust my cat to know when there's a storm in the air, but I won't let him . . . " Jeremy looked around and then picked up his hammer. "I won't let him help me fix this wheel. That takes skill and reason."

"Cats aren't supposed to fix wheels," Taggart said with a laugh. "And men aren't supposed to catch mice."

"To each his own, you mean."

"Yes. We all have our purpose, no matter how seemingly important or insignificant. None of us knows enough to really judge the worth of another, let alone how he fits in the grand scheme."

"Or the grand illusion," Jeremy relit his pipe.

"Every illusion has something behind it."

"Maybe," replied Jeremy. "But what might be back of that?"

"That's not for us." Taggart touched the other man's knee. "We have enough to deal with here."

"'Tis true enough, I suppose." He puffed a moment on his pipe. "So, what are you going to do with the German boy?"

"I have him staying with Ogma."

"Ogma?" The other Druid looked curiously at Taggart, then his beard quivered with laughter. "You really don't trust the boy, do you?"

"It's not just a matter of trust." Taggart stood and stretched his legs while he spoke. "It's a grand place to keep Rolf out of view; not many go around spying on Ogma. He is the most observant man on the Island; what he doesn't see, he hears, for all secrets finally find their way to the gravedigger. Ogma, if need be, can extract secrets from the dead."

"Like most people on the Island," the other Druid also stood, "I care to see Ogma as little as possible, although he'll have the final say about that sooner than I wish." He pointed his pipe at Taggart. "But everything you've said is true enough; I can't think of a better man to get the job done."

"No, Jeremy, there isn't."

"Ah well, more's the pity that he is so unpleasant."

"Some would say that he has an unpleasant job."

"I don't know, Taggart; at least no one talks back to him."

"Maybe having Rolf for a while will change him." Taggart reached for the staff he had laid against the turf pile. "If he is there for long, that is. This thing will be done in the next few days, and what happens beyond that is a question."

"Ogma won't change, whatever is done." Jeremy tapped out his pipe and placed it in a pocket. "I'll see you to the gate then. You'll be having a long day of it to get us together."

"Yes, I'm going to have to use the motor to cover the Island."

"Pah, ugly things, stink and noise." The two men walked past the barn and along the rutted track. "They should never have let the dirty things on the Island; horse and wagon are good enough."

"It will be welcome transport today, Jeremy, when I must do things quickly. I'm fortunate that there is no one on the Calf to summon."

"Say what you will, Taggart, you won't get me in one."

"There are so many people now, Jeremy, that they can't all live in the same villages and towns. They cover more land; you need new ways to get to them. Only fools try to stop the change."

"And old men."

Taggart smiled. "You've a while yet before Ogma prepares your final resting place. Think of the pleasure you'll give him."

"Nay," Jeremy shook his head, "the man's too cold for pleasure."

When they passed the garden, Taggart stopped for a moment. "It looks as if you have a good crop this year."

"Aye, very good. We'll start to bring it in next week." He paused, looking across the field. "If next week there be."

"We'll all do our best to make your harvest worthwhile, Jeremy." The Head Druid shook his hand. "Until tonight, at the usual place and time." He took a last glance across the neat fields, then turned along the rugged track through the stunted brush. It was not yet eight as he hurried back down the road.

It took Taggart nearly the rest of the day to see the remaining ten members of the Druid council. He had to cover the width and breadth of the Isle of Man, from Mull Hill to Bride, and over the mountain to Knocksharry. He had visited Jeremy first because he was the eldest Druid of the council. Now the only order he followed was determined by the distance of the other Druids from the meeting place. Although he assumed the others already had a forewarning, he knew they would not have guessed about the specific meeting necessary for this evening. Therefore, the Head Druid went first to those men who had the farthest to travel, so they could have as much time as possible to get ready. These lived in secluded hamlets and small villages. One chose to be by himself along the shore of Ramsey Bay, while another lived with his family in the woods near Greebo Castle. The youngest Druid lived in Douglas, not far from the House of Keys, while yet another lived in Castletown near the walls of Rushen Castle. As always, Taggart had to chuckle as he came to Druidale, the more so because the Druid who lived near there had no sense of humor at all. He was forced to hear at nearly every meeting some reference—usually unflattering—about being the Druid from Druidale.

It was close to dusk when Taggart finally returned home. He rested for a couple of hours, falling into an immediate deep sleep. He awoke refreshed and had a substantial meal, having barely eaten all day. He was feeling comfortable now, his plans made as he traversed the Island. He unhurriedly dressed for the council, slipping the long white gown over the clothes he already wore. He ran his fingers over the massive gold torque before he put it around his neck. On a smaller man its weight would have been uncomfortable, but Taggart liked the feel of the heavy gold collar. He wound a leather cord three times around his waist before tying it at the front. Allowing the billowing sleeves of his gown to slide back from his wrists, he reached to the top of a cabinet and took down the staff of an Archdruid. It was as tall as himself, a thick oak staff intricately carved with oak leaves and winding mistletoe vines. Spaced along the lower part were raised circles of hazelnuts. The final four inches at the base of the staff were encased in lodestone. The knob of the staff was a large carved acorn lying on its side, that he occasionally used as a handle and that had, in rare past times, taken on the functions of a club.

Taggart put the white hood up over his head and left his home. It was a brisk half-hour walk to where they held council, and he was always punctual. Tradition decreed that the Head Druid arrive last, and upon his arrival the meeting immediately began. As a younger man, Taggart had suffered through two Head Druids who always came late. He had changed that when he was appointed leader of the council, and this was just one of many changes that made Taggart well liked and respected among the other Druids. He moved inland, through light woods and rough pasture land, until he reached a narrow river, in places no more than a stream. He followed a path along its bank for fifteen minutes, until he came to a bend in the river that almost curved back upon itself, before turning toward the north.

He left the path and crossed a slightly marshy area until he came to a stand of towering trees. He walked a couple of minutes more through the trees and came into a wide meadow, roughly the shape of a circle. The meadow was surrounded by trees, and in one corner a clear-water spring bubbled out of the ground. A number of large, irregular-shaped stones were scattered around the deep spring, and among these stones stood the other Druids. They were also robed in white flowing gowns, with hoods over their heads. They all had silver torques around their necks, and some chose to wear cords about their waists, while others did not. Many of the Druids had heavy beards, and one or two still found it peculiar that a traditionalist like Taggart chose to break with this tradition. Some held oak staffs, as long as the Head Druid's but much less ornate, while the rest had shorter sticks, no more than a yard in length. The youngest Druids had rods made of hazelwood and were assigned a lesser role in the council, though they had as much opportunity to express their ideas.

As the eldest, Jeremy had the duty to step forward first and greet the Head Druid in the ancient Manx tongue. Then, one by one, the others greeted Taggart in the old language and formed a wide circle around him, leaving a well-defined space that led to the spring. As each Druid stepped into his place in the circle, Taggart nodded his head and shook the person's hand. When the circle was complete, Taggart walked slowly to the sacred spring and dipped the point of his staff into the deep water. He then held his staff outright and, standing on one spot, slowly rotated in a circle, pointing his staff at the tall oaks surrounding the meadow. When this was done, he placed his staff once more in the water and returned to the circle of Druids. He went from one to the other, from youngest to eldest, lightly tapping each one over the heart with the tip of his oak staff. When he finally reached Jeremy, he returned the elder Druid's greeting, then went to the center of the circle and lightly tapped the soft earth. It was time for the council to begin.

The Head Druid looked up at the moon and began to speak. "I know that none of us had planned to meet until the festival of Samhin, a little less than two months from now. But, as all of you must have felt, Manannan's protective mantle has slipped from the Island, and we are in dire trouble. Somewhere . . ." He paused, seemingly trying to peer through the gloom. "Somewhere close to us is the start of a Reign of Fire. Not just to us and our small island, but the whole earth. Due to the times we find ourselves in, I am certain it is connected to this war, and that madman, Hitler. As you know, the Monster of Berlin screams about the purity of the old race, twists aspects of our ancient lore for his own ends. With all the power that he possesses, it is possible he has made some contact with the bloodier parts of our history and beliefs and may indeed be unleashing some terrible destruction. We will discuss what is to be done. We will form our council in the sacred grove and tend to no other matter. The time is now."

With those ritual words, the Head Druid walked along a wellworn path winding among the oak trees. At the base of one tree, he drew back a cover to reveal a stack of tapers. He took one and lit it and from its flame proceeded to light the others. As each was lit, one of the Druids came into the grove and took it from Taggart's hands. They did this one by one until all the Druids had their own light. They then clustered in a small circle, a rough stump or slab of stone for each to sit on, and began their discussion.

Taggart began by telling them all that had passed. He mentioned Fenella's dream, which seemed to be the start, and what happened the night of the full moon. There were murmurs when he related the actions of the unicorn, for none had ever seen the beast. There was surprised silence when they learned that Rolf, and his distant ancestors, came from Radasbona, for all knew the legends of the Manx Druid who went there centuries ago. Although groans of sympathy occurred when they heard Rolf was staying under the watchful eye of Ogma, there was again shocked silence when Taggart told of Katherine's prophecy. They had all experienced the troubled feeling of the last few days, and now substance had been given their fears. When Taggart finished speaking, they immediately began asking questions. Jeremy spoke first, and he quickly asked what all the others were now wondering.

"What do you think is going to happen, Taggart?"

The Head Druid paused a moment, looking at the oak grove surrounding them. Most of the trees rose six feet or more before they branched out into a tangle of limbs. The leaves had few weeks of life, and as Taggart looked up, he could see the occasional star, and pieces of the moon, sliced up by the sharp-edged leaves. He slowly lowered his gaze and looked at Jeremy.

"I don't know."

"Have you made any guesses?" one of the younger Druids asked.

"It isn't a time to guess, lad. It's a case of all or nothing, and we can't waste any time on mistakes. It's better we do nothing and be ready to act on a moment's notice. I was hoping that our council would get rid of any guesswork."

The Druid who lived by Ramsey Bay and was accepted as being one of the most knowledgeable spoke without looking at the others. "If we cannot follow supposition, then we must deal solely with the facts. The Head Druid has given us many facts, but few of them seem to join together. Katherine's prophecy has ended any doubt that disaster is going to happen. The German boy is joined to us through his ancestors but is also, through his uniform, connected to the most evil power in the world. I agree with the Head Druid that Hitler may indeed have use of forces that would enable him to bring ultimate destruction; it is no secret that he and his court delve into the realms of the supernatural. This German soldier is the key, so he must be watched closely. Although one would not wish Ogma upon anyone, I concede that he is the best choice for such a job. But, if I may stray from the facts for a moment," he at last looked around at the other Druids and finally let his gaze rest upon Taggart, "it is my opinion that not only is the German boy the key to finding out about this unknown destruction, he is probably himself a part of this deadly act. Whether he does it wittingly or unwittingly, we not only need his help, but we may have to stop him."

A long silence occurred after this speech, and Taggart could sense there was not much left to be said. A few of the Druids asked a question or two, but all agreed that without more information, there was not much they could do. Their final decisions were to stay close to the area so they could meet quickly and, most important, to join the powers on the Island together in one single force. From the unicorn and the other beasts, the lore of the ancients and the present unseen sources, unified action would be needed. With these decisions agreed to, the tapers were extinguished, and the Druids left the sacred grove as they had entered it.

XI

WHEN THE small animal leaned forward to take a drink, the trickling stream brushed its whiskers and tickled its face. With a noise like a sneeze, the creature backed away and shook some drops off its nose. It turned and looked questioningly to the tall beast beside it. In the darkness, even standing so close, its weak eyes could not perceive much more than a hazy white form. It pressed closer to a slender leg and rubbed its snout along the firm shape, closing its eyes at the pleasurable sensation. It gave a quiet sigh and moved sideways under the body of the other creature, feeling safe from the unknown and unseen of the dark.

The sheltered glen was secluded as no other part of the Island, impenetrable to those not called, a last refuge found only by instinct, at a time of both knowing and needing. The beasts had not the cumbersome burden of thought; but acted as destined, from the time creation began the now-shrinking cycles. A waft of wind moved more than just leaves. Time itself was abandoned when the creatures of the ages grouped in the quiet hollow of the holy.

A white head sloped, and the splash of ivory in the deep current drew red and silver fish from springs and seas. They leaped over the horn to curve gracefully back into the turbulent froth, spraying many of the other beasts with glimmering water. Fish of strange shape and hue turned the liquid into sparkling arcs. The smaller animals backed from the stream, shaking the flashing drops from skin and fur, taking shelter behind their larger brethren. Even weak eyes, accustomed to deep burrows and nocturnal wanderings, had to look away from the frothy torrent that cascaded over the spiral that had summoned them.

Wingbeats slashed through sharp pointed leaves, and magnificent birds came to rest among the waiting animals. Small fowl with light-colored feathers mixed in the flutter with grand black ravens and metal-gray eagles, whose talons dug into the earth with massive power. Some of the smaller birds lit on the backs of the larger creatures, cocking their heads from side to side so nothing would be missed. While waiting, many took the time to preen themselves, beaks tugging at misplaced feathers. The large birds, casting huge shadows of midnight upon the earth, walked among the other beasts with stilted movements, slightly awkward out of the freedom of the air. A few of the seabirds, their sticklike legs vulnerable to a misplaced hoof or lumbering paw, walked into the dazzling stream where bird and fish, knowing their places, avoided one another. Most of the birds were settled, waiting, when a final flicker of feathers descended from the night sky, its rich color visible through the gloom. Even the hawks, with razor beaks and tearing claws, paused to look as the blood-red dove landed on the unicorn's back.

Now, through the trees, mammoth beasts could be heard, the next-to-last members of this vast community. Bull and antelope, stag and boar, giant deer and four-horned Loghten sheep—all came calmly through the secluded oaks, each hoof or claw almost silent upon the earth. They took their places with all other manner of creature, each equal in the majesty of life. Hare felt at ease by the side of the hawk, and the hedgehog curled between the lion's paws. The unicorn turned from the stream to face the darkest spot. Four-footed yet winged, the awesome living thing with an eagle's fierce eyes moved slowly to stand beside the white shape. All stood silent as the final myth made itself known and was made welcome, as were all the rest, no creature needing to beware the flash of the dragon's tail.

With all assembled, three people came from the wood, and the unicorn walked toward them also, stopping beside the woman who reached out to touch him. Brigid's fingers stroked his ghostly mane, while the red dove fluttered from his back to land on Katherine's shoulder. And Taggart, standing between the two women, held forth his oaken staff and spoke a single word. Their unity was one, and all their massive power was life itself.

XII

A STORM threatened as the slender man came closer to Taggart's house. Although still tired from the council meeting held not many hours before, the young Druid from Douglas hurried along the main route and skidded slightly as he turned onto the twisting rough road. His bicycle lurched toward some bush, and he felt a painful slap across his right ear from the branches. He straightened the wheel and kept pedaling, feeling less sure of himself as he went along the last mile to Taggart's house. Being the youngest member of the group, he felt intimidated by the Head Druid. Now he was also uncertain that he had anything that was important enough to rouse Taggart out of bed. He had no obvious facts to present, yet the times seemed to demand that one follow feelings as much as fact. And the foreigner in Douglas certainly caused strange feelings.

Nigel—the young Druid—had first noticed the stranger three days ago, standing near the House of Keys. Many people stopped to look at the building, which was old and picturesque, but in these days they quickly moved on, for most of the newcomers were soldiers and sailors, not really interested in the historic sights offered by the small port. Because Nigel lived nearby, he passed the House of Keys almost every day and, being deep in thought, he had paid little attention to the man across the street. It was only when returning home, as he came to the base of the Jubilee Clock, that he gave in to the nagging suspicion that had been with him for quite a while, and he abruptly turned around. Back along the Promenade, another man quickly stopped and began to stare through the wire fence, pretending to watch the Italian and German internees take their exercise. It was the same man Nigel had seen at the House of Keys, medium height, thick-set and approaching middle age.

Having a Druid's great suspicion of coincidence, Nigel knew he was being followed. He headed down Victoria Street, and through a series of quick maneuvers, back-trackings, and entering buildings by one door and leaving by another, he returned to his own home. He watched carefully for hours as he did his other work, but he never saw the man near his house. Next morning, as he once again passed the House of Keys, the man started to follow. He was so unobtrusive that half the time Nigel was certain it was only imagination and shadow he saw sliding into doorways and alleys. Still, he took extra care when he returned home that evening and again saw no one near his house.

On the following day Taggart had arrived to tell him about the Druid council meeting, and, having little more than bare suspicion, Nigel had not bothered to mention the man. He did, however, refuse Taggart's offer of a lift in the car, so they would not be seen together. As he himself left later in the morning, the man was once again near the Keys and this time followed him quite openly, never near enough to be approached, but always there, in constant view. Nigel spent a good half-hour to reach his home in a surreptitious manner, waiting until after dusk to do so.

But this morning, when he looked out the window, the man was directly across the street from his house. Nigel was forced to sneak away, climbing across some back roofs to do so. From an old friend who would ask no questions and tell nothing to anyone, he borrowed a bicycle. He had taken every precaution he could think of, even going a few feet out of his way and doubling back along a disused track through a swale, before he finally reached the road to Taggart's house. Now he stopped at the end of a straight stretch in the road and waited ten minutes, until he was certain no one was behind him. He then quickly traveled the rest of the way and was soon outside Taggart's. He hesitated a minute, then leaned the bicycle against a tree and walked to the front door, which he tapped gently, and then more loudly when he realized Taggart was probably asleep.

When the door was opened, he could tell by the look on the Head Druid's face that he was both tired and surprised to see him. Nevertheless, he was quickly admitted and was soon sitting in a chair across from Taggart, telling him of the things that had been happening, and of his suspicions about the man he had found across from his house a couple of hours ago. Taggart sat through the story without speaking, but when the young Druid was finished, he asked his questions quickly.

"You say that he was a foreigner. Where do you think he was from?"

"Across the sea, America or Canada most like."

"Why do you say that?"

"From his clothes. He has much better clothes than most people from hereabouts, or from Europe. Fancy, you know, not for farming or labor."

"And one day you hardly knew he was there, and the next he was everywhere you went."

"Without any doubt."

"Then he wanted you to see him—to know that you were being followed?"

"Yes."

"But he didn't want to talk to you?"

"Never tried, not even once. I stopped a few times yesterday to let him come up to me, but he just stopped himself. I started walking back to see him a couple of times, but he made himself scarce."

"Then it wasn't you he wanted."

"What do you mean?" Nigel sat straight in his chair.

"It sounds as if he had to make certain you were the right person, and when that was accomplished, he made himself known to prompt you to action."

"But I was there whenever he wanted. What could . . . "

"He wanted you to lead him to something."

"What?"

"If he knows you are a Druid, there could be various things. The most probable, however, is that he wanted you to take him to me."

"Then I was right in taking so much care when I came here this morning?"

"From the sounds of the man, Nigel, you could not be careful enough. You're certain that he—"

"Oh yes," Nigel jumped from his chair. "I'm sure of that—I don't see how he could have followed me out of Douglas, let alone get anywhere near here."

"Just to be safe, Nigel, we'd best take a look." Taggart took his normal staff and together they went outside. It was not yet raining, but the air was thick with moisture as they walked down the dirt drive a short distance. Taggart stopped and pointed to the bicycle, leaning against a tree as Nigel had left it.

"You should have laid that down in the brush. It's an advertisement of where you stopped."

"I never really thought." Nigel went over to the bicycle and placed it on its side farther away from the path. He quickly rejoined Taggart and they continued down the slight slope. "I didn't think it was necessary."

"Men who deal with cautious things should be cautious about everything they do," replied Taggart. "It can be that one thing in a thousand that ruins all the rest." They walked in silence for a few minutes until they came to the straight stretch of road where Nigel had waited and watched before continuing on to the house. "I think we had better leave the road and go on through the brush where we're less apt to be seen."

"He couldn't have come this far," Nigel protested.

"What any man can do is unknown," replied Taggart, and they walked beside the rough road, keeping silent and unseen in the brush. A quarter of an hour passed before they reached the main road, where Nigel's skid marks were still plainly visible. Taggart said nothing, but the young Druid silently berated himself for not brushing them away. The two men turned along this road and started walking toward Douglas, keeping well to the side in pastures and thinly wooded glens. They walked for nearly half an hour, climbing over an occasional fence or jumping a shallow stream. They saw only a handful of people on the road, none of them the man who had so bothered Nigel.

"I'm sure he couldn't even have followed me out of Douglas," said the young Druid in annoyance, when he slipped while crossing one of the streams and water went into his boot. "He'll never get here."

"That's what the mayor of Paris said about Hitler," replied Taggart, with a slight smile. "It looks as if we will soon be drenched anyway, so you needn't worry about your foot." He pointed to the heavy clouds with his staff, and indeed a few splats of rain fell from time to time. "Anyway, exercise is always good, for the mind as well as the body." They continued for another half a mile until Nigel touched the Head Druid on the arm and motioned with his other hand.

"This is where I came out to the road from the marshland, you know, that old rut one or two of the farmers use when the summer's extra dry, thinking it's a shortcut. I was lucky to get through, damp as it is now." Nigel started to turn down the shallow path, but Taggart stopped him.

"No, we'll go on a piece. There's a hill not far off, and we can look across the whole *reeast* without being seen. And," he added with a smile, "without having to go through the damp ourselves."

A few minutes later they were climbing a small hill, and from the top they could see the area that Nigel had double-backed through to elude anyone following. They kept low, moving on hands and knees, until they reached the crest, where they had to lay flat because there was no cover.

"I feel like an American cowboy," said Taggart. "The ones you see in those moving pictures at the cinema."

"We'll cut them off at the pass," replied Nigel.

"You don't sound much like John Wayne."

"Well, I feel something like him, crawling around up here like this," said Nigel. "I'd much rather be following our old traditions and run screaming down the hill, flashing our swords with piercing yells . . . "

"And stark naked," chuckled Taggart.

"It would certainly put a good scare into . . . " Nigel had started to turn toward the Head Druid, a smile on his lips, when his head snapped back. "Good God of Man," he whispered. "There he is."

Taggart looked quickly and caught a glimpse of movement through the tall grasses. He motioned Nigel to keep quiet and continued staring down the hill. It was indeed the man Nigel had described, and he was doggedly following the almost nonexistent trail through the rough ground of the *reeast*. He moved slowly and methodically, looking closely at each foot of ground, moving steadily along the trail that Nigel had left. Taggart had been right in his feelings about this man, and he gave a small smile. Nigel could not see far beyond his own experience and youth, and although very bright, he as yet did not realize what a man of skill and determination was capable of. Taggart turned to see the young Druid scowling down on the man.

"I don't believe it," Nigel hissed. "Bloody bastard."

"Don't be upset, lad. What you did would have been enough to stop most men, even men from here on the Island. That yon man has reached this far is a credit to him, and no discredit to you."

Nigel turned to the Head Druid, feeling somewhat better. "It still doesn't seem possible. What will we do?"

"I think," said Taggart, "that instead of creeping around up here, we will fulfill some of your ancient Celtic desires and go striding down the hill to meet the man."

"Do you think it safe?" Nigel whispered back. "Don't misunderstand me; I'd like nothing better than to shorten his years with a good fright. But if it is you he's after, he might wish to harm you, and if he has a pistol, we'd be at a disadvantage."

The Head Druid had been thinking along the same lines, but while he was listening to Nigel, his eye had been attracted by some slight movement behind and to the left of the man below them. A patch of white briefly showed from time to time, screened by the grasses, stalking the man. Taggart was decided in a moment.

"We'll go down; it is safe enough. The way your friend is coming, he would probably reach my house in due time anyway. We may as well keep that piece of information from him. You can, if you wish, give a good rousing yell to get his attention, and maybe lop a year or two off him. But no wild dash with blazing eyes. Come along then." They both stood, Nigel with a stern set to his jaw. "Go to it, lad," said the Head Druid, and he gave the younger man a nudge.

"CLAGH NY KILLEY AYNS CORNEIL DTY HIE," Nigel bellowed, surprising even Taggart with the power of his voice. The man down below, bent over and looking in the grass, straightened with a start and wheeled around abruptly to stare up the hill. The Head Druid saw a look of satisfaction in the young man's eyes, and also, far off, the spiral point of what he felt was a nod of approval. Nigel took forward place, the ancient position to protect his leader, and they walked quickly down the side of the hill, making a straight line for the man, who hesitated before he started to move toward them. If he found the sight of the two Druids menac-

ing, he gave no sign, and in a minute they were face to face, the man staring past the young Druid to look at Taggart. Nigel quickly spoke, bristling with antagonism.

"What do you want?" he asked, still keeping between the man and the Head Druid. "What are you doing here?"

"I'm here because you've led a merry chase."

"Who are you?" asked Nigel, surprised at the man's candor. "How were you able to follow me out of Douglas, let alone out here?"

"Much of my job is following people, watching where they go and what they do. And who they do things with." He kept staring into Taggart's eyes. "Sometimes that is most important."

"But I still don't know why you're here," persisted Nigel.

"I don't want to appear rude, young man." For the first time he looked at Nigel. "But time is short and this cat-and-mouse gets us nowhere. You're a Druid, a practitioner of one of the oldest existing religions. I must talk with your leader, who I presume is the tall man standing behind you." As Nigel's mouth gaped, the man once again looked over him into the Head Druid's eyes. "My business concerns the war, disaster, and a Wehrmacht Hauptleutnant called Rolf Scholl. Anything further I have to say must, I think, be solely for the Archdruid."

"You can't . . . " Nigel was at a loss for words, "can't possibly know these things. You aren't even . . . "

"I'm afraid there is little time for this." The man looked past Nigel and into the older man's face. "You are the leader, the Archdruid, aren't you?"

"We don't answer any . . . " began Nigel, but a hand touched his shoulder, and he turned around, perplexed.

"It's all right, lad. When you confront the truth, it's always best to admit it." He looked calmly into the eyes of the stranger. "Yes, I am who you say."

"We can help each other."

"Then we shall talk," Taggart stepped forward to take a closer look at the man. "It would be nice to start with your name, and how you come to know these things."

"Don't be offended, young man," the stranger glanced back to Nigel. "But this conversation is solely for the Archdruid and me."

"That's not possible," Nigel began to protest. "I can't leave you two alone. How do we know that . . . "

"I have no intention of harming the Archdruid. We are both on the same side, and he is in no danger from me."

"Will you allow me to search you?" asked Nigel.

"I'm open to any reasonable request." The stranger undid his jacket and raised his arms. Nigel mimicked the type of search he had seen in movies and found nothing. He was just turning to tell Taggart so when the stranger opened his hand to reveal a small pistol, pointing in their direction. Nigel stood motionless for a second, then made a quick decision and leaped back in front of the Head Druid.

"No, no, that won't be necessary," said the stranger, as he turned the pistol toward himself, gripping it by the barrel and handing it over to Taggart. "I just want to prove that you have nothing to fear."

Nigel quickly took the gun, then gave it to the Head Druid, who placed it in a pocket of his tunic.

"Where'd you have that damn thing?" asked Nigel.

"Oh, well concealed—nicely hidden you can be sure, although your search was none too expert."

"All right," said Taggart. "Nigel, you can go back for your bicycle, and then return here to see if anything's needed."

"You'll be all right, alone?"

"I'll be all right. And I'm not quite alone."

The young man looked puzzled, but he said no more and started along the hill. He had only gone a short distance when the stranger called.

"Hey!"

Nigel turned back and looked at him.

"What was that horrid thing you yelled at me when you started down?"

Nigel gave a grin and shouted back, "It meant, 'A stone of the church in the corner of thy house.'"

"But what does that mean?"

"I'll let the parson tell you," said Nigel and continued on his way.

"You're a parson, too." The stranger smiled. "I thought I was good at disguises. Well, 'parson,' what does it mean?"

"It's a curse," Taggart explained. "In the old days—and sometimes not so long ago—people took the stones from ruined or disused churches to put in their own foundations when building homes or barns. Many thought this was a desecration and bad luck, thus a curse. But enough Manx folklore—who are you?"

"I go by many, many names."

"Since you say we must help each other, why not tell me your real one? As a change."

"All right." The other man smiled. "I'm Mr. Stephenson."

"The world is full of Mr. Stephensons," replied Taggart. "A few here on the Island."

"Be that as it may, I am one of them." The man shook his head. "And I haven't told many people that much for years and years."

"All right, Mr. Stephenson," the Head Druid's face was grim. "You obviously know about things that interest me, so—"

"We're not alone," the man interrupted Taggart. "You said to the young man that you were not alone. What did you mean?"

"Here," Taggart stretched a long arc with his arm, "on this Island, with me, there are many things you may never know."

"Yes," the man looked suddenly old. "I can sense that." He ran a hand in his thinning hair. "I realize there are things I cannot understand, and I have come to accept that fact." A smile crossed his face again. "There are two things, however, that should not be difficult. May we leave this damn swamp before it rains, and," he stared into the glittering green eyes, "you have me at a disadvantage, for I have yet to know your name."

"Taggart." The Head Druid pointed his staff up the hill. "I'm called Taggart. We can go along there and find some shelter under a tree, if it starts to rain."

"An oak tree?" asked Mr. Stephenson.

"Considering our conversation, any help should be appreciated." The tall Druid's face softened a bit, and they walked up the slope, passing the place where Taggart and Nigel had been.

"How long were you watching me?" asked the man.

"Four or five minutes."

"Is that all?" The man looked puzzled. "I had the sensation that eyes were observing me for well over half an hour. You get a feeling for things like that in my business. I wonder . . ."

"Yes, Mr. Stephenson, your business." Taggart turned to look at him. "What exactly is your business?"

"Modern parlance would class me as a spy. I take some offence at the word, but I suppose it's accurate nevertheless."

"You are not, I take it, an ordinary spy?"

"Just as you are not an ordinary Druid." Mr. Stephenson gave a low chuckle. "I never really imagined I would find myself in a situation where any spy—or especially a Druid—would be ordinary."

They came to the main road and walked along it a short distance, stopping under the first suitable tree they found.

"This may not be necessary," said Taggart. "It seems as if it's starting to clear."

"Any improvement is welcome," Mr. Stephenson answered.

"Now we begin," said Taggart, handing the small pistol back to the shorter man. "What do you want with Hauptleutnant Rolf Scholl?"

"I don't know." The man did not remove his gaze from Taggart's eyes as he put his gun away. "There is a war going on and he is an enemy soldier—that should be enough."

"You were behind that search for the supposed Germans?"

"Yes." The smaller man smiled. "I don't know how he got away from us that time. I should have come myself, and not left things to Major Ross. He came back babbling about crazy women and I don't know what all. I think this Island affects people."

"What do you mean, you don't know why you want him?"

"Bits and pieces," Mr. Stephenson frowned. "His name, or some reference to him, comes up in bits and pieces of information that never quite come together. He's connected in some way with . . ."

"With what?" Taggart's voice was hard.

"With a . . ." Mr. Stephenson's face showed indecision for the first time. He looked closely at Taggart, trying to judge. "He seems to be dealing with great destruction."

"What do you mean?" Taggart stood even closer.

"There is the potential for a type of bomb." The other man paused. "Have you ever been bombed?"

"Here on the Island?" Taggart asked. "Once or twice, it seemed by mistake. And of course, the other night. But I myself have never been near such a thing when it fell."

"There are plans for a type of bomb, an explosion, such as would . . ." he stopped again, wondering whether the other man could believe this. "One of these things, just one, coming from only one airplane, could level a city like London, turn it into nothing." He saw some type of recognition in the other man's eyes and decided to go on. "Or, if one were big enough, it could destroy this whole Island, turn the length and breadth of it black."

"Fire," whispered Taggart.

"What was that?"

"Everything would turn to fire," the Head Druid was mumbling.

"Why yes, of course. Great firestorms, terrific things. So you do understand what I'm talking about?"

"The last time it was flood." Taggart's eyes snapped back to Mr. Stephenson. "Hitler—does he have such a thing, this bomb you're talking about?"

"No—not yet—we don't think so." The man did not understand all of what Taggart was saying. "That's why I'm here."

"Here?" Taggart became composed. "But there's nothing on Man."

"Rolf Scholl is here." Out of habit, Mr. Stephenson lowered his voice. "And you have a ferry that within three or four hours can get one to Liverpool, one of the cities in Great Britain where we are trying to make one of these wretched things ourselves."

"There's a chance Hitler might get the use of this—this bomb?" asked Taggart.

"A very good chance; it's a race between him and us."

"And if he got hold of it first?"

"Oh, that bastard would bomb everything in sight without a second thought," Mr. Stephenson said tonelessly. "Without much of a first thought, I suppose. The man can't be satisfied."

"And what of Rolf?" asked Taggart.

"I am party to much information, Taggart." The man paused, searching for the right way to put the situation. "Before the war started, back even in the mid-thirties, it was apparent the direction in which Herr Hitler was headed. Apparent, at least, to those who wanted to know, like Mr. Churchill and certain others, President Roosevelt included."

"You sound as if you know both men," interrupted Taggart.

"I deal with them directly. I last saw Winston five days ago. There are, of course, no records, and I doubt there ever will be."

"Oral tradition has much to be said for it," smiled Taggart.

"Yes," Mr. Stephenson nodded. "The less put on paper, the better. One of the reasons the Germans will lose is that they have everything down on paper and stamped with their silly eagle. It could have all been stopped, you know—years ago. This isn't a new war, but the continuation of the last." Mr. Stephenson gave a sigh. "So many chances lost." He lapsed into silence again, and Taggart waited patiently. Stephenson looked up, the past gone from his eyes. "Over the years we have built up an efficient and effective network of people all across Europe. There are few Nazi secrets we know nothing about. That the Germans are after this horrid bomb, we know. That they are snooping around Liverpool, we know, although we aren't sure who they all are. That Rolf Scholl is somehow connected to all this, we suspect, but we don't know how. We assume the Germans feel it is easier to send information from the Isle of Man than from England, and they're right. A sub could come up anywhere along this coast, or a seaplane could land, especially on the side facing Ireland. All we have to work with on Man itself is Rolf Scholl."

"There are things about him," Taggart paused. "Things about us and the . . . the order of our existence on the Island, that you cannot discover through your network of surveillance. Yet you in your way and we in ours are dealing with the same problem, searching for a similar solution. And you have brought me information I did not have, so I acknowledge the success of your methods." Taggart gave a small smile. "You are no doubt familiar, Mr. Stephenson, with situations where you must work in a haze, dealing, no matter how reluctantly, in the realm of trust and . . . of necessity, ignorance."

"I believe I know what you mean," replied the other man. "We call it doing the best with what you have."

"There are things I can and cannot do," replied Taggart. "I can't let you find Rolf—not because of him, but because of what can be exposed through him, things that have nothing at all to do with the problem at hand. I can, however, assure you he is never out of our sight; I can let you know anything pertinent he may do or say. I can keep in touch with you through Nigel—the young man you followed. He'll let you know anything that happens; we won't keep anything from you that concerns our mutual problem. And also, Nigel can tell me of any important information you may gain. I must ask that you do nothing further as regards Rolf and do not attempt to deal any further with us. I am, I'll admit, surprised that you found out about Nigel. It makes me respect your ways."

"It wasn't easy," Mr. Stephenson smiled. "If he's your youngest, you have a crafty bunch." He quickly became serious. "All right,

I'll agree to everything you say. Trust is a short commodity in my business, but I feel all right about you. And young Nigel is bright enough to keep us safely in touch. One thing I forgot to mention is that we suspect something is going to happen very shortly."

"Less than four days," said Taggart.

"How do you know that?" The other man was shocked.

"We have no more than four settings of the sun," replied Taggart. "And none of them are guaranteed. Take my word."

"Our information suggests tomorrow or the next day," said Mr. Stephenson. "Highly classified and most secret it is." He held his hand out toward the Head Druid. "Your ways and mine, Taggart; you've convinced me now that they're leading to the same end. I know little of your beliefs, even less of what may be going on around me here, right now. But I don't doubt your power, and I'm relieved to have you with me, and not against me. We might pull this off yet."

Taggart placed his large hand into the strong hand of the other, and they shook on their deal with mutual respect.

"You may feel out of place among us, Mr. Stephenson," the Head Druid released his hand. "But the same cannot be said for Mr. Churchill. He was once initiated into our ways. Ask him whether he remembers August 15, 1908, at Blenheim. He was a young man then, and the whole thing was far too theatrical by half —none of our group here on Man had anything to do with it. Still, an honorary membership is better than no membership at all. A man such as yourself, dealing in these modern times, may yet be surprised by the power of the old ways. We have come a great distance, after all."

"In my business, Taggart, where a surprise can kill, we learn to reach the point where nothing surprises us." Mr. Stephenson laughed. "I'll even believe in the little people if they'll help us beat Hitler."

"They will," answered Taggart. He turned to look down the road. "Here comes Nigel. I'll just have a few words with him, and you can return to Douglas together. Tell him how you can be reached, and I'll make certain he stays near a telephone." The two men stepped across the ditch. "It really is starting to clear; you should have a nice walk back." After a brief conversation with Nigel, the Head Druid watched the two men until they were out of sight.

XIII

ALTHOUGH THE threatened rain did not come, the sky was slow in clearing, and by late morning only occasional patches of blue broke through the gloom. Though not much rain had actually fallen, the grass was still wet, and the old woman grumbled as she tried to keep her long skirts out of the damp. Alice had offered to come, but the old woman ambled out of their cottage with a few curt words and went on her way. She did not like getting her skirt wet, but she preferred the cloudy sky to the heat of the sun. She had never liked hot places, and the older she became, the more she enjoyed the coolness of autumn. During the winter months, Alice was always finding windows to close. The damp, cool mists of the Island made the old woman very content.

She came within sight of a rough shack and grunted her disapproval. It was little better than a hovel, and although she had had to go to many poor places in her time, the people in them usually made some attempt to make their homes pleasant, even if it were nothing more than a scraggly plot of flowers near the door. But this place was worse than ill-kept; it appeared as if time had been spent making it as disreputable as possible. The lands were overgrown, and there were heaps of rubbish everywhere. The walls were stained, with occasional cracks appearing between the stones. Even the thatched roof had a quilt of hasty repairs. She shuddered to think of living in it.

"You ought to be ashamed, staying in the likes of that," the old woman called. "Come out o' the bushes, you gray little devil; it's me you've been watchin' since I turned off into this cursed place. Yon *tholtan* is not any better than a pig sty." She stopped for breath and glared around her.

"Then you'll be feeling right at home," the voice sneered behind her, and Ogma came from the brush, shaking water from the branches. "Why couldn't young Alice have come today—at least she's something to look at."

"Aye, and that'll be only what you're capable of—looking. You're disgusting as it is, without such thoughts."

"Leastways I do have thoughts," Ogma came up to stand beside the old woman. "That's more than anyone has done for you in many a long year, you can believe that or not."

"Times be that there was more than just thinking done about me—Alice is proof enough of that." The old woman shifted her bulk to look at him more closely. "I can't see where there's any proof that you've done more than thinking all your life."

"Oh, I've been discreet in my time, old woman." The gravedigger came closer to her and lowered his voice. "No matter who you see, you can never be quite sure how they got here. Some people, let me tell you, could be surprised about their own children."

"There's lots of talk because the air is free," replied the old woman, holding up her skirts as she started toward the house. "Now let me see the German lad, that's why I've come." She stepped over some broken tools. "Have you ever thought of clearing out the place and living like a human?"

She pushed the door open and went into the small cottage. There were only two rooms; the front was a combination of a kitchen and living room, while a doorway at the back led to a smaller room used for sleeping. The old woman squinted in the gloom and saw there was as much mess inside the house as there was furniture. Rolf was seated at a battered table, eating some cold food and drinking tea from a chipped cup. When he glanced up to see who it was, a look of relief crossed his face. Even the old woman was a welcome change.

She turned to Ogma, who had followed her in. "Get us some

light, then. I can't see enough to look at his shoulder."

"With you he's just as well off in the dark."

"Never mind that." The old woman was feeling tired. "Get us a lantern and then leave. Being in the same room as you is making *me* feel sick. You're supposed to be watching for people coming, anyway."

Ogma grumbled, but he retrieved a rusty lantern from a corner and lit it, placing it on the table. He turned to Rolf with a concerned look on his face and said in a loud whisper, "Don't worry, lad; if the old bitch does you in, I got a nice deep pit waiting for you. You've seen it yourself, and I'll throw in a box for free, seeing I've grown accustomed to you. What can old friends do, eh? I'll even comfort your lass for you." Ogma gave a snorted chuckle and went out the door.

The old woman placed the lantern on the cluttered table while Rolf unbuttoned his shirt. As she helped him take it off, he looked toward the door.

"Herr Ogma, he acts to me in a strange way, yes?"

"He's not a normal person," the old woman said, undoing some of the bandages. "God made a mistake when that one was born."

"He does not seem to like anything," Rolf winced as the old fingers prodded around his shoulder, feeling the stitches.

"Ugh, they're good—she sewed you good." The old woman reached into one of her pockets. "Oh, that one," she inclined her head at the door. "It's more than 'not liking' with him. He hates everything that isn't corrupt or full of despair." She brought a small box of powder out of the pocket. "If he has any heart, it's as black as the pits he digs." She spread a little of the powder over the wounds. "It was a sad lot that fell to you when you had to come here." She cut some fresh bandages. "For all that he isn't, it was a good idea. What do you do with a Jerry lad in the midst of a war —you bury him." She put the clean cloths in place with strips of tape and then started fixing on the other bandages.

"How long am I to stay here?"

"Don't know, Jerry. I just do the patching up; it's himself that makes all the decisions."

"You mean Herr Taggart?"

"None other. Me and Alice take care of what we can. And Ogma cleans up after us if anything is left over. We all have our place in the grand scheme, I dare say."

"You have the certainty of that?" asked Rolf.

"Certainty?" The old woman gave a tired laugh. "When you reach my age, you find out you're not sure of anything. You start out young on certain hope, and you end up on shaky hope." She gave a final smoothing to the bandages. "There lad, how does it feel?"

"It does not hurt so much," he replied. "It is getting better."

"Aye, that it is. Body is a remarkable thing, if you ever stop to think about it." She returned her tools to the pockets of her skirt. "Let's get your shirt and jacket back on and then get you out into some fresh air." She helped him put his arm through the sleeve of both garments and then adjusted the sling around his neck. "There, that'll do till Alice comes for a look."

"The more people who visit, the better I feel."

"I've heard that you don't lack for company." She blew out the lamp and gave a sigh. "You young ones—it's all as you want, and there's no telling you any different. How things really are only comes with age. It's too bad some of that intensity couldn't be spaced out over the years. All I really look forward to now is a good night's sleep—and more than thankful that I still get it." She looked around for a place to put the old bandages and finally rolled them up and tossed them into the black fireplace. "I imagine I could be putting them in his cupboard and he'd not notice. Pah, what a place. Come on, lad, and be thankful it isn't going to rain, or you'd be stuck in here all day." She followed him to the door, kicking out in disgust at some pile of rubbish on the floor. Rolf turned at her curse, but she shooed him out the door like a chicken. "Fresh air—as much as you can get." They went out, the old woman refusing to close the door in the hope of letting a little clean air into the house. They went part-way down the path, where Rolf stopped and turned to her.

"This is as far as Herr Ogma wishes me to go."

"What?" The old woman looked up sharply. "I suppose he knows what he's doing, but it isn't much exercise walking back and forth to here. Still, better than a cell. All right, Jerry, walk around where you can, but don't do too much. And if it dries up a bit, sit out somewhere in the sun. But don't get a chill, mind."

"Yes, I will do all this." Rolf felt more at ease with the old woman. "Will you be returning soon to see me?"

"Alice will be along tonight. Once a day is enough of this for me. You're a special case, you see."

"Do you know if anyone else . . . " Rolf paused for a moment.

"If I am to have any more people to visit me?"

"Ah, the lass." The old woman gave a small smile. "You should be as concerned with the healin' as you are with the girl." She patted his shoulder, not unkindly. "The shock won't be too great on me if I hear she's been comin' to see you." She was quiet a minute, then looked up into his eyes, her round face creased with concern. "You two met under the moon—you might have been touched too much by it. You don't know yet that everything doesn't work out just because it feels right. The dreams I've had . . ." The old woman looked away, staring over his shoulder at a large area of blue sky. "I'm being silly—it's like talking to the stones. You don't find out except by yourself." She turned and started down the path. "Of course she'll be here, Jerry; the sun came up this morning, didn't it?" She picked her way around a clump of damp grass and was intent on missing the bushes on either side, so she did not hear the footsteps falling in behind her and gave a jump when a voice spoke close by her shoulder.

"And the sun will be setting tonight, too, so what does any of it mean?" She twisted around to see Ogma grinning at her. "Don't get mad, I dare say I did a heap of good, scaring some of that fat off you. Not that you deserve it, feeding Jerry that swill."

She tried to ignore his talk and turned back along the path, hitting at some branches that brushed her arm. "You'd be better off leaving your nonsense alone and cutting back some of these bushes. A person can hardly make his way through them."

"Then he's that much easier to hear, isn't he?" Ogma stayed close behind, talking to the back of her head. "So that silly lass will be here, will she, and I'll have to watch the two of them fussing around each other again, touching and whispering like—"

"So don't watch," the old woman snapped. "It's no concern of yours one way or the other. You're supposed to make sure nobody finds him, is all—he's got little enough pleasure around here."

"And why should he expect to have any pleasure?" Ogma almost spat at the old woman. "Especially with her?"

"And why shouldn't he have some pleasure—with the lass or no?" She abruptly stopped, and her bulk made him stumble into the bushes so he wouldn't walk into her. "There's none of it around if he has to stay with you; it's like being buried alive." She turned her small eyes onto his face. "And it's more her than him that's botherin' you."

A muscle twitched across his cheek, which he hid quickly with a false smile. "Now who'd want his own daughter going around with one of the enemy?"

The statement, instead of shocking the old woman as intended, made her snort with mirth. She had to brush some of the thin white hair out of her face as she laughed. "If William Crovan could hear you say that, he'd be digging your grave with your own head. I brought the lass into the world, you forget, and seen her grow. There's none of your dirty blood in that girl, Ogma—and this had best be the last word ever heard about it."

"But there should have been," Ogma's face had gone blank, and his voice was almost a cry. "Every time I see her I think that. She reminds me of her mother, when she laughs, the way she holds her hands together when she walks fast; she looks like Fenella did at that age—and I hate him every time he touches her." His breath came in gasps. "Taggart shouldn't let her near here."

"You should be over that nonsense."

"What would you know of it, you fat old bitch."

"I weren't always fat . . . or old." She pointed a stubby finger at him. "You go moping about something that's a dream—something that's never happened or ever had any chance of happening. You can't lose what you never had; you have to have someone for that —like I did. He's been dead for twenty years—you know, you put him under yourself. I've never wanted another since him. That's what it means to lose someone, not this crying over a dream that went sour in your belly and stayed there. And there was me daughter and son-in-law, gone down in a ship and never found. You wake out of a sleep some night with that in your head, and you'll find something to carry on about. Something real, nay like this wasted time over Fenella. You two was never meant, I tell thee." The old woman wiped an eye that was starting to sting and turned away from the man.

Ogma stood, his mouth open and his eyes unblinking, hearing all the old woman had to say. "You've been above ground too long, old woman." His open mouth turned into a grin. "I'm more than willing to take care of things for you—you can believe that or not."

"I won't be wanting your horrid old hands on me, Ogma; you've gone too queer these last few years. I'd never be able to trust you.

This carcass may be old and fat, but I don't want you poking around with it. I've got my eye on a nice cabinetmaker in Laxey, and Alice knows of it. Not that I'm planning to die just to please you."

"Any death pleases me."

"More sad that, then." She started walking away from him. "Get to the lad before Berrey Dhone spirits him away." She did not look back at the gravedigger and so missed his single finger thrust at her retreating figure. She was lost in her memories and did not even bother to step around the wet grasses.

XIV

"I'M OFF to see him," the voice came through the bedroom door.

"Go on, call her back," William gave his wife a slight push with his hand. "Talk to her."

"There's no point to it, she won't . . . "

"Go to it, before she's gone."

"And what am I going to say?" Fenella's voice was exasperated. "You can't talk about feelings like they . . . "

"Brigid." William's loud voice cut off his wife's words, and she glared at him as footsteps came toward them.

"You can do the talking, then," she said and moved away from the bed.

"We both will, if need be," he replied as the door opened.

"Will you be wanting anything?" asked Brigid as she came toward the bed. "It's starting to clear and we won't have to stay in that horrid little shack." She was looking from one to the other, her face animated. "If he didn't tire so much I could stay longer, but Alice's grandmother said that I could only see him a couple of hours." Brigid went and sat on her father's bed. "You know, she and Alice aren't as bad as you make out." She gave his pillows a shove to fluff them. "What do you need?"

"There'll be nothing to be getting for me, girl." William looked into her face and then turned away. "Your mother has something that she's been meaning to talk to you about."

"Oh aye, William Crovan, put it on to me."

"Well, you're her mother."

"And I wasn't the doing of it by myself." Fenella came back to her husband's bed and sat heavily beside Brigid, causing William to wince as his leg moved. "The man will just not leave well enough alone—as if any of this will do any good."

"Any of what?" asked Brigid. "What's the matter?"

"Well, girl," her father began. "It isn't as if . . . "

"Oh, William," his wife lost her patience. "For God's sake don't go into any of your backward explanations that try, with one sentence, to smooth over the mess made by another. Tell the lass point-blank and get it done, so she can be on her way, because on her way she'll be no matter what's said here."

"Fenella, you're not making this—"

"The man doesn't think you should be going to see Rolf," Fenella said sharply.

"Now that isn't quite what I—" William began.

"Not see him?" Brigid's head had been turning between her mother and father. "Why on earth not?"

"See what you've had a go at," accused William. "You've got her all upset and it will be even harder to make her see sense."

"Sometimes I don't know which is most maddening," said Fenella. "The fact that you're a man, or the fact that you're you." She put up her hands as William and Brigid started to speak. "Shush, the both of you." She turned to her daughter. "We're not going to try and stop you; if the Head Druid sees fit to let you, right and well. But we both think that you should be cautious, although I dare say for different reasons."

"But Rolf wouldn't do anything to harm me."

"There are many ways to harm a person, Brigid. Now your father, thinking like a man, has some fears for your honor."

"Father!" Brigid's eyes snapped to him. "Rolf would never do . . . "

"Agh," William shook his head. "Don't be telling me what a young man is or is not able to do. I know the feelings and the forces, and things can get away from you, bad shoulder or no."

"What you say is true, William." His wife turned to Brigid with a small smile. "But it seems to me I kept you in your place until both the time was right and I was good and ready." Her voice took on a gentler tone. "No, and you weren't lacking in persistence, either."

"Well, I can take care of myself," Brigid said.

"Try not to be angry with your father, although I'm the first to know that it's easy enough to do, with him and his ways." Fenella looked at her husband and back to her daughter. "He also forgets that you have much more to be responsible for than other women, and that the decision is one that affects far more than you yourself. Your time has not yet come to lose your powers. You realize that, don't you, Brigid?"

"Of course I do, mother." Brigid looked into the older woman's eyes. "There is no chance of my forgetting myself."

Fenella reached over and took her daughter's hand, giving it a squeeze that was returned with equal strength.

"Good." William nodded his head. "Good, I'm glad we got that rid of. Now let's get on with the rest of it and let her get out of here," he said.

"Let *us* get on with it?" Fenella gave a snort. "I suppose you mean let *me* get on with it, like I did just now."

"Well, you did a good job, and the girl isn't too angry. You've always been a better talker than me."

"Since my good name is taken care of, what is it now?" asked Brigid. "Am I not to be holding hands, or any other nasty business?"

"Harmless pleasure and friendship are one thing, Brigid." Her mother paused, looking for the right words. "What we ask is that you be cautious with Rolf, to be sure that . . . "

"I've already said that nothing will happen."

"Oh, your mother doesn't mean that way," put in William.

"No, Brigid, don't misunderstand me—all that was your father's nonsense." Fenella paused again. "It would be wise not to become too emotionally involved—not yet." She hurried on when she saw that her daughter was about to speak. "When all's said and done, we still know very little about Rolf. He's a stranger and—"

"But he saved my life."

"Yes, I know that, but—"

"And he saved the unicorn," persisted Brigid.

"Yes, you're right, he did both things." Fenella gave a sigh. "But also, neither of those things would have happened if he hadn't been there. Had you gone to the unicorn as you intended, you both would have reached the woods before the bomber came, and nothing would have happened. All Rolf really did was correct the damage he himself had made."

"But you dreamed he was coming."

"Dreams can bring danger as well as good."

"He's from Regensburg; his ancestors were Druid."

"He's also a soldier of Hitler's army."

"The unicorn let Rolf see him."

"None of us fully understand the unicorn, Brigid; you know that as well as I."

"The Head Druid trusts him; he lets me go and visit as—"

"Girl," her father's voice cut in. "Taggart makes sure that Ogma watches his every move, even when you're there. Rolf is a question, and until there's an answer, there'll be no chances taken."

"Brigid," her mother's voice was calm but insistent. "We don't even know why he's here. Has he ever told you?"

Brigid looked confused. "No, he never talks about it—we never think of talking about it. We talk about ideas, and what we think, and what the future will be, and he asks me questions about the Island and my life, and I tell him what I can. I never tell him things that people—other people—are not supposed to know." She thought a moment. "And he never asks me about things like that, either. And we're silly quite a lot; we say things that would sound quite quite foolish to anyone else. And he has this game he plays with me." Brigid's eyes lit up and she giggled. "He pretends he doesn't understand what I'm saying—and you know, his English really is good—and he'll make me say some things three or four times, especially if it has something to do with how much I like him: '*Vos ist?*' he says in a deep voice, 'what do I mean?' He can be so silly." She stopped talking and looked up, as if surprised. "Dear, I suppose I sound silly now."

"Well," began William.

"Nonsense, girl," Fenella cut in, giving a sharp look to her husband. "You sound like someone who's found a friend and is having a good time. Your father and I could be quite daft in our day—him especially when he was on that old horse of his. If he'd had his way, you would have been conceived on that horse."

"Fenella!" William's voice boomed in embarrassment.

"Shush up, you old troublemaker," Fenella laughed from deep in her throat. "It's true enough, so don't take on so. We wouldn't have to be going through any of this talk if it weren't for you, so you may as well be shown up a little too." She turned back to her daughter. "What two people do together is never foolish. Now, we've kept you long enough, so go and cheer the lad up. No one should have to spend a day alone with Ogma, unless he's one of the little man's clients."

"And even that would be unpleasant enough," put in William with a sour face.

"You know I wouldn't do, or say, anything wrong," Brigid said, looking at them both.

"Oh, we know that right enough, don't we, William?" Fenella looked pointedly at her husband, and he was forced to grunt his agreement.

"Aye, of course," he muttered.

"But I do ask, Brigid, that you be cautious with your feelings. It's not anything that we have against Rolf, but the fact that we don't know enough about him, that worries me. If things turn out right, then you'll have all the time in the world to get to know him. And if it does come about that the two of you are intended, then all that can occur in due course."

"I'm sure there couldn't be anything bad about him," said Brigid.

"Too many questions," her father warned, almost to himself. "Still too many questions around his head."

"I can ask him some things," Brigid hesitated, "if you like."

"That's not necessary," Fenella said quickly, before her husband could speak. "We don't want you being a spy; it's not your way. Just put a rein on your feelings, and that's enough done for now." Fenella gave her daughter's hand a tap. "Now get going, before you're caught up in more talk and the whole day disappears in words."

Brigid kissed her mother, and her father, giving a playful tug at his beard, then ran toward the door. She turned to speak, but Fenella put a finger to her lips and shook her head, so she went down the hall and out into the sun without a word. She hurried around the house, went along a short path beside the garden, and then took a shortcut through some woods to reach the road. She looked up and smiled at the disappearing cloud, and at times she ran, taking one or two twirling dance steps as she did. The day was turning lovely, and she was having happy thoughts about sitting out with Rolf, together on a rickety piece of planking that Ogma had set up near the trees. Although she knew that Ogma was always close, he did not hover over them, and she suspected that the Head Druid may have said a word or two to him about it. She did not understand, or much care, why Ogma acted the way he did, as long as he left them alone.

Thinking of Rolf made her do a few more dance circles, her arms outstretched and her long hair flying across her face. In the midst of a turn, she caught a glimpse of a figure on the road ahead, causing her to stop self-consciously and brush the hair out of her eyes. It was Alice's grandmother, but the short woman had an uncharacteristic smile on her round face.

"Don't be stopping on my account, lass. I've just been thinking of my man and the years ago." The old woman came closer and stopped in front of Brigid. "You won't believe it to be seeing me now, but we used to take our flings with the coming of Saturday night." She gave a small sigh. "Ah, he was a high stepper, that one; weren't no one could keep a pace with him. And there's many a Mheillea when he'd kick up the dust right in the harvest field. You bring it back, lass, God bless you. To dance again . . ."

Brigid saw the look in the old woman's eyes and held out both hands toward her.

"What?" The old eyes were momentarily puzzled, then a gleam formed in them. "Och, nay, nay lass, I'm far too gone in years." She looked around her. "And it's not a Shebeen we'll be in, but a public road." She hesitantly held up her short arms and Brigid gently took the wrinkled hands in her own. "It's locking me away they'll be doin', if we're seen." She gripped the girl's hands, and Brigid led her in a slow circle, feet lightly touching the road as the couple went around once, and then again, the old eyes shining and Brigid's hair gently moving in the breeze. One more time, the old woman's skirts brushing across the earth, and then they stopped. Both were laughing, and then the round face looked up at Brigid, years gone from the eyes. She put her arms around the young woman's waist and gave her a tight hug.

"Thank you, lass." She dabbed at some perspiration on her forehead. "I supposed it's being on the way to the Jerry lad that's making you so light with your feet." She paused. "With our feet."

"How is he?"

"Doing grand." The old woman shook her head. "But he's not ready for any dancing just yet. Get him out in the sun for a while, though, and away from the gloom of that hut."

"Yes, that's what I was going to do. Although I'm not staying any more than the two hours, as you told me."

"It's turning a nice day; you can be with him a bit longer if you want, as long as the lad doesn't tire."

"Another half-hour?"

"Use your sense, girl." The old woman took a breath. "You want him healthy more than anyone. If he gets a look of strain on his face, or the shoulder starts to ache more than usual, it's time to get him laid down and leave him be. It's no pleasure, I know, to have to stay in that shack, but it's rest he needs more than anything. Any bed is comfortable when you're tired."

"What do you think of him?"

"What do *I* think of him?" The old woman snorted. "Ugh, what a question to be asking. I think he's a silly moon-touched man with a bad shoulder. And also, I think that whatever sins he may have done in all his life, he's paid for them threefold by having to stay with the likes of Ogma. A more unpleasant wretch has never come from land or sea."

"The gravedigger puzzles me," said Brigid. "He looks at me with strange eyes."

The old woman thought for a moment, then decided to say nothing. "He's treating you like everyone else, measuring you for a box is all. Now get on and see the Jerry lad, and don't take him to no dancing."

"I won't do anything. We'll just sit and talk, maybe walk a bit."

"He'll be all right, girl, don't over-fret yourself." The old woman looked up into Brigid's face with a twinkle. "Go on, now."

Brigid gave her hand a squeeze, then started hurrying toward Ogma's house. She had not gone very far when she was startled to hear a laugh behind her. She turned in time to see the old woman, her skirts lifted off the road, give a short series of kicks with her feet and then continue on her way, singing in a rough voice. Brigid smiled and turned toward her own destination, going all the more quickly when she realized Rolf would be expecting her by now.

In ten minutes Brigid was turning off toward the gravedigger's house. She almost ran down the path and only slowed near the end when Ogma came out beside her.

"You make too much noise," he growled.

"I thought you liked to be able to hear people coming," she replied, looking at him but not stopping.

"I'll hear you come, right enough, no matter what you do, you can believe that or not. I don't take so kind to the whole of Man hearin' you come thundering through the brush. Hard enough to keep Jerry out of the way without your leading people here with the noise."

"I'll be more quiet the next time. You see, I'm late, and—"

"Aye, you do that," he glared into her face. "Silent as the grave, that's the way I like to have it." Ogma grinned and took out his pipe. "And a grave's where Jerry will be if you don't quit getting him all excited."

"What do you mean by that?" Brigid's voice was sharp.

"Teasin' him up like—you know." He took his time with the matches, looking at her over the bowl of the pipe. "Coming around here and being with him. He's a weak lad and should be getting his rest. I don't know why you come around to see him anyway. With all the men on the Island waiting to get into your—"

"The Head Druid says it's all right, so all right it is." Brigid stood with her feet apart, staring down at the gray face. "Now tell me where he is and we'll end off this unpleasing bit of talk."

"Aye, Taggart says it's so, doesn't he?" Ogma's gaze never left her eyes. "So I can't be held responsible for the results, can I?" He took his pipe from his mouth and jabbed toward the right with it. "He's down back, on my old bench. Fool's been waiting twenty minutes or more."

She started going where Ogma had pointed but spun around, her eyes full of anger. "If there's a fool staying at this house, it's not Rolf Scholl," she snapped. She turned her back to Ogma before he could say any more and hurried around the side of the house, coming to an overgrown field that had once been a large garden. Rolf saw her immediately and got to his feet to come toward her, but she waved him back down and ran across the rest of the field, shaking her head.

"You're supposed to rest. I can stay longer if you don't get tired." She sat beside him and told of meeting Alice's grandmother on the road. "I was held up by talking to her, so that's why I'm late," explained Brigid. She did not mention the dance, for she thought the old woman might be embarrassed. Neither did she mention the talk with Ogma. The little man's unpleasant presence was around them all the time, and she did not intend to add to it. Instead she inquired after Rolf's shoulder, whether he had been able to sleep, whether he was eating all right (he made a face at that), and other questions about his well-being, finishing that part of their talk by telling him that as soon as he was able to take care of himself, he was going to be sent to a small village near the north where he could wait out the war.

"It's where one of the Druids lives," she explained, "And he can use some help on his farm. He's about my father's age, and quite nice, so it won't be an unpleasant place. And I'll still be able to see you a lot. But we've got to be doing something about your language. The way you speak English makes . . ."

"My English is being better," he protested.

"Oh, your English is being better," she replied with a grin. "But you're not talking it proper like a Manx."

"That is not the way I was instructed in school," he said.

"So what of it?" Brigid laughed. "That's not the way I was taught in school either. It's after you get away from there that you learn to speak it right. You're not expected to sound like the King, grand man that he might be. You're supposed to talk like us simple folk, so no one will look at you twice."

"Maybe I will start to talk like Herr Ogma, yes." Rolf put a nasty grin on his face. "You can believe that or not."

"Shush," Brigid giggled. "Be careful or he'll hear you." She looked around quickly. "St. Maughold help us if you ever start to sound like him. One horrid little man such as he is enough."

"You do not like him?" asked Rolf.

"He doesn't like me," answered Brigid, "or anyone else as far as I can tell. The only time he likes people is when they're dead."

"Brigit," Rolf cautioned with his hand. "He will hear you."

"Let it be, then." Brigid's face was flushed. "The horrid little man hears everything. I'm sure they talk to him from the grave." She looked around, expecting to see his face in the trees. "All things have their dark side," she said. "And for us it's the likes of him."

"What do you mean?" asked Rolf.

"He has his job to do on the Island, his part to play in our beliefs." She paused a moment, looking at Rolf. "Not all the powers of the Celts are high thoughts and good deeds. If there were only decency in the world, we'd none of us be having any problems, would we? There wouldn't be this war going on, or no type of injustice. But there is, and we've got to deal with it to keep things going."

"You mean Ogma is evil?" Rolf's voice was low.

"Evil?" Brigid looked slightly confused. "Oh no, I wouldn't say that, he's not really evil. His duty is to the Head Druid, and he can be trusted to do his job." She thought a moment. "But he's not good, either. He revels in the squalid. He's like a maggot or some insect that lives on filth, cleans it up; you find the creature revolting, but where would you be without it? Ogma has to deal with unpleasant things, it's true, but I feel that he enjoys his work far too much. I don't know whether the man was chosen for the job, or the job has made him what he is. Ogma has always been there for me and it seems he always will be."

"We sometimes have to do what we do not wish," Rolf looked away.

"Oh, Ogma doesn't mind the doing of it," Brigid smiled weakly. "This is silly, my going on about him, and I promised myself not to mention his name. It must be having him so close that does it." She jumped quickly to her feet. "Let's have a bit of a walk, then. Alice's grandmother says you're to have some exercise while you're out, as long as it's not too much." Rolf stood and Brigid lightly took his hand. They walked slowly around the parameter of the field, Brigid watching with care that none of the branches from the encroaching forest brushed against them and jolted his bad shoulder. They followed the track around the side of the house and went along the path to the point where Ogma had said Rolf should stop. They stood talking here a few minutes, then turned back to the shack. Rolf said that he was thirsty and was going in to get a drink. Brigid stopped him, arguing that the water in the house was probably days old. She said that she would draw him a pail, and as he protested, she led him to the well behind the house. The pail was already in the water, so she bent forward and pulled it up, hand over hand. Although the crank was rusty and unusable, the pail was brand-new, which surprised her. She held the pail on the stone rim, and Rolf cupped his hand and drank. Brigid also took some swallows of the cool water, then let the pail splash back into the darkness.

"You are strong, yes?" said Rolf, wiping his hand on his leg.

"I'm strong enough, aye," she said, flexing her arms. "But I'm not too unsightly, with bulging muscles."

Rolf looked puzzled for a moment, then his face lit up in memory. "Bulging—oh yes, to swell." He looked at her. "To be truthful, Brigit, it was not the—the bulge, yes—it was not the bulge of your muscles that I was looking at when you bended over for the water."

Brigid turned with a laugh. "Am I going to be hauling the pail up again, Rolf Scholl, so I can cool you off?" She grabbed his hand. "Come, you'd best be sitting down, before you get over-tired, even if it's only your imagination that does it." They walked to the rough plank and sat. They didn't speak for a while, and Brigid was lost in thought. She was wondering whether she should mention anything about the conversation she had had with her parents. It was something she had been thinking about all afternoon with him. She did not want him to feel that she did not trust him, but the fact was that there were reasonable questions that deserved answers.

"Rolf," she began, "I haven't told you that my mother and father didn't really want me to come and see you."

"When did they say that, Brigit?" His voice was flat.

"Before I came here today."

"Why? Do they not trust me?" He looked down at his feet. "Do they think that you are not safe to be with me?"

"No, Rolf. It isn't really that. They don't think that you . . ."

"Herr Ogma is always around, yes." Rolf looked in her direction. "He would never let me do anything wrong to you."

"They're not afraid for me in that way, Rolf." Brigid took his hand. "Well, my father did mention something—but that's the way fathers always worry about their daughters when men are involved."

"Yes," said Rolf slowly. "I think I understand that."

"Good," Brigid forced a smile. "Good. It is just natural, being concerned about the young man I'm seeing." She stopped for a moment, then decided to plunge ahead and get it over with. "What is really bothering them, Rolf, is why you're here at all."

"Why I am here?"

"Yes, on Man. We are at war, you know," she added quickly.

"And you, Brigit?" He turned and looked at her face. "Is it a problem with you why I am here? Do you wonder at it?"

Brigid returned his look a moment, then spoke quickly. "Yes, Rolf, it bothers me some. The feelings in the air are sometimes not good. I can tell that something is troubling the Head Druid. There was even a Druid council meeting last night, which is very, very strange. Your coming here does not appear a chance happening to many people, and when you refuse to tell anyone why you are on—"

"I have a job to do—I have told you that, Brigit." He looked away and gazed at the trees on the other side of the field. "I am still an army officer, I have a duty to do. There would be no honor with me if I told you."

"Rolf, what difference does it make?" Her voice was raised. "You can't do anything now; you can hardly walk around this field, let alone fight a war."

"I cannot tell you my job, Brigit." He looked back to her, and his face softened. "I can tell you that it has nothing to do with your home—with the Island. And certainly nothing with the Druids, or the . . . or what happened on the shore that night. I had no knowledge of such things before I met with you. And when the job is done I can tell you everything, and we can forget all this."

"When?" She jumped from the bench, her back to him. "Why can't you forget it now?" She turned, staring down into his eyes. "You still plan to go through with whatever it is, and you having no more strength than a new calf. This is all madness." She shook her head angrily and started storming across the field, but then she swung around abruptly and returned to stand over him again. "What am I going to do about you? A person can't be goin' just on feelings, you know. There has to be trust, and for trust you've got to have honesty. I can't let anything happen that could be a threat to the Island, to my way of life, to the things I am responsible for."

"But I am not a threat." Rolf stood beside her.

"They don't have Ogma watching over you because they think he's lonely. The Druids didn't meet because it was a fine night for a wee chat." Her face was flushed with emotion, her hands moving quickly to emphasize each point. "Taggart isn't moving all over the Island and doing God knows what just for the exercise." Her voice was loud now. "And mother doesn't have dreams, and all the beasts on the Island—all of them—don't come together—" She stopped short, her eyes blazing. "And all of it since you've come. You're the eye of the gale, Rolf Scholl, and I'm glad for all of us that you can't do your job, or whatever it is that is upsetting everything. And when the time is past, and all is done, then we can forget."

"But my work has nothing to do with what I have discovered on the Island. Nothing." Rolf put his fingers to her face and touched her cheek. "Do you not believe that? I would have nothing to do with the hurting of you."

"Rolf." She took his hand in hers. "It appears that you have powers beyond the ordinary five senses—that you're one of us, no matter how far in the past the connection was made. You must feel what is going on around you."

"Ja," he started, "I can feel . . . and I have seen. Brigit, there are different . . . " he paused a moment, then continued. "Different types of reality. When I am finished—have finished forever—with my old way, I can then start to be with your people. I have to finish with the old—my job—before I do this." She started to speak, but he shook his head. "No, let me to finish, please. I have felt what you describe, and that I was meant to come here. I think what is most important is the meeting of you and me. Together we will strengthen the power. I think this is what causes all the problems; your people do not want to accept a foreigner to be part of them, espesz . . . especially a German during the war."

"What nonsense, man," she removed her hand from his. "There's no one more likely to be accepting what is supposed to be than the Druids—that's part of their beliefs. And as for your being a German soldier having anything to do with it—that's all of your own making; you're the one going on about your job and your duty. None of us here sees you as a German soldier—not any more. We see you as some sort of relation, a part of our past come back to us."

"If I am meant to be here," insisted Rolf, "then I am meant to do my job. It's a part of me just as the things on the Island are."

"I might as well be talking to a bump on a log." She put her hands to her head and started pulling on her hair.

"Brigit," Rolf reached over to her, startled. "What are you doing?"

"It's what they'd be at in the old days." She gave her long hair some more tugs. "When a young lass went insane, it was pulling it out by the roots she was." She gave a snarl and bit at his hand. "And if anyone is driving me into madness, Rolf Scholl, it'll be yourself in all your stubborn glory." She slapped his hand away and turned her back to him, her hair in a jumble. "If I gave a screech like I'm feeling right now, I'd be scaring all the birds off the Calf." She stood silent for a minute, her hands made into fists by her sides. She turned slowly and looked at Rolf. "I'll have to be satisfied that you're in no shape to do anything about anything, won't I?"

"Are you angry at me, Brigit?"

"Of course I'm angry at you. What'll you be thinking, that I do this for my looks?" She took his hand and started leading him to the shack. "It doesn't mean I don't like you." They walked the rest of the way to Ogma's house in silence and stood a minute in front of the open door. "Go in now and get your rest. The day has surely tired me out."

"You will still come to see me?"

"Yes. Yes, of course I'll come. Now go lie down." She watched him enter the gloomy room, then turned and went down the path. Ogma shortly appeared behind her, and she stopped to speak.

"You'll be keeping a good eye on him," she said.

"As if he was a prize corpse," chuckled Ogma. "You can believe that or not."

Brigid hurried for home without another word.

XV

"I EXPECTED her to become more angry still," said Fenella as Taggart paced the room in front of her. "But she seemed to accept that I had better be telling you what Rolf had said. She seemed almost relieved, in fact. She doesn't want anything happening to the lad, and I don't think she knows what to do."

"And he didn't tell Brigid any more of what the job might be, where he was supposed to go, or when?" asked Taggart.

"No, he only kept repeating that it would not hurt the Island or damage our way of life."

"He's a bit young to be knowing that," said Taggart.

"They both are. I'm sure I didn't give as much trouble when I was her age," added Fenella.

"Yet I imagine that you did," Taggart smiled.

"At least I stuck to a Manxman," she laughed. "If only we had brains when we're young."

"To know too much deadens the feelings." Taggart stopped his pacing. "I received a note that Jeremy wants to see me, so I may as well go by way of Ogma's." He gave a small smile. "Do you want to come?"

"I can be answering that right fast enough, but I suspect it won't be necessary. You know it well that I don't." She got out of her chair, ready to leave. "Brigid doesn't know why Ogma takes on at her so, and I don't see any sense in telling her." Fenella followed the Head Druid to the door. "You'd think he'd forget and let it rest."

Taggart opened the door, stepping back to let her go ahead. "Ogma doesn't forget anything, especially if he feels he's been wronged." They walked quickly along the lane.

"He has no reason to feel wronged," Fenella said. "I did nothing to encourage him, and after I met Will there was no question of whom I wanted."

"That's not quite the way William puts it," said Taggart.

"Well, to be sure, I did a little teasing with him." Fenella smiled in memory. "The man was so sure of himself that he had to be put in his place a bit. Even with my games, I don't think that he ever had much doubt."

"If one man could want you so much," put in Taggart, "then it shouldn't be a surprise when another man feels the same."

"But after all these years—the man's not reasonable."

"You can't reason with feelings; isn't that what you said to Brigid? It's just as true in Ogma's case."

"He shouldn't be taking it out on the girl," she insisted.

"No," Taggart agreed. "Of course not. I'll have a word with him. It's unfortunate that having to deal with Rolf and Brigid—and through her, with you—has brought all this up again. He's never done anything as concerns you for years now, has he?" asked Taggart.

"No, not since the girl started going out on her own. He's never really done much since I've been married—except for that song he wrote about Will." Fenella laughed out, "That was a piece of work, that was."

"How do you know of that?" Taggart asked. "And what did William have to say when he heard it?"

"Och, you think I'm mad? As far as I know, Will's never heard it. He'd have beaten Ogma with his own shovel, you know the pride that's in him." Fenella looked over at the Head Druid. "Oh, that Ogma's a sly one; he made sure I got a copy when Will was out on the fishing. I found it tied to the well handle one morning. I tore it up right away, but it did give me a laugh."

"They still sing it in some of the pubs," said Taggart.

"It was done with feeling, right enough," replied Fenella. "It'll probably just keep on going, become part of the great Manx folklore. It's funny to think of Will as being a ballad in a hundred years or so—and him never hearing the thing."

"That's just as well," chuckled Taggart.

"Yes," Fenella agreed, "and I'll be hoping it stays that way. Although done long ago, it could still cause trouble." She looked over to the Head Druid. "And I'm thinking that we have enough of that right now—so it feels, at any rate."

"Yes," replied Taggart. "Whatever is to happen is trouble such as we have never known."

"The first war—in my time—never gave these feelings."

"That was a war of kings. It was different, a dying of the old ways. Now we change or perish."

They spoke very little the rest of the way to the main road, and after Taggart told Fenella to give his regards to William, they went in different directions. Taggart followed the main road for a time and then cut through some fields and woods, until he came to a rougher road. As he walked along at a fast pace, he wondered whether there was some action he was not taking that he should, or some event he had overlooked. Where did the hand of fate halt, and his ability to change things begin? Rolf now had strong attractions to the Island, which might help to dilute the crisis when it occurred. It would probably be best if he were left alone and allowed to act out his role.

Taggart turned onto the narrow track that led to Ogma's and was surprised to see how long the shadows were. It was obviously quite a bit later than he thought; that happened when many things occurred at once. He went around a clump of bushes and came upon Ogma, packing some tobacco into his pipe.

"You're not as quiet as usual, Taggart."

"Do I hear a touch of reproach in your voice?" The Head Druid smiled.

"Don't like things being made too easy," he lit his pipe. "It'd be easy to start getting slack." He moved the pipe from one corner of his mouth to the other. "Not that you're as bad as the old fat one —that's like hearing a truck coming at you." He fell into step beside the Head Druid. "It's been too busy a day; I'm not used to so many people that can move around by themselves. Conversation is a trouble, I prefer it when they can't answer back." Ogma followed Taggart to the door of his house. "Will you be wanting to talk with Jerry about something?"

"Is he inside?"

"Aye. Been there since the girl left." He took the pipe from his mouth and grinned. "She got him so worked up that he's probably in there playing with himself now."

"Ogma," the Head Druid turned to look at the small man. "I'm used to your ways and also know what's bothering you. If you want to keep working at this foolishness, all right—a man's entitled to his feelings. But you've no business to bother the girl about it. She's done nothing to you and cannot be made responsible for what's gone on in your past. Lay the blame where it's deserved, at your own feet."

"She could have . . . "

"There's no more to be said of it," the Head Druid cut him off. "We have problems enough to deal with," he pointed to the door. "Now, how is the boy?"

"The last I looked he was asleep."

"We'll leave him be then," Taggart turned from the door. "Has he said anything to you that might be of help?"

"He had quite a set-to with the lass."

"Yes, I know. He seems determined to go ahead with his 'job' and insists that it holds no threat to us."

"You should let me tie him up and be done with it. I'm good at putting people in their place, you can believe that or not."

"If I knew that was the right thing to do, Ogma, it would solve all our problems. But I think he'll help as much as hinder, as he has already." Taggart started back along the path. "There's nothing that he's said?"

Ogma walked beside him, puffing on his pipe. "No, there's nothing been said to me that tells what he's doing here." The small man scratched his balding head. "There is something a bit strange, though, if you stop to think about it."

"What might that be?" Taggart was interested, for Ogma was a very shrewd observer.

"Is Jerry an orphan?"

"An orphan? No, I don't think so." Taggart traced back in his mind over the things that had been said. "His mother . . . his mother was killed in a train accident." Taggart was silent a few moments. "Yes, it is apparently through her that Rolf is descended from the Manx Druid, for it was his mother's sister who had some of the gifts of second sight. He mentioned it before they cut the bullet out of him. Why do you want to know?"

"It isn't what he says," Ogma looked up into Taggart's eyes. "It's what he isn't saying. If it were any from Man in his place—especially at his age—they'd be talking about missing their family, or wives, or lovers, or whatever. I've seen at funerals that it's the family that carries on the most. If you don't have family, it doesn't bother you so much. That's why I asked about his being an orphan—he's never mentioned his father or any brothers and sisters—he's always on about that town of his, and the places in it he'd visit."

"Never mentions his father?"

"No, not once—it's not normal."

"You're right, Ogma; it's something to think about."

Taggart was silent for a minute, wondering whether there was any importance to the fact. Rolf had definitely mentioned his mother's death, but whether his father had been killed at the same time—or any other time—that too should have been mentioned. "Maybe it means nothing more than that he's a misfit like you," suggested Taggart.

"Oh, there's none likely to be like me," said Ogma. "Jerry's got too much trust in him to be any good in my world. He thinks he'll go on, one two three, playing his part and getting the things he wants in nice little pieces, adding all up to a proper and happy life, and that he'll die in the end with a sweet smile of satisfaction on his face."

"We all think much the same when we're young, Ogma; it's not such a bad thing to have dreams."

"How can you," Ogma asked, stopping on the rough path, "with all that you know, say something like that?"

"I can still see both sides," Taggart stopped also. "There is a bounty of pleasurable things on earth, and in this life. It's not a weakness to enjoy them."

"Pah, 'tis all dust from the footsteps, it just makes things a bit bearable, to try and cover all the sighing and groaning that we'd be naturally doing. To be sure there's some pleasure, but it's ha'-penny to a pound with all we have to put up with. You dig underneath, Taggart, you dig underneath it all, and you just get the blackness, you get to the despair that is at the bottom of life."

"We may end in a black hole," replied Taggart. "As you well enough like to keep saying. But we do not have to live our lives in one, except by our own choosing. Someone puts you in that hole when you're dead, but you climb into it yourself if that's where you spend your life. It seems to me, Ogma, that you spend as much time trying to make yourself wretched, as most people spend hunting for enjoyment."

"If I'm a fool, then they're as much a one."

"It must be small consolation," said Taggart.

"I don't need much consolation," the grin came back to the small man's face. "But when I do, I can get it fast enough. When it's my turn with them—all the strivers and believers and chasers of that enjoyment and happiness they've been after their whole lives—when I straighten their jackets and comb their hair, when I put the lid over them and fasten it down—nails or clasps makes no matter—when I do all that, is when I get my feelings of pleasure, because it's then I know that I've been right. Say what you want Taggart, I'm the one that remains, not them."

"I can't help feeling," said the Head Druid, as he started walking, "that they're still better off than you are, Ogma."

"Different points of view," said Ogma, "is what makes life." He walked beside the tall man for a time, then stopped where Taggart had first seen him. "I'd best not go any farther if I want to keep a good eye on the Jerry. Not that he could get very far the way he is." He took the pipe from his mouth. "And that's something else to be thinking about, his being so weak and still planning on his job. It can't be all that hard if he still thinks he can do it."

"His insistence about it had crossed my mind," agreed Taggart.

"He won't be having much strength for weeks," added Ogma.

"Regardless," said Taggart, "don't underestimate the lad. If he says anything at all, or . . ." Taggart smiled, "doesn't say something he should, let me know of it as soon as possible."

"I'll be as fast to your door as if I've heard there's been a death, you can believe that or not." Ogma grinned as he turned and started back to his house.

The Head Druid started walking quickly. His long strides took him through more fields and across a road or two until he came to the main road, which he hurried along until he came to the turn-off to Jeremy's farm. In another five minutes he was at the gate of the small farm, and he stopped to listen. There was no sound, so he went to the door and knocked. When there was no response, he knocked more loudly.

"Taggart?" The voice came from behind the barn.

"Yes." The Head Druid went around the building and saw Jeremy sitting on the peat pile, as he had been a couple of days before.

"Just getting the last rays of the sun," said the elderly Druid. "Come and sit beside me; you look tired."

"It's been a rushed day." Taggart went and sat down by the old man. "We keep getting the sunshine, and all your turf will soon be nice and dry."

"Aye, true enough." Jeremy sat silent for a moment, then took some folded pages out of his pocket and spread them flat on his knees. He looked at the papers a moment, then passed them over to Taggart. "Take a look at this. Got them from the wee house, going to use them for toilet paper—lucky to get anything with this war."

Taggart looked at the creased papers. They were pages from the Manchester Guardian, about three weeks old. They had yet to be cut into squares and Taggart glanced at the front page. He saw nothing unusual; it was practically all war news. He started to turn the page when Jeremy stopped him.

"No lad, it's on the first page." Taggart looked up, puzzled, and Jeremy gave a small smile. "You know how I never read the newspapers, never have all of my life. I don't mind books, especially history and the like, but never the papers—a waste of time. My sons get them, though—I've never been one to push my beliefs down their throats. Well, one of my sons, Peter—that's the one with the shop in Castletown—he went over about a month ago, and when he was in Manchester, he picked this up. I usually do the cuttin' of the pages once a week, never really paying any attention to what's in them. Look at the pictures sometimes, though, and that's why I saw this." Jeremy leaned forward and jabbed at a photograph at the top of the page.

Taggart looked again at the paper. "It's a picture of Hitler," he said.

"That's the bugger, right enough," said Jeremy. "I've been hearing the name all these years, but I never saw what he looked like before."

Taggart looked from the picture to Jeremy, and back to the

picture. It was a head-and-shoulders shot of Hitler, with a story about his latest speech, still saying he wanted peace with Britain. The Head Druid looked at Jeremy one more time. "I don't understand; what's important about this?"

The old Druid stroked his long beard, his fingers sometimes getting lost in the white hair. Then he pointed to the picture again. "I met the bastard once," he said. "Even spoke to him."

Taggart looked away, his face showing confusion and doubt.

Jeremy smiled and touched the other man's knee. "Don't look worried and think I've gone off my head." He gave a small laugh. "That's one of the benefits of having a beard, lad; people can't read your face as easy." He tapped the page again. "You know me and faces, Taggart. I never forget one."

"That's true." Taggart had to agree; the old Druid's memory for people was a legend on the Island. "But when . . . "

"That's what I've been trying to remember," said Jeremy, leaning back against the turf pile to be more comfortable. "It was before the war—the first war, the war to end all wars—but it took a while to get the year right. When you've had as many years as I, they all come together, and you have to stop to keep them separate. It would have been March or April of 1913, probably March, for the weather was mostly nasty."

"Where?" Taggart asked.

"On the other side," said Jeremy, "in Liverpool. I've been spending most of the day trying to remember everything I can, so I'd be accurate in the telling." The old Druid paused for a moment, took his pipe out of a pocket, but replaced it as quickly. "I don't remember why I was there, maybe for the trip more than anything; I still liked a bit of travel in those days. I was walking around in the early afternoon, puffing on the pipe, so I might have just had a lunch—I like a smoke after a meal. Feeling good, a nice day, and I didn't carry all the aches and pains around that I do now. Anyway, I noticed a man across the pavement. I was right opposite the Bluecoat Hospital, and this man was looking up at the sign, then looking down at a piece of paper in his hand. Skinny chap; his clothes were loose on him. Then he started looking around him, up and down the street, and back at the piece of paper. He looked around again and saw me walking past on the other side. There was no one else near, so he called and crossed the road toward me."

"What did he say," asked Taggart, "when he spoke across the street?"

"He yelled out, 'Hello'," replied Jeremy, "in a very thick accent, so I figured he was a foreigner right away. You didn't see many people from other countries in those days, except the sailors off the ships. So I stopped, and he hurried over. He moved in a nervous way; his legs almost seemed to be jerking. He was a young man then, of course, I suppose in his early twenties. He took hold of my hand and shook it like a pump handle. He was almost exploding with energy, like a sparkler the children use on Guy Fawkes night. He had terrible English, almost nonexistent. Somewhere after a harsh 'pardon me' and a lot of muttering and hand waving, I heard the word 'lost.' I repeated the word, and his mouth became a big smile, and his eyes turned into blue diamonds flashing in my face. I've heard the talk on the wireless that he can hypnotize people, and it just may be true, thinking about those eyes now. *Ja,*' he said, '*ja, ja, ja,*' and some more German, and then 'lost.' He showed me the piece of paper, and his hand shook. I took it from him and had a look. It was some sort of map he was trying to follow."

"A street map?" Taggart wanted to know.

"Oh no," Jeremy snorted. "Nothing so fancy as that. It was a crude map on some cheap wrapping paper. I could make out some of the street names, but the rest of it was foreign to me; German, I expect. Oh, one or two place names were in English—the hospital was one of them—but all the others were beyond me. I still don't know whether he ever got there." Jeremy stopped and gave a sigh. "It's a funny thing, you know."

"What is?"

"I was just thinking—you do too much of that when you get old, lad. The 'what might have happened' sometimes gets more important than what really did. Silly way to think. But you know, I could have stopped it all right then. If I had shoved him under a tram, or into the Mersey, or just snapped his neck—I was a strong one then and he was such a thin bag of clothes. And there'd be none of this war going on, all those people still alive, none of this business on Man causing us trouble."

"But you had no reason," said Taggart.

"That's not quite true," Jeremy looked away.

"What do you mean?"

"You know me, Taggart, the way I am." He looked back at the

other man, slowly raised his eyes to meet the dark green ones. "I've always been the most practical Druid, never been much for 'feeling' things, or dealing with the Otherworld. That type of thing I've left to people like you, or the girl and her mother—and yes, her grandmother—or to Katherine and her kind. But this time—this once—I got touched by a bit of the power—we're all supposed to be capable of it, you know, once in a while. I never realized until now, until I'd seen that damned thing," he jabbed a finger toward the picture. "I never realized that my feeling was right."

"Why?" asked Taggart. "What did he do?" The Head Druid's eyes went back to the creased picture in front of him.

"Oh, he didn't do anything—or say anything for that matter; I couldn't have understood him if he had. In fact, once he saw that I was going to try and help, he couldn't have been more grateful; he was almost frantic to make me understand what he wanted. He wasn't troublesome or threatening like that. But there was . . . " Jeremy stopped speaking and glanced over at the newspaper. "I'm trying to say this exactly, like the practical man I am, and not be vague, but that's hard to do with what you feel." The old Druid gave a shy smile, hardly visible through his dense beard. "Katherine tried to tell me about it once. Her exact words were: 'Feelings are feelings; there's nothing to be said about them.' Smart woman, right enough. You shouldn't be waiting too long about her, Taggart."

"I know."

"Anyway," Jeremy went on, "the thing was, when he talked or looked at you, he made you feel inferior. Even though he looked right at you, right into your eyes, he was also looking through you, seeing something else at the same time. He was so sure of himself, that no one else was quite real to him. That's the feeling he gave; he was completely one with himself."

"That doesn't necessarily make a person evil," said Taggart.

"No, you're right, it doesn't," Jeremy nodded his head. "But it does make the person inhuman. When you have no time for other people, then all your energy goes into something else. Such people usually go from one extreme to another, and it was nothing hard to see that this man was never going to be a saint, no matter what he felt himself."

"You felt his evil?"

"No, just the emptiness." Jeremy's voice grew hard. "But I could also see how this void would be filled."

"It wasn't up to you to finish his existence."

"Maybe not," said Jeremy. "But we'll never really know that, will we? I was given a chance."

Both men were silent for a long time, not looking at each other but gazing at some neutral object: Jeremy at his house and barn, Taggart at the setting sun. A chill was settling over the yard, and a slight wind blew the coolness against them. After three or four minutes, the Head Druid finally spoke.

"And that was the last of it?" he asked.

Jeremy looked up, startled. "What?"

"That was the last you saw of him?"

"Oh no," the old man shook his head. "That wasn't the finish of it. I was with him for another fifteen or twenty minutes. I said that I couldn't read much of his map or tell where he wanted to go, but I could make out some of the street names. It happened that one of the street corners wasn't that far away from where we were, and in the direction I was going, so I felt that the least I could do was take him there."

"Even feeling the way you did about him?"

"Oh, I was uneasy right enough, being with him. But it was also fascinating—just to watch him. All these ideas, my reasons for feeling the way I do, never came till much later. Some of them I don't think I realized until today, when I've spent most of my time thinking about it."

"Did you suspect that he was mad?"

"Yes, without any doubt. Even then you could see it in him. All that intensity, it was none of it normal. But he wasn't mad in the sense that he didn't know what went on around him; his eyes might have always seen something you and I don't, but they still never missed anything."

"Where did you go?"

"Heh, I don't remember that now—it was just a street corner, after all. I had a difficult time to make him understand that I wanted him to come with me. At last I just took him—a bit forcefully—by the elbow, and half-pushed him in front of me. I was, after all, much stronger and he was just a young man; he didn't even have that silly little mustache then." Jeremy stopped and laid a finger along his upper lip, which looked so incongruous with his full beard that Taggart burst out laughing, causing Jeremy to laugh also. "Yet they say the women worship him," Jeremy wiped his eyes. "Ah, it doesn't make any sense, but then, women never do."

He gave a sigh of bafflement and went on. "After he started walking he kept nattering away in German, keeping up a conversation, yet from time to time grinning foolishly when he realized that I couldn't understand what he was saying. I'd point out one or two places and mention their names, and he'd look at them and nod vacantly. Once in a while he seemed interested in a building, and his face would light up and he'd ramble on, pointing at things and sometimes even touching the stones. But these bits of interest came and went with the quickness of a gust of wind. Once he took the map and pointed to an X on it, in the opposite direction from which we were going, and said the word 'brother.' I don't know what he meant, or maybe I just didn't hear him right.

"Once, when he was rattling on," Jeremy gave a loud laugh, "and he finally paused for breath, I started replying in Manx Gaelic, with a loud voice like I was pronouncing from the pulpit. He gave me such a look, as if I'd swelled like *Cú Chulainn*. I don't know whether I sounded so absurd, or whether perhaps he did see the humor of our talking to each other—anyway, he started to laugh, and I laughed with him. I don't think it made him talk any less, but I felt that I'd done what I could.

"We walked on together for about another five minutes, and then I touched his arm and pointed to a street sign. He looked up at it, and down to his map, and then back to the sign. His face shone and those eyes began to sparkle, and he grabbed my hand again and started to shake it up and down. *'Ja ja ja,'* he said, and then *'Danke, danke'* without even looking at me, but gazing at the sign and then at the map. Then, with a very formal handshake—using both his hands to clasp my own—he turned and walked away." Jeremy paused a moment. "I haven't the faintest doubt that as soon as his back was turned, he forgot about me completely and never thought of me again."

The yard was streaked with shadows now, and only the top parts of their bodies were in the sunlight. Jeremy stood and stretched, reaching his arms above his head. He looked down at Taggart with a wink.

"All that talk's made my throat feel like one of those slabs of turf. How would you be looking on a wee mug of *jough?*"

"Brewed by yourself?" asked Taggart.

"Aye. I don't waste my time buying any of the stuff."

"Then I know the ale will be good and strong." Taggart stood beside the other man. "I won't say no—just out of politeness, you understand." He followed Jeremy across the yard and they went through the narrow back door into the kitchen. It was small, with a few cupboards along one wall, a black stove in a corner, and a brown, scarred table near the window.

"Sit down, lad," said Jeremy, "I won't be a minute."

Taggart sat at the table, placing in front of him the pages of the newspaper he still carried. Jeremy went to the cupboards and bent to open the one nearest the corner. He took out a thick, reddish-colored jug, and, collecting two mugs from an upper cupboard, he returned to the table and sat opposite Taggart. He pried the plug out of the neck of the jug and poured the two mugs full to the brim.

"Traa dy liooar," said Jeremy and took a gulp of his ale. Taggart smiled and drank some of his. The old man did make the drink strong, and it raced down his throat in an agreeable way.

"I'm not sure how you mean that," said Taggart, putting the mug on the table. "There's time enough for what?"

"Why, lad," Jeremy stroked a drop from his beard. "I haven't been telling you this story for the nice bit of history it makes."

"No, I didn't suppose you were." The Head Druid took another drink of the ale, and Jeremy refilled his mug. "What do you think is the importance of your meeting the man?" Taggart tapped the picture in front of him with a finger.

"Why, it's the connection." Jeremy put down his drink and looked Taggart directly in the eyes. "It erases any doubt as to what the problem is. It all centers around the German boy, and the job he has to do." He could still see the doubt in the dark green eyes staring back at him. "It wasn't just by chance that I met this murderous bastard." Jeremy picked up the picture and glared at it. "He looks such a fool."

"Jeremy," Taggart began, "we already know that Rolf is the key to this whole problem."

"Yes, but now . . ." Jeremy paused and took another sip. "But now the wheel has come full circle. My encounter with Hitler and my connection with Rolf join them both together through me— through what I am. Meeting with . . . " he shoved the paper back, ". . . with *that,* was a warning, and we're not warned of people who are harmless." Jeremy saw understanding dawning in the Head Druid's eyes and pressed on. "You've been wondering if Rolf might be just a pawn, not really capable of evil himself. I'm positive that this connection with Hitler—where maybe I am just a pawn—proves that Rolf *can* be very dangerous, that what he may do is capable of creating great evil."

"Rolf is not the innocent he seems," said Taggart.

"Oh, he may be innocent enough, but he's none the less dangerous for that." Jeremy poured himself some more from the jug. "But innocence isn't all that helpful in this world. He probably does really think that his job can't harm us, but he doesn't realize that we can never be sure of all the consequences of our acts. Some place two hundred years ago, a man may have introduced his friend to his sister, and today their great-great-grandson is trying to destroy the world. Could that man ever imagine such a consequence of his act?"

"Ogma may be right," Taggart finished his drink and refused any more. "Perhaps we should just lock the lad away for the next few days. It would take care of any immediate threat."

"As far as we know," added Jeremy.

"Yes," Taggart smiled. "As far as we know." He looked at the picture one more time. "You really believe that your meeting with Hitler was a portent of what is happening now?"

"Portent?" Jeremy grinned. "Is that one of Katherine's words?"

"Yes," Taggart answered. "She believes that such things can be very important—if one understands what they mean."

"Aye," agreed Jeremy. "And I'll be thinking that she's right. It may have taken over twenty-five years for the seed to come good, but here it is none the less. I'm not a Druid for nothing, and if Katherine calls it a portent of things to come, then a portent it is. The things have certainly come, haven't they?"

"Yes," Taggart gave a wry smile. "At least I certainly hope that nothing more is to happen."

"As I've pointed out before," said Jeremy, putting the plug back into his jug, "you've always been a cheerful one."

"Your jug of *jough* always brightens me."

"Ung." The older Druid stood from the table. "Well, enough's been had if you're starting to think of worse things than we've already got." He walked across the room and put the ale back in the cupboard. "You should learn to be content with disaster and not ask for anything more."

"I'll try to remember that." Taggart also stood from the table. He went to one of the small windows and peered out. "It's starting to get black, and I've things yet to do." He paused a moment, craning his neck to look up into the sky. "Some stars, though, and the moon will be rising later on." He turned to the other man. "I prefer to do things in person when possible, but there's no time for that now. I'd best use your telephone."

"Pah," the old man snorted. "I wish I'd never let the boys talk me into getting it. You don't get to hear what a person really has to say unless you can see his face. Every time that little bell gets to clamoring, I—"

"Spare me one of your sermons about the proper days that have gone by. Modern things can be useful if they're treated properly. In most ways we're better off in the present than in the past."

"Matter of opinion, that is." Jeremy went back to the table and sat. "You'll be knowing where the damn thing is."

Taggart went through a small room and came to the living room at the front of the house. In a bottom compartment of the radio stand he found the telephone, and he rang for Nigel's number in Douglas. There were the usual clicks and burrs, and after a short pause he heard the young Druid's voice at the other end of the line. After asking whether there was any new information and finding there was not, he told Nigel what he wanted Mr. Stephenson to do.

"Ask him whether he knows—or can find out—anything about Rolf's father; it may help somehow in dealing with Rolf and his job. We are now convinced that the job and whatever Rolf's actions may be will lead to some terrible disaster, and I think there can be no doubt that it must be as important as what we discussed this morning. And as an afterthought—though not as important—ask whether he knows of any reason why Hitler would have been in Liverpool a year before the first war."

Taggart put the telephone back in its place and returned to the kitchen, where he found Jeremy looking at the newspaper.

"I'm going to see Katherine, if I'm needed for anything."

"All right, lad, I'll remember."

Taggart was just about to close the door behind him, when he turned back to the old Druid. "Don't brood over the picture; we're doing all that we can." He was surprised when Jeremy smiled.

"Don't worry about me." He tapped the photo. "I'm going to put this to good use."

Taggart went into the night with a chuckle.

XVI

BRIGID WAS anxious to get home. The night was full of noise, sounds she had never heard and did not understand. The whole Island was restless; wherever she had gone she had sensed it. The unicorn had forced her far afield for hours, as distant as the Cloven Stones near Baldrine. They had never been there before, and he paced around the shattered rocks in an odd manner, as if hunting for something in the earth. Brigid stayed by his side, trying to sense what was wrong, but he did not give her any sign. His actions were of years ago, his manner toward her as to a child with much to learn.

Their night had ended there. He refused to leave the Cloven Stones. When Brigid tried to insist that he come with her, his eyes had shot sparks and his teeth nipped at her hand. In confusion she stepped back, and his white head shook, the horn pointing out the direction she must take. She was angry and turned her back to stride away, not once glancing behind. She walked defiantly through the village, little caring who saw her, forsaking the secrecy of their walks. But there was no one about; each door was barred, for Brigid was not the only one who felt the unease of the night.

As she walked toward her home, she was uncertain about the movements in the trees around her. There was constant activity; neither ground nor air was at peace. It was more than just the beasts, though she could sense they were agitated enough, passing through the darkness with much flurry and fluster. The meeting of the night before had brought them all together, but now they were joining on their own, preparing for some action in which she was not a part. With this arrangement of creatures, from the smallest to the most fantastic, there were forces she had never seen—the legends of Man and its myths coming to join and to aid. Brigid felt that she was barely tolerated as she moved quickly through the turbulent night, the unseen powers parting to let her pass but closing quickly behind, impatient for her to be away.

Brigid finally came to her more familiar part of the Island and almost began to run, she so wanted to be home. The commotion in the forest was less, and she wondered whether perhaps she should mention nothing to her parents. Any discussion might bring up further doubts about Rolf. She did not want to start debating about him again; all she had to answer her father's arguments were her feelings, and they never had any weight against logic. Brigid was sure that even her mother was now far more cautious about Rolf. Although Fenella still believed that he could be trusted with the secrets of the Island, the Head Druid had apparently convinced her that Rolf was a great threat in some other way. Brigid had to admit that she herself was feeling uneasy —not that she really doubted Rolf, but she could not close her eyes to the unrest around her.

By the time she came in sight of her home, Brigid had decided not to disturb her parents so late at night. When she entered the hallway, however, she saw light coming from under the door of the room where Rolf had stayed. She had noticed nothing outside because of the blackout curtains and was quite surprised. She knocked lightly on the door and opened it. Her father was propped up by pillows with a book in his hands, while her mother sat in an easy chair near his bed, patching the pair of pants he had been wearing the night of the bomber attack.

"And what will you two be doing, up this late at night?" She was annoyed because she knew why they were still awake, waiting together for her to come home, something they had not done for years. They were no longer sure she could keep in control of the things happening around her. "Especially you, father," she added. "You should be getting all the sleep you can to heal that bad leg."

"I'm in bed enough as it is, girl," he said gruffly. "Don't you think I'm getting more sleep than I need?"

"You've been out longer than usual," said Fenella, not looking up from her sewing.

"He went as far as Baldrine," answered Brigid.

"Oh," her mother seemed startled. "That is a distance."

"We've never been there before." She looked at them both, wondering whether to go on. She decided that she would; things were as well done first as last. "Did he ever take you to the place?" she asked, looking toward Fenella.

"No." She stopped her sewing.

"He acted very strange." Brigid went over to her father's bed and sat at the foot of it. "He made me come home alone."

"The Cloven Stones are still an unpleasant place," said Fenella.

"Aye," added William. "Where we Celtic heathens were converted."

"Now Will," his wife glanced at him. "That makes a good story and fits into Christian convention is all. A small adjustment we don't mind making. It still has the agony around it of being a place of sacrifice."

"But why would he go there?" asked Brigid.

"It's a place of power." Fenella looked closely at her daughter. "Where there's terror and death, the earth becomes very strong. It wasn't just the unicorn that was going there tonight, was it?"

"No." Brigid's voice could hardly be heard.

"It attracts like a magnet, that place." Fenella kept staring at her daughter, for she had to make her understand. "There are things we people have no control over. Last night, when you and Katherine and Taggart met with all the beasts, you became a part —perhaps an equal—but in no way the master, of the strength of the ages that is moving on the Island. Taggart may supply the reasoning, Katherine gives us warnings, and you are our link to their link, but in the end we depend on those powers that are meeting tonight. They have their own ways, far beyond our understanding. Your father and I could feel that going on, as I suspect most Manx can—there won't be many out and about at this hour. That's why we were waiting up for you—we just wanted to make sure."

"Do you think he was angry with me?" Brigid asked.

"I don't know," said Fenella.

"If all this is happening because of Rolf . . . " Brigid began.

"Maybe it is, maybe it isn't," said her father. "We just have to go along as best we can."

"There aren't any answers, anymore," said Fenella.

"He let Rolf see him," insisted Brigid. "He saved his life."

"Yes, but Brigid," her father gave a sigh. "They helped each other. Don't you see, they're even now. Clean slate."

"So we just wait?" asked Brigid.

"Yes." Fenella put her sewing things away in a box. "We just wait."

Taggart was surprised by the intensity of the Island and stood undecided amidst the rush and murmur, wondering whether he should call another Druid council. Should they not be part of what was happening, even though they had had their own joining of power just a short time ago? He walked on slowly for a while, pondering this problem, then stopped abruptly. He realized that the question was really its own answer. Just as he and the Druids had had their meeting the night before, now it was the time for the others to do the same. If somehow he were caught unprepared, they would give him warning when to act. There was unease on the land tonight, but he could not sense any danger. The time was not yet arrived.

He felt it best to get clear of the woods, to allow the night its privacy. He continued quickly to his destination, through forest and across fields that began to glow in the light from the rising moon. The way was familiar, and as one who was used to moving in the dark, he had no trouble finding the road that led to where Katherine stayed. Like the sun, the moon did not reach through the massive trees that lined the winding path. It was difficult to see the narrow entrance between the two dark oaks, and Taggart hesitated until he saw a glimmer beyond that guided him into the clearing. As he went closer, he saw that the well was a circle of light, the water shimmering and frothing as if electrified.

When he approached and looked down, seven fish leaped high from the surface and arched back to the water, splashing him with sparkling colors. He turned around, his tunic streaked with rainbow. A movement from the cave where Katherine stayed had caught his attention, and as he watched she came out of the entrance. She wore a long flowing gown—the purple color of clouds. Her luxuriant black hair fell freely across her shoulders and down her back. A wide silver belt was linked around her waist, and a heavy gold cube hung from a fine chain around her neck, touching her breasts as she walked toward him.

"It took such a night to bring you?" she asked.

"The night played some part," he said, stepping toward her. "But though it is a time for the unexpected, you are surely not surprised that I wish to see you?"

"You should see me more often than you do."

"I know." Taggart stood beside her and took her hand. "That is what Jeremy told me earlier today."

"That kind old man."

"Do we speak of the same person?" Taggart smiled as he bent close, lips touching her cheek. "Jeremy's as hard as nails."

"He's always been kind to me." She led him to the well, the light glancing off the cube at her breast. "Perhaps he attempts to make up for the way he feels you neglect me."

"Do you think I neglect you, Katherine?"

"Thoughts aren't needed, Taggart. I know you do." She turned from him and looked into the water. "But I also know that you don't do it because of lack of affection."

"No, of course not." He sounded surprised. "I . . ."

"You feel a great duty to your work." She paused and continued to stare into the water. "And a closer relationship with me would lessen the time you should spend on your responsibilities."

"As usual, you have described the situation perfectly." Taggart gazed over her shoulder. "As you know, my tasks are not the kind I can put away when evening comes and forget until the next day. There are no weekends and no holidays as most others have. I think that a strong relationship between people needs more time than I can give."

"Shouldn't both the people involved decide that?" she asked.

"I'm so used to making all the decisions." Taggart gave a small laugh. "One gets trapped into thinking the same way all the time." He touched her shoulder. "Of course, you are right. But what of the reverse of that coin?"

"Your job, you mean?"

"Yes. Just as I wonder whether I could treat you properly, I fear that I might not devote enough attention to my duties. My feelings for you might detract from the work I must constantly do."

"Being what I am, Taggart, I would never let that happen." She turned her face up toward his eyes. "I would be far more help than a hindrance."

"You seem to have both our parts thought out," he said.

"All except the answer."

"You cannot guess that?"

"Yes, but only guess. My sight of the future stops at myself. It is, I imagine, a safeguard of sanity."

"It seems odd to me," said Taggart, his fingers stroking her hair, "that at this time, when I face the most stress I have ever known, I have the greatest need to be with you. If my own argument held true, then I should have no time to be thinking of you. But you are more in my thoughts, not less." His fingers moved along her neck, brushed against her breasts as he weighed the gold cube in his palm. "The symbol of perfection—no matter which way you look at it, it remains the same. An absolute completion." His eyes bored into her own. "That is the way I feel when with you—as if I were finally complete."

"I have always felt that with you, Taggart." Her voice was low.

"Yes . . . I . . . " he looked away from her. "I may never have wanted to admit that before. I have always thought of needing someone as a type of weakness."

"Strong men often do," she said.

"It may have taken these troubles—this night—to show me that I can't do everything. There's a large place left vacant for you, Katherine; I see now that you are the only one who can fill it."

"My one hope, Taggart, is that we haven't left it too late."

"With what is going on around us," Taggart looked off into the darkness, "we have at least one night."

"And then?"

"You're asking me?" Taggart smiled. "I work with what I have; it's you who deal with the future."

"I've had enough of the future." She turned from him and looked into the sparkling water. "It's been like this all evening, magic waters and magic fish, as if all the stars had fallen together. I've never seen the power this strong, Taggart. It must go its own way, for I can have no part of it. It is not our night to deal with any of the things around us."

"We are left to ourselves?"

"Yes."

Taggart looked down on the back of her head, then put his arms around her, his fingers lightly caressing the tips of her breasts. He felt a beginning hardness as she turned to face him, and as they kissed his hands slid along her back, stopping at her swelling flesh as he pressed their bodies closer.

A fish leaped with a grin.

XVIIII

"AND HOW were you sleeping, lad? Any more used to my humble place? Does your affection for it grow with passing time?"

Rolf stirred on his hard cot, looked through the gloom to see the gravedigger standing near him. "What is the time, Herr Ogma?"

"Well now, you've let yourself go quite a while this morning. It's pressing ten; you must have been having some pleasing dreams." The short man gave a wink. "I'll bet the girl had more than her ears burning last night, if that were the case."

Rolf ignored the comment and shoved the thin covers off as he swung his legs from the bed. "I felt that it was a very strange night; is that not so?" He stood, lightly touching his wounded shoulder. "I almost felt dizzy, as if I were rolling down a hill or falling from a type of cliff." He looked through a grimy window to see sun shining. "It was like preparing to swim from an unknown beach with the water stretching into the distance and being afraid of what might be waiting under the water." He glanced quickly from the window. "Did you sleep all right—did you not feel any of what I have said?"

"I slept well enough." Ogma looked troubled for a moment, then hid it with a fake grin. " 'Course, I didn't have any women on my mind, so I was keeping my hands above the covers."

A perplexed look crossed Rolf's face, then he turned his back to Ogma. "I will go out and have a wash," he said and started toward the door.

"Don't be too long about it; we've got one to put down today. Old Agnes Skillicorn finally let the cancer take her. Been fighting it for weeks, for the good it done."

"It is better to fight than to give up," said Rolf.

"It all comes to the same in the end." Ogma hacked off a piece of cheese for his lunch. "We're sticking her under, aren't we? Today or a month ago, it all comes to the same. Hers is just one more *crosh* we'll be planting in the *rullick*, equal to all the rest, you can believe that or not."

"It is a duty to fight for one's life," said Rolf, as he went out the door. A chill was still in the air and he shivered slightly at the corner of the house, for he had not put on his jacket. A tub of water was placed a few paces from the well, and he scooped some over his head and into his face. He wished he could do a more thorough job, but it was too much trouble getting his shirt off with one hand. He was also afraid of getting the bandages wet. He would wait and ask the old woman to help him. He was too shy to ask Alice and he refused to ask Ogma for anything. The man was always talking about Brigid, making crude remarks. After his job was done, he would ask the Head Druid if he could move elsewhere. In the midst of these thoughts, as he reached for a cloth to dry his face, he heard footsteps and turned quickly.

"How is the shoulder this morning, Rolf?" asked Taggart, as he walked toward the startled man.

"It is better; I do not feel the pain as much."

"Good." Taggart stopped by the well. "You seem to be healing quickly. It helps to be young."

"Excuse me, Herr Taggart." Rolf decided not to wait.

"Yes, Rolf, what is it?"

"I was wondering," he looked around to be certain that Ogma was not near. "Would it be possible for me to stay somewhere else —to leave here as soon as possible?"

Taggart's face showed some surprise. "I thought you would last the week."

"It is not about me," Rolf finished drying his face. "Such a place as this," he indicated the shack with his hand, "and such a person,

I have lived with much worse. A rough place and rough people are no terrible thing for me." Rolf looked away from Taggart's face and adjusted the sling. "It is when he talks about something else —saying things that he has no right to say—that I feel I should strike him."

"I'm afraid you'd be no match with that arm."

"I have the temper, Herr Taggart, when I am pushed."

"Well, lad, remember that being here is better than being in a British camp. If you had had the time to know Ogma, he would not bother you as much." The Head Druid smiled. "Maybe." He turned away from the young man. "Just don't pay him any mind. As long as you know what he says is a lot of foolishness, he should not get to you."

"I do not mean to make trouble."

Taggart almost laughed. "No, maybe you don't, but you surely aren't helping any—and I'm not talking about Ogma."

"You do not understand, Herr Taggart."

"No, I don't, Rolf—not yet. I'm doing my best to find out, however, before it is too late."

"I am no threat to you." His voice was shrill.

"Yes, you are." Taggart half-turned to Rolf. "A threat to me, to Brigid, and to every person and thing we hold dear."

"That is not true." Rolf came toward the Head Druid, his eyes wide with frustration. "It is not true at all. Why will no one believe me? It is such a small thing I am to do. It is nothing more than to take—" He stopped abruptly, looking confused. Rolf turned from Taggart and walked away. He called over his shoulder, "It will soon be over and everything can be forgotten."

Taggart watched him go and sit on the rough bench, staring at his feet as if in deep thought. The Head Druid had no doubt about his sincerity; it was apparent that Rolf felt his job was innocent enough. Taggart turned and went around to the front of the house. Ogma was waiting for him, sitting on the doorsill, puffing on his pipe.

"Got Jerry going, did ye? I heard him ranting from inside."

"You tend to exaggerate, Ogma."

"Oh aye, I may a mite."

"He said he was going to take something."

"You must be good, Taggart; I haven't got a thing out of him." Ogma took the pipe from his mouth. "Hardly ever talks to me is a fact. Silent bugger, to be sure."

"You go on too much about the girl," said Taggart.

Ogma looked up at the Head Druid, then changed the subject. "What's he got to take, then? And where?"

"That's what I'm wondering," replied Taggart. "He didn't have anything but his uniform and pistol and his papers and things in his pockets. We have all that now."

"Burned the uniform," reminded Ogma.

"Yes. So there's nothing there."

"Might have something hidden in the woods," said Ogma. "It were strange he had nothing else with him that night."

"Even so," Taggart was almost thinking out loud. "He can't carry much the way he is."

"Strong lad," pointed out Ogma. "And he's doing his best to get his strength. Sleeping a lot."

"That's natural enough," said Taggart.

"Not quite," the gravedigger put his pipe back into his mouth and talked around it. "He sleeps and rests whenever he can, yet I heard him ask young Alice for something to make him sleep last night. He's trying to sleep more than's natural. Wasn't up till almost ten this morning. I tell you, he's trying to get as much strength back as fast as possible. He's up to something."

"Did Alice say anything?"

"No, she gave him some powder to put in his tea. He said that his arm hurt some in the night and he didn't sleep well."

"That sounds reasonable, Ogma."

"As far as it goes—maybe. But the powder didn't do him much good last night. He could feel everything that was going on outside—you know what I mean about last night?"

"Yes."

"Aye." Ogma drew loudly on the pipe, then took it from his mouth. "It wasn't a night to be in the graveyards, you can believe that or not. I was glad enough to be at home, with all that going on. I've never felt anything like it, and I've . . ." His voice trailed off, and he stared at the ground. Then he looked up at the Head Druid. "I'll give credit when it's due—you know I'm honest enough for that." He paused again as Taggart nodded his head. "Well, the Jerry knew what was going on last night—not the details, of course; none of us knows too much about that. But the feelings he had, the dreams that he told me about, they were right with what was happening. Most people would just know something was going on, something they should leave alone. But he knew more than that, so maybe he is right for the girl. Maybe he can become one of us."

"If his job doesn't ruin him," said Taggart.

"Or us." Ogma got to his feet. "Why don't I just lock him up until the time passes?"

"If you did that, we'd not know whether we'd really stopped things or just done a bit to delay them." Taggart put up his hand as Ogma started to speak. "No, I've been thinking about it a lot. Whatever his job, he is still our only link to the trouble that's coming. And after last night—you be sharp out for him, Ogma. We can't have much time left."

"Things are rushing, right enough," Ogma agreed. He tapped his pipe out against the doorframe and put it into his shirt pocket. "I'd best get the lad and take him off to the boneyard; we've got a pit to dig for old Agnes. I can't get him to dig, but I might think up something to keep him tired. He's not so hard to watch at the *keeill*, either."

"You'll have him there the rest of the day?"

"It doesn't usually take that long at a digging."

"But you could stretch it?"

"Oh aye, 'twould be easy enough. Why do you want him kept there? One place is as good as the other."

"There'll be more pressure on him if he thinks that he's expected to stay in a place doing something. Around here, at your house, there's more chance of getting away undetected."

"Not much there ain't. Not from me he won't."

"As you say." Taggart suppressed a smile at the small man's indignation. "But even if he just feels that he is under some pressure, he might get anxious and make a mistake; people in a rush do. And if he makes a blunder, it might be easier for us."

"Put a bit of a screw on him."

"That's right."

"But not too much."

"No. I don't want him forced into anything drastic. That might even make things worse."

"I don't think he'll bite, Taggart; he's a cool sort—except when he's sniffin' around the girl. Still, I'll do my best."

"I don't doubt your abilities," said Taggart. He glanced up into the sky. "The sun seems to be moving fast today; that's no doubt due to my getting up later than usual." He looked quickly back to the gravedigger. "I've received a message that I'm wanted in

Douglas, so I'm going straight off. I'll be taking the car, and if something happens, get in touch with Jeremy and he'll let me know."

"Do you have time to do something else?" asked Ogma.

"Yes, the message wasn't urgent."

"It's not much," said Ogma. "Young Alice or her grandma is supposed to come and look at Jerry. Would you stop by and tell them we'll be at the *keeill?*"

"Certainly," said the Head Druid. "It won't take but a few minutes. You can move fast in a machine."

"Machines." Ogma gave a grunt of dissatisfaction. "Soon they'll have them digging the graves; they got them everywhere else. Things have gone downhill ever since they started the cycle races in naught-seven. Stink and noise is all they are—we end up with machines doing everything, and what will be the use of having people?"

"Well," said Taggart, as he turned to leave, "there is one good thing to be said about machines."

"And what might that be?" asked Ogma with a frown.

"They don't complain."

As Ogma watched the Head Druid leave, he grumbled under his breath. He then went into the house for the lunches he had placed in the pockets of his coat and a jug to get water from the well. He debated whether to wear the coat or not, then put it on and went out the door. As he went around the house, he was startled to see the bench empty. He put down the jug and took a quick look around the field, peering into the woods on each side. He was just getting ready to call Rolf's name when he heard a noise behind him. He spun around in time to see the door of the toilet shed open and Rolf come out, buttoning the front of his trousers. Rolf looked up to see Ogma staring at him, and he felt very uncomfortable. The little man had a way of looking as if he knew what a person was thinking. Rolf walked past him and went to the tub of water, where he washed his hands. Ogma took the jug to the well and pulled up the pail. He put the jug in the pail and waited a minute until it filled, then let the pail drop back and put a cap on the jug.

"I've got our lunches," Ogma said, patting his pocket. "And this is what we drink, so we'd best be on our way. It's never nice to keep the dead long above ground."

"It is not often I have met a man who likes his work as much as you," said Rolf, as they started to move around the house. "I wish you were as happy about me as you are about the digging."

"Well, lad, I'll be telling you." Ogma stopped a minute to get his shovel. He started to hand it to Rolf but changed his mind and gave him the jug of water instead. "The thing I like the most about my job is the finality. When you hammer down the dear departed and pack them away, it's all done and finished, if you get my meaning, no loose ends." He turned to stare at the wounded man. "You, my lad, are trailing as many loose ends as a rotting shroud. There's not the satisfaction in being with you as there is with a corpse. For me, the answers are given when I put them in the box, but when I look at you, all I see are a lot of questions hanging in the air."

"If you knew these answers, then you would like me."

"It's not a question of whether I like you or not—you get enough of that foolishness from the girl. But I will feel more comfortable when I find out what you're about and all this trouble you're causing is put to an end."

"There is no trouble," Rolf insisted.

"No trouble?" Ogma made a grin with his mouth, but his eyes were hard. "Now that's what Mr. Hitler kept telling the rest of the world and for a long time he was right; there was no trouble—for him."

"Herr Ogma, that is not . . . "

"There's nothing to be said, Jerry, unless you're going to be telling me what's going on and how to stop it. You may not have noticed, panting around after the girl and all, but I'm a bit of a skeptic. Now Taggart is smart, but he's too trusting at times, and he takes you at your word, even though he's being cautious. And as for the girl . . . "

"Brigit?"

"Aye, Brigid." The small man's face clouded over. "She can go by her feelings—just like her mother did—but it's not a way to make a judgment. I won't give a set of grave clothes for what either of them think."

"I have the trust of the unicorn, that is . . . "

"Yes—the beasts. Well, I don't understand the beasts. As far as I know, they all could be against you as much as for you. I don't think what was going on last night happened just to give you a welcome, though—you can believe that or not." Ogma glared at

Rolf, and at last the young man averted his eyes and looked at the road. "Aye, look away, Jerry, it doesn't make any difference. I've seen what I thought I would, something I've seen there before."

"What do you mean?" Rolf glanced back at him.

"In your eyes, that look has been there before. Doubt—you're starting to doubt what you're going to do. And that makes me worry just a bit more." Ogma started to walk more quickly. "Come along then, don't keep the dead waiting."

Taggart was still smiling as he approached Douglas, remembering how Alice's grandmother had not liked the idea of seeing Rolf in the graveyard. She claimed that she was not superstitious, which Taggart felt was true enough, but she did not want to be in a graveyard and with Ogma at the same time. That would certainly be just cause to give the hand of fate itchy fingers.

The Head Druid left his car a short distance from the Promenade and walked toward the docks. It was past noon and many were going for their lunch. Even with the bustle of wartime, the pace of Douglas was unhurried; people did not seem unduly troubled. They had not seen many tragic effects of battle, except for the occasional ship alight and burning after being torpedoed. Taggart moved through the crowd, ignoring the glances his unusually tall body often drew. He was used to stares when he went to places where he was not known. He suspected that this was one of the reasons Mr. Stephenson had wanted to meet him on the docks and away from the central part of town.

As Taggart came near the water, he saw Nigel at a distance, looking at the ships in the harbor. A gull screamed as the Head Druid approached.

"You won't often see the likes of that, lad."

Nigel turned, a puzzled expression on his face.

"There hasn't been so much traffic in the harbor since the last war," continued Taggart. "It's a shame that it usually takes some sort of disaster to give us a spectacle. We're not enough moved to excitement by the common. I think that is why peace is so quickly taken for granted once it is attained."

"There's a thrill in seeing all those ships," said Nigel. "Coming from different countries, and going far away."

"The romance of war," suggested Taggart.

"That's an odd way to put it." Nigel thought in silence for a moment. "It seems like a contradiction, but there really is something glamorous about battle."

"Yes," agreed Taggart. "Except for those in it." The Head Druid turned away from the ships. "Speaking of the war, where is your friend and faithful follower, Mr. Stephenson?"

"He was here until just a few minutes ago, and then some military chap came and talked to him, and they went off together. He of course didn't tell me what any of it was about; getting a piece of information out of him is like eating peas with a knife. Not that he doesn't answer my questions, and as polite as you please about it. But after a minute or two, you find out that he really didn't tell you anything at all." Nigel turned to look along the Promenade. "And for such a nondescript person, he seems to have the ear of everyone on the Island. Do you know where I met him this morning? Standing on the steps shaking hands with the governor. I thought he wanted to meet me at the governor's house because it was a point of reference, not because he was staying there. It must have been the governor's number he gave me to call." The young Druid's face was flushed with excitement. "And there always seems to be an army officer hovering in the background, ready to do whatever he wants. It's like being with royalty."

"You've been with him much of the time?"

"More or less constantly since we left you yesterday. He goes away for a half-hour or so when the officer brings some message or other. But he's soon back again. And just as he never really gives an answer, so he's always trying to find out things about us and what we do. Very careful questions, though, nothing straight out. It was getting so that I didn't know whether I was telling him anything important or not, even with the most innocent-sounding things he'd ask."

"And how did you handle him?"

"I started lying about everything," said Nigel.

The Head Druid burst out laughing and placed his hand on the young man's shoulder. "From what you say, it doesn't sound as if you had much choice."

"It's true," Nigel insisted. "After ten minutes with your Mr. Stephenson, I didn't know whether I was coming or going."

"Well, you're up against a master with him, lad. It's his job to know everything and he's been at it for years. Be glad the man's on our side."

"I'm not so sure he is."

"Aye. Well, at least as far as winning the war, he's with us. You're right in thinking that he wouldn't mind knowing as much about us as possible, but for now he's more interested in the German lad, and we can help each other there. War can form strange families."

"Speaking of families," said Nigel, "here comes your brother now."

Taggart turned to see the heavy-set man coming toward them, his hands in his pockets, his shoulders slightly hunched. He stopped beside the two men and looked up into the Head Druid's eyes.

"You'd make a hell of a target," he said.

"I presume that's a professional opinion."

"In my job you don't have much else," Mr. Stephenson smiled. "And speaking professionally, my opinion of you has gone off the top of the board." He looked over at Nigel. "I'm afraid it's time for the Archdruid and me to talk alone."

"I don't mind," said Nigel and then, under his breath to Taggart, "I could do with the rest."

Mr. Stephenson waited until Nigel was out of hearing range before he spoke. "You say he's your youngest?"

"Yes, that's right," replied Taggart.

"Then you've got quite a crew. I've been at him all morning and got next to nothing."

"So I've heard."

"The poor fellow didn't want to lie," Mr. Stephenson smiled. "It was rather refreshing to see someone feeling bad about that sort of thing. It's been a long time since I've seen anyone act guilty because of the lies he was telling me."

"And," said Taggart, "I imagine it has been a long time since you yourself have felt that way."

"Duplicity becomes a way of life after a while." Mr. Stephenson flexed his fingers. "That's why it's a bit unnerving to deal with you, Taggart. The things you wish to remain hidden you make no pretense about, and everything else is open season. In my business, I'm used to people hiding everything about anything. I, myself, am that way, and it's hard to break the habit."

"That sort of thing isn't necessary with me," said Taggart. "And more important, I suspect we have no time left to play the finer games of secrecy. If my suspicions are accurate, tomorrow's sunrise will find the deed done."

"I wonder if you need my help at all," said Mr. Stephenson, unable to conceal the surprise on his face. "You seem to know everything I'm about to tell you. If I thought you worked that way, I'd suspect you were plugged into my sources of information."

"Any help makes things easier," replied Taggart. "And you can be assured that I work from my own sources . . . " he paused, " . . . of knowledge."

"How would you like a nice, leisurely walk over to Onchan Head?" asked Mr. Stephenson. "I've found that one gets a lovely view of the town from there—as I'm sure you well know. Also, it's a long walk, and I have a lot to talk about. The sea is a lovely thing —the wind and waves quite nicely drown out voices."

The two men started to walk northward, following the gentle curve of the Promenade. There was a stiff breeze blowing across the water, and the ships dipped and groaned at their moorings. The salt smell was strong in the air and flocks of gulls circled overhead; the war was being good to them. There were few other people along the walk, and soon Mr. Stephenson began to speak.

"I don't mind admitting my admiration, and I won't deny my curiosity." He glanced sideways at the Head Druid. "So I hope you'll be able to tell me, whatever put you on to Rolf Scholl's father? It's something we should have found ourselves—and probably would have with time. But there was never any reason to go hunting him out."

"It was something the man—an observant man—who is looking after Rolf told me. The lad never mentioned his father, though he had talked about his mother, who is dead. This was strange to both of us, something out of the ordinary usually deserves an explanation, as you no doubt well know." The other man nodded without looking up. Taggart went on. "No man minds credit, but I don't want to give the wrong impression. I don't know anything about Rolf's father and only vaguely suspected he might have something to do with all this. Up until now, that is."

"I'll try to keep things as uncomplicated as possible," said Mr. Stephenson. "Do you remember that I said we had some reports about Rolf Scholl's being mixed up in this bomb business?"

"I remember only too well," replied Taggart.

"Yes, of course. You see, the strange thing was, many of the reports had no relation to each other. A few of them made sense, but on the whole, they wouldn't add up. Something else we noticed was that much of the time, when Rolf's name was mentioned, there was some other code word used. At these times, nothing made any sense at all. It was as if they were talking about two different people."

"Two different people?" repeated Taggart.

"That's right."

"Two Rolf Scholls?" asked Taggart.

"Right again," said Mr. Stephenson. "I knew you were the type to catch on quickly."

"Is the real one here, with us?" asked Taggart.

"Oh yes, there's no doubt about that. He's real enough."

"Then the other one is the fake."

"Oh no, he's real enough, too."

"How can that be poss—" Taggart began, and then understanding showed in his eyes.

"I think you have it, Taggart," Mr. Stephenson smiled. "There really are two Rolf Scholls."

"Father and son?" asked Taggart.

"Exactly so," said Mr. Stephenson. "You have it perfectly. We are confronted with *Rolf Scholl und Sohn*—it could almost be the name of a wine company."

"Their import and export is much more deadly than a case or two of white wine."

"Much," said Mr. Stephenson. "We think the old man's got his hooks into something that could make us all give up drinking permanently. And that he's on the move with it—and you're quite right, it will probably be tonight."

"And what's Rolf—our Rolf here—got to do with all this? We would never have suspected him capable of dealing with such a bomb and its resulting horrors."

"As far as we can find out," said Mr. Stephenson, "he probably doesn't know what he is doing."

"A bit of explanation would be appreciated," said Taggart.

"I'll do my best. Not that we know everything, of course, but we've pieced together a story that makes sense. One of the problems of having a large organization, far-flung across the world, is that oftentimes it takes a while for the right hand to know what the left is doing. That is why it took someone such a long time to put both Rolf Scholls together.

"Rolf Scholl senior is a scientist and has had a position at Munich University for many years. He is also a fanatical Nazi—he seems to have become one shortly after his wife's death. Now he's not a genius by any means, which is why we haven't kept that close a watch on him. But he is competent enough and it seems he's out spying around. We've finally traced him to Liverpool."

"Liverpool?" The Head Druid's voice was gruff.

"Yes," replied Mr. Stephenson, pointing into the distance. "Just across the way, in a manner of speaking. We're certain the son of a bitch is in Liverpool, but we can't find him anywhere. We've strengthened the security around our people working on this damn bomb, but it might be closing the barn door after the horse has been spirited away."

"You surely had protection there before," said Taggart.

"Oh yes," said Mr. Stephenson. "Of course we did, but Liverpool was rather low on the list of priorities. If he was in Liverpool all this time without our knowing, then who is to say what he's been able to do?"

"Have the British discovered such a bomb?"

"No, not yet."

"Then there's no secret to be taken," said Taggart. "The man can't steal what doesn't exist."

"That's true as far as it goes," agreed Mr. Stephenson. "But you see, we don't know how advanced the Nazis are. They might put together what they already know with what Scholl may have stolen and end up with a nice big bang."

"You think that is possible?"

"Sadly, it is very possible," said Mr. Stephenson. "We've had far too much trouble because we've underestimated Mr. Hitler and his cronies. Barbaric they are, but there's also a lot of intelligence there too. They didn't get where they are through luck."

"He must be stopped."

"Most definitely," said Mr. Stephenson. "That's where your Rolf comes into the unpleasant picture."

"Yes," said Taggart. "What is his role in all this?"

"Again, there are pieces missing." Mr. Stephenson took a folded paper from his pocket. "We don't know much about the son—you can't keep tabs on every German officer. But it is fairly obvious that his job is to guide the father across the Island." He opened the paper to reveal a map of Man. "From the radio messages we've been able to uncover, his father is supposed to land right here." He pointed at a section of coast on the map and Taggart looked closely.

"Why, that's where the bombs fell the other night."

"Yes," said Mr. Stephenson. "It's almost exactly the place."

"We Celts are very suspicious of coincidence," said the Head Druid, as the other man put the map away. "I presume you are going to tell me more about that bomber."

"You see, Taggart," the heavy-set man had a slight flush on his face, "spy work is far from foolproof; we're all a bit touchy about it, don't like to admit mistakes and that sort of thing. The bald truth is that we haven't spent too much time worrying about Liverpool. We had a lot of radio interceptions, but since none of them seemed to add up to much, no serious attention was paid. But after the bombing—strange enough in itself—and then after finding traces of the Germans in the area, we started going over everything again. It now appears that Scholl the father was supposed to land that night . . ."

"When we were bombed?"

"Yes," said Mr. Stephenson. "We don't know whether the bombing was a mistake or not. As you say—too much of a coincidence. We speculate that the Stuka was flying some sort of cover for the boat they were coming across on—one of those small fishing boats, what do you call them?"

"Nobbies."

"That's right, nobbies. We figure the pilot saw something on the shore—God knows what, that part's damn queer—and tried to signal the boat but couldn't. Radio didn't work or lights didn't flash or whatever; we don't know. So he reverted to dropping his bombs in desperation—especially if he did see something on the beach. The explosions could be seen for quite a distance, and the . . .

nobbie was warned off. They probably figure the whole thing will be accepted as an isolated incident, and after a couple of nights they're ready to try it again. The big boys in Berlin will be interested to get that sort of stuff as fast as possible."

"You said Rolf doesn't know about the bomb."

"No, probably not. He's a mystery to us, as I said; no records about him. We've only come across his name in these radio reports. But we do have records about his father and in there we found something interesting. I told you the old man is a rabid Nazi, but in his file we came across some Gestapo reports about his son. This concerned a time before the war—thirty-six, thirty-seven— and before he joined the army. They weren't clear, but the son was in some sort of trouble with the Gestapo. He either protested against the state or wouldn't do something they wanted. It seems the father and son are very fond of each other in spite of everything, according to some snide remarks in this report. The old man had enough sway to keep his son out of trouble and packed him off to the army. We suspect that their being used together in this operation is a test of their loyalties—the Nazis love to do that sort of thing. But since the son is the one in doubt, it's unlikely he knows how important the job is. To him it's a simple task of getting his father across the Island and nothing more."

"And how is Rolf supposed to find his own way across an Island that he's a stranger to?"

"Oh, the boy's been here two weeks at least—if not longer. He sneaked in from Ireland. Man's not a wide island, you know; you could walk across it in a day. I imagine he's taken his good time and kept to the back roads."

"He was never near that beach before," said Taggart.

"Are you sure?"

"He would have been noticed."

"It's a closely watched area, is it?"

"In a manner of speaking."

"Well, if the boy felt unsure about the place, he probably stayed away until the very last night, so he wouldn't draw attention to himself. He wouldn't worry about a short distance; he could check that out rather quickly."

"About the bomb—couldn't his father have said something about it?"

"Oh, he could," agreed Mr. Stephenson. "But he wouldn't.

There's lots in this business I don't tell my own family, as much for their own good as for anything else. If it got out that the old man was a talker, he'd be in lots of trouble, as well as anyone he happened to tell things to."

"So what we really have," said the Head Druid, "is a lad who is helping his father—whom he likes a great deal—get back to the safety of his country."

"If you don't mind my saying so," Mr. Stephenson stopped to look up at Taggart, "you seem to be going out of your way to whitewash the boy. Yes, what you say is probably true; the boy's nothing more than a guide who doesn't know what his old man's up to—but he's still a German soldier, and we're in a war. I don't see where ignorance is all that important; he's very dangerous, regardless."

"You only see him as an enemy soldier," answered Taggart. "To us he can become much more, but we must be certain of him; we must feel that he can be trusted. A man who would knowingly do such a horrible thing could not be trusted."

"He may be his father's son," said Mr. Stephenson.

"Yes." The Head Druid paused a moment. "But we're hoping that he turns out to be his mother's."

Mr. Stephenson looked questioningly at the tall man, but he saw that he was not going to get any further explanation. "Well, I dare say you have your reasons." He started walking again and looked out across Douglas Bay. "I suppose they concern some of those things that you don't wish to tell me. I never seriously thought that the boy could have any part in your beliefs." Mr. Stephenson glanced up at Taggart. "You'll want to keep the boy when this is over and done?"

"What do you mean?" asked the Head Druid.

"Well, it's going to be difficult to explain why he isn't being arrested when we stop this thing."

"We?" Taggart glared down at the other man.

"The army. I'm going to have so many troops there that—"

"No," said Taggart. "You must let us do this our way."

"That isn't possible." Mr. Stephenson halted abruptly and stood in front of the Head Druid. "Now look here, Taggart." His voice was firm, bordering upon anger. "I know you're doing your best to help me without betraying your own interests, but you must realize there are limits to how far backward I can bend before I snap. We aren't just dealing with this Island and whatever beliefs you and your people may hold. If the boy's father has the makings of that bomb, it could heap destruction on much of the world. That's the scale of things I'm working at, Taggart."

"All actions must have a beginning," said the Head Druid. "They all have their small start." Taggart chose his words carefully. "If such a start is here, I can assure you we will stop it. Rolf's father and his secrets will get no further than the beach; that is an unqualified guarantee." Taggart smiled. "You must try to realize that what I stand for, the powers I deal with—though perhaps intangible to you—have centuries of knowledge and events behind them. Worldwide actions are not new to us; we here on Man are a part of something larger. You may put it to chance that this event is to happen on Man—I do not. It is quite possible that the bomb may be only secondary in importance, that Rolf has the potential for something far greater."

"What could be greater than blowing up Europe?"

"Saving it."

Mr. Stephenson shook his head. "I don't know, Taggart. You're asking an awful lot. It's not in my line of work to go on faith, you know."

"I believe I have already proven the abilities of our ways," said Taggart. "We are getting along together well; I would not like the idea of our becoming at odds with one another. That would just be one more problem to overcome when the time is already short."

"Taggart, it's not that I doubt your intentions, but you're asking me to go shooting with a blindfold on." He looked out over the water and walked for a couple of minutes without saying a word. At last he turned his face to the Head Druid. "Everything you've told me has been accurate; it's true that we wouldn't know what we do now if it weren't for you." He paused for a moment, then spoke again. "All right, we can keep out the troops—but I'll have to be there."

Taggart had been watching the street ahead of him, but now he turned a steady gaze to Mr. Stephenson. He quickly saw by the smaller man's expression that it would be useless to argue. "All right." He put out his hand and Mr. Stephenson shook it.

"I realize there may be things that you don't want me to see or know about, Taggart. Try to remember that I'm a man of great discretion when need be. As far as you and I are concerned, I have no desire other than to stop Scholl from delivering anything he might have."

"Then you'll leave Rolf alone."

"Yes—he's nothing to us. I presume you won't have him running about spying on things."

"He'll completely disappear," said Taggart, "where he can do no harm. And where no harm can come to him." He paused a moment and then asked, "What do you plan to do with his father?"

"Oh, we'll pack him off to a secure place in the middle of nowhere over in Canada. He might have things to tell us."

"Well," commented Taggart, "that will certainly get him out of the way."

"Oh, Canada's a lovely place to put people, all right. Even if they escape, they have nowhere to go."

"Something you can't say of Man."

"No," agreed Mr. Stephenson. They walked on in silence a while, until Stephenson gave a short laugh and looked at the Head Druid. "I almost forgot all about it. One of your little afterthoughts —I don't know how you get such facts. You wanted to know whether Hitler had any reason to be in Liverpool." Taggart nodded. "Well, the mad bastard did. He had a brother living there before the first war—owned some sort of pub or café. Crazy Adolf might have gone there looking for money. Now the brother has a posh bar in Berlin. Why did you ask?"

"One of the Druids met your crazy Adolf there in 1913."

"And that has something to do with this?"

"By our ways, it means that Rolf's father has got what you think. Evil begets evil."

"You know," said Mr. Stephenson, as they turned to walk back, "sometimes you make my job seem very simple."

XX

LATE AFTERNOON shadows were thrown across the narrow path as Taggart walked the winding slope. He was anxious to see Katherine and the other Druids, whom he had summoned as quickly as possible after his return from Douglas. Mr. Stephenson had promised he would know immediately when any information arrived to say that Rolf's father was on the move. Everything pointed at tonight from both their sources; thus Taggart had decided on the present meeting. He had also agreed that Nigel should stay with Mr. Stephenson and act with him when the time came.

Taggart paused a moment before going through the two oaks, then turned to enter the clearing and stopped again when he saw Katherine. She came toward him, her white garment brushing across the ground.

"Are they all here?"

"All but Jeremy," she said. "I'm waiting for you both." She stood before him and took his hands in her own, lightly holding them as she gazed into his eyes. "The others expected you would want to see them after last night, though perhaps not as informally as they are now."

"Some of them enjoy ceremony," agreed Taggart. "But I think our last council was enough."

"Do you have some new information?"

"Not really. I've found many reasons, but we are still left with everything revolving around Rolf. The main question is whether he can break from his old ways."

"Do you think it possible?" she asked.

"I've always felt anything is possible, Katherine, and what I've learned today just makes me more convinced. There's a madness —such a madness—developing in the world."

"When a people go mad, 'tis the sane who are locked up."

"In such a world, it'd be a pleasure to be locked away." The voice startled them, and they both turned to see Jeremy coming through the trees. "Then you wouldn't be caring about what went on." He came closer and stood beside them. "I hope you'll change his ways somewhat, Katherine. I've tried to warn him about his pessimistic ideas—he's starting to sound a wee bit like Ogma, a sad state for anyone."

"You're asking the wrong one to change me," said Taggart. "She's the one that sees things getting worse."

"Now Taggart," she looked over at Jeremy with a smile. "You interpret as you like, but I just see things as they're going to be; I don't try to say whether they are right or wrong."

"You see, Taggart," Jeremy was grinning, "you've got to do what you can, but let the rest take care of itself. Start worrying about everything, and you'll soon be one of those mad people— or on the borderland, as is Ogma."

"All right, you two," Taggart looked from one to the other, "I'll stop talking doom and disaster."

"That will be nice," said Jeremy. "I hear enough of that on the wireless."

"Anything to stop you two optimistic preachers."

"Who do you mean?" Katherine winked at Jeremy. "What do you think the man is on about?"

"He was having too much of my *jough* yestereven and is not quite over it. The ale makes a man prone to imagining things."

"He does look as if he hasn't been getting enough rest, I'll admit," commented Katherine.

Taggart almost laughed out loud when she said that, and he noticed a look of understanding coming into the old Druid's eyes.

"Maybe a combination of both things has left me the way I am," he said. "There's no telling these days what can happen to a man as he innocently goes about his business. A person can hardly be blamed for the peculiar things that may unexpectedly befall him."

"Yes," said Katherine. "It must be the times we live in. How else to explain the complexities of the innocent man?"

All three had smiles that went beyond their words. Taggart at last spoke, almost to himself. "Innocent or not, complexities there are." He looked from one to the other. "I'll save most of what I learned today to tell you and the others together. But one thing stands out and I'd like your opinions. It appears that Rolf has been on the Island for two weeks, if not more. Obviously none of us knew about him until the night of the bombing, but the beasts have tolerated him, giving us no indication of his presence. It seems to me that they want him to go ahead with his plans, so we should not try to stop him."

"Taggart," Katherine touched his arm. "The boy is surrounded by destruction. The beasts have their own ways; we can never be sure that our reasons are their reasons."

"She's right." The old Druid looked into Taggart's eyes. "We've gone too far apiece to start taking chances now. If the lad is meant to go through with his job, then he will, what we do or no. But we have our part to play also, which is to act as we normally would —with caution."

"But it will be almost impossible to get away from Ogma," said Taggart. "What if we've been too effective? I was wondering whether we should tell him to loosen his grip."

"You learn many things getting to be my age," said Jeremy, "though you never seem to learn enough. And one of those things is that second-guessing never works. It's a waste of time that leaves you no better off. As long as you've spent the time thinking things over, you do your best and leave it be." Jeremy tugged at his beard. "Now I'd be the first to spare anyone Ogma's company, but the time isn't right."

"The boy needs watching," insisted Katherine. "It would be what you'd normally do."

"Yes," agreed the Head Druid.

"Then until you're really shown different, keep him the way he is."

"Aye," said Jeremy. "We'll be having troubles enough when things start to happen."

"All right," said Taggart. "I'll leave things as they are. Now we had better go and tell the rest."

XXI

ALICE'S GRANDMOTHER put three spoons of tea into the pot and placed it on the counter, ready for the stove. She already had a kettle of water boiling and hoped that Alice would not be much longer, for she was tired and wanted to go to bed. She took two cups and saucers from the shelf and placed them on the kitchen table, along with cream and sugar. She also took a plate of small cakes she had baked in the afternoon and put it with the rest. When everything was ready to her satisfaction, she dragged a chair over to the window, put out the lamp, and pulled back the blackout curtain. Patches of cloud obscured the moon from time to time, and the old woman watched the misshapen shadows slither across the trees. It had been dark for half an hour, and she was glad that Alice now took the night rounds. Still, she liked looking at the moon and stars and sat gazing from her chair, occasionally nodding. She kept watching along the back path where Alice usually came and at last saw the beam of her torch. She put the curtains back in place, relit the lamp, and hurried over to the kettle, where she poured the water into the teapot and placed it on the stove. She was returning the chair to the table when the kitchen door opened.

"I've just put it on, 'twill be ready short."

"Thanks, gran." Alice slipped off her knapsack and put it on a small table near the door, where they kept many of their medical supplies. She removed the drugs from her case and took them to their small pantry, where she unlocked a cabinet and placed them carefully on their proper shelves. She locked the cabinet again, and by the time she returned to the kitchen, her grandmother had poured the tea and was waiting at the table for her.

"Any trouble?" she asked, as Alice sat across from her.

"Nothing much." She took a sip. "One of the Cubbin boys was thrown by his horse. Had to set his wrist. And the Mylchreest woman—the one in trade, not the fisher's wife—got a boil on her dainty arse and is making a real time. The Jerry's still got pain, but he was so glad to see me he didn't complain much about it. I told you he asked me to come and see him first, before I went to the others. Must be desperate for company." She bit into a cake.

"Don't blame him," said the old woman. "May as well be in hell as stayin' with that runty bastard."

Alice smiled as she went for more tea. "Other than that, there wasn't much different from what you saw this morning." She came back to the table and took another cake. "Oh, I forgot, old Samuel Radcliffe got too much o' the water o' life in him and took on a bunch of Tommies—they tried to beat the shit out of both ends at the same time. He'll not be moving for a week or two."

"The old fool—he was doing good there for a while."

"Aye, not a drop for three months was what his son said."

The old woman took a bite of cake. "I thought I was seeing you weren't alone, coming back home," she said.

"No, I wasn't."

"Would it have been Ramsey Killip?"

"Yes." Alice avoided her grandmother's gaze and had a sip of tea. "He walked me from the village."

"You like the lad?"

"You know I do, gran."

"Aye, I know it." The old woman took a drink and put her cup noisily in her saucer. "What I don't understand is what you're waiting for. The lad's been keeping company for over a year now."

"I just want to be sure is all. I don't jump on my feelings the way Brigid does."

"Well, don't keep young Killip waiting too long. He's a nice lad and it's time you were getting married." The old woman finished her tea. "I don't expect bombs to fall like with Brigid and the Jerry, but you ought to know by now."

"Yes, gran." Alice smiled at the old woman but thought it was time to change the subject. "Speaking of Jerry . . ."

"Yes?" her grandmother asked, reaching for another cake.

"What are you thinking about his shoulder?"

"It's doing remarkable for what happened to it. The healing is grand."

"That's what I was thinking," said Alice, as she took their cups to the sink. "Everything looks good to me, yet he keeps complaining about the pain—says it keeps him from sleeping. He asked me for more sleeping powder tonight."

"More?" The old woman stopped eating her cake.

"Yes." Alice spoke across the room. "He asked for some last night, too. He was almost apologizing for causing trouble."

"Now, that is strange." The old woman turned to look at her granddaughter. "He was asking me for some this morning."

"Did you give it him?"

"Yes." She paused, staring at Alice. "He said he was very tired at the end of the day and might forget to ask you for it."

"Maybe he forgot getting some from you," Alice said.

"Maybe." The old woman was thinking. "You're right, I didn't think the wound should be hurting that much." She stood up from the table. "How much did you give him?"

"Enough for a good sleep."

"Aye, so did I."

"His shoulder isn't that bad, is it, gran?"

"No."

"You don't think he's trying to kill himself?"

"Nay—the lad's not the type." The old woman absently brushed away crumbs. "Anyway he's got no reason, what with Brigid and all."

"It could be nothing," said Alice.

"Aye, it could be." She looked at her granddaughter. "But if Jerry didn't use any of the powder, it's something else."

Alice looked sharply at the old woman. "If you put all that powder together, you'd get enough to put out a horse."

"More than enough for that fucking corpse-lover."

"What do you think?" Alice walked over and stood by her grandmother. "Is he up to something?"

"Could be as you say, girl, he's just forgot."

"And his wound *will* be hurting some—can't help but do that for a while."

"That's true." The old woman was silent once again, thinking more deeply than ever. She suddenly looked into Alice's eyes. "There was something else you said."

"What?"

"How long ago did you leave him?"

"Let me think." Alice looked confused. "I went out at seven, and with all the others . . . "

"You saw him first—that's what you said."

"Yes. He asked me to, being with Ogma and all. And he said he was going to bed early, from working all day."

"How long ago?" her grandmother insisted.

"Well, there was him, and the others, and all the walking, and when Ramsey brought me home, we weren't in any hurry." She saw an impatient look come into her grandmother's eyes. "All that and the time I've been here, it'll be getting on to four hours since I gave him the—"

"Aye, aye." The old woman started pacing. "If Jerry did keep all that powder, it would put a man out in less than half an hour."

"Oh gran, do you think he did?"

"Not a hard thing to do in that gloomy shack; they'd probably have tea or whiskey or even a drink of *jough*—easy enough it would be to talk Ogma into some drinking."

"Surely Ogma would be looking for—"

"Looking for what? He wouldn't have reason to suspect the Jerry had something like that. He wasn't near us when I gave the lad some this morning."

"Ogma saw me give him some last night," said Alice. "I remember that, right enough. Rolf did act funny, but I thought he was just embarrassed at asking for it in front of Ogma—not wanting to let on a weakness." The young woman's eyes widened. "But tonight, he asked me for it when Ogma went out to get me some water when I was changing the dressings."

"So, as far as the dwarf knows," the old woman stopped pacing, "Jerry only had one dose, which he took last night. He's got nothing to look for, has he?"

"No, I suppose not," Alice sounded subdued.

"It could still be as innocent as a baby's smile."

"But you don't think so, do you, gran?"

"Ah, we'd best not take a chance, no matter what I be thinking. You know yourself the hustle that's been on ever since Jerry arrived. And last night you weren't lingering on the path with young Killip but were home right quick and glad of it. All that wasn't going on just to save your purity." The old woman's smile faded as quickly as it began. "We'd better be letting himself know, just in case."

"The Head Druid?"

"Aye, it should all be in his hands. If it's nothing, then there's no damage done. But if our doubts turn true, then the Jerry might have as much as three hours on us to do whatever it is he came here for." The old woman went over to the door and took her coat off a peg. "I'll head off to Ogma's house and you get Taggart on the talker—tell him what we think."

"No, gran, I'll go. It's so dark out there now—you use the telephone, I'll be faster on my feet."

"Nay, nay." Her grandmother opened the door. "Taggart might be wanting something important done and that's when he'll be needing fast feet. And you're tired, too; it's best you get some rest in case you have to go."

"Here, at least take a torch." Alice handed it to her grandmother. "Shall I tell him you're going?"

"Yes," the old woman called over her shoulder. "He'll probably pick me up in his motor." She went quickly down the path.

Taggart was pacing expectantly in his living room, waiting for some word from Nigel and Mr. Stephenson. He spoke occasionally to Jeremy, who sat in an easy chair by the window. Taggart greatly valued the old Druid's judgment and was comforted to have him so close at hand. In the midst of his pacing from one end of the room to the other, a harsh ringing interrupted his thoughts and almost startled him. When he answered, he was very surprised to hear a woman's voice. After a few short questions, the Head Druid told Alice she was right in calling and then asked her to go to Brigid's house and tell her to hurry to Ogma's. Taggart put the phone in its cradle and turned to Jeremy.

"He may be on the run." Taggart picked up the telephone again to contact Nigel. "Alice thinks he might have saved up enough sleeping powder to put Ogma out. Her grandmother is on her way there now." He got Nigel on the line and, after telling him the story, found out in return that Mr. Stephenson had just been called away once again, but that Nigel would inform him as soon as he returned. Taggart put the telephone away and gave a sigh.

"They're like all other machines," said Jeremy. "All they bring is trouble."

"You're going to have your share of trouble, then," said Taggart, as he reached for his heavy staff. "We'll have to take the motor to get on to Ogma's."

The old Druid muttered, "I hate the thing."

"We don't have a choice," said Taggart, as he opened the door. "If Rolf is gone and has as much time ahead of us as young Alice thinks, then we have to act quickly."

"Aye." Jeremy got out of his chair. "You're right about that. The damn machine is fast, I'll grant." He followed the Head Druid out of the house and around to the side where the car was. He grumbled as he got in, and Taggart eased down the drive, breaking regulations by turning on his headlamps. "You'll be getting us bombed," said Jeremy.

"There's no time to go creeping," answered Taggart as he sped along the roads. "We won't be on the highway long enough to make much of a target."

"Then your speeding will get us killed."

"To think you were calling me a pessimist," said Taggart.

"If the gods wanted us to drive, Taggart, we'd suckle petrol at our mothers' teats." He looked at the trees rushing past the windows, jumping from the roadside in the glare of the lights. "This just isn't a natural way to travel."

"Neither are boats," replied Taggart.

"If they go under I can at least swim. This damn thing crashes and we'll be finishing our trip in the Otherworld."

They drove a few minutes longer in silence, and suddenly a squat figure appeared in the beam of their lights. Taggart came up beside the old woman and stopped. She peered at them, then switched off her torch and got into the back without a word. She breathed heavily and it was evident she had been walking quickly. After a couple of minutes, she finally muttered a few words.

"I'll be feeling the fool if we're off chasing a will o' the wisp."

"Don't be bothered," said Taggart. "Whether you're right or

wrong, I'm feeling enough of a fool for both of us for not thinking of the possibility. I really felt that there was no way he could get past Ogma."

"He's good at keeping the dead," said Jeremy, "but he might have forgot what it's like dealing with the living. There's no way you could think of everything, lad."

"We're not yet sure if I'm right," said the old woman.

"I think we're sure," said Taggart, glancing into the rear-view mirror. "It's just that we're not *certain,* and that will happen as soon as we reach Ogma's. I can feel the whole thing falling into place."

Taggart turned onto another road and small stones started clanging against the underside of the car. The way was narrow, and some of the larger bushes scraped against the doors. In a few minutes they reached the path that led to Ogma's house. Taggart turned the vehicle so it pointed in the direction they had just come and then shut off the engine and lights.

"There's not a mark on you, Jeremy. You survived it well."

"No great thanks to your driving," answered the elderly Druid. "And the night's not over."

The old woman was the first out of the car, and she started along the overgrown path. "I may as well lead," she said, "I got the torch." The two Druids followed closely, circling around the haphazard clumps of brush that grew in the narrow path. There was an occasional muttered curse from the old woman as some branch slapped against her, but otherwise none of them talked. Shortly they came to the dim outline of the shack, reflecting pale in the moonlight, and the old woman's torch shone on the door, which was closed. She stopped and turned to Taggart.

"What do we do—knock?" she asked.

"It'd be best, in case we're wrong." The Head Druid reached past her with his staff and rapped loudly. When there was no response, he struck the door even more soundly with the end of his staff.

"Best be careful," said the old woman. "You'll be bringing this sty down on us."

Taggart glanced quickly at her with a small smile, then hit the door one more time. He waited a moment and turned again to the old woman. "I'm right in thinking that there's no back door to this place."

She gave a snort. "Only if all the rats got desperate at the same time and decided to leave together."

"Aye. Then we'd best take a look." He grasped the latch with a shove and the door swung in on rusty hinges. "Give me the torch and I'll go first." The old woman handed the light to him, and he bent his head as he went in the door. The strong beam picked a path through the gloom and Taggart entered, shining the light from one part of the room to the other. When he saw nothing but furniture and junk, he carefully crossed the floor and entered the smaller room at the back. He moved the light from the bed to the cot and back to the bed. He then returned to the open door and spoke to them.

"You'd better come quickly." He led them across the cluttered room. "It looks like you were right. The lad is gone, there's no telling how long ago." They entered the sleeping quarters and he shone the light on the vacant cot and then back to the bed, where Ogma lay curled on his side, facing out into the room.

"Everything has its good point," said Jeremy, as the old woman went to the bed. "I've been waiting for years to see Ogma with his mouth closed." The old woman cackled as she looked him over.

"How is he?" asked Taggart.

"Don't be getting your hopes up," she said as she raised one of his eyelids. "He's far from being one of his own corpses yet, though it's going to take some doing to get him on his feet—if that's what you're really wanting to do."

"It's a tempting thing to leave him be, lad," said Jeremy.

"He might come in useful to us tonight," answered Taggart. "Even though it will be a disappointment for you two." He looked down at the old woman, who was feeling Ogma's pulse. "What do we do about getting him up and about?"

"Hard to say." She let his arm fall back on the bed. "Don't know how much powder the Jerry gave him. He looks deep; must have been quite a bit." She looked at the Head Druid's face. "You get him up on his feet," she gave a wide grin, "and I'll start slapping him around."

Taggart handed his staff and the light to Jeremy, then bent and swung the small man's legs off the bed. He grabbed Ogma under the arms and stood in front of the old woman, holding the gravedigger almost as if he were a puppet. She started to slap his face while Jeremy held the light on the scene. She hit him on one cheek and then the other, sometimes hard enough to make his head move. She paused now and then to lift up his eyelid, then started to strike him once more.

"Come along, you shrunken bastard," she muttered. "How much work will you be putting me to, anyway?" She stopped a moment, flexing her hand, then started on him again. In a couple of minutes there was a sluggish response. Ogma's head twitched a couple of times and his breathing became louder. "See if you can get him walking around," the old woman said to Taggart. "If we get him moving any, we'll take him outside into the fresh air. It's a wonder one don't suffocate natural in this place—maybe Jerry just wanted to get away from here to breathe."

Jeremy walked into the other room and Taggart followed the beam of light, dragging Ogma as he went, although the gravedigger's legs had started to jerk about. Jeremy tried to pick a safe route through the mounds of clutter, but even then Taggart stumbled and almost fell on top of Ogma. The old woman sat in a chair to rest, and in a few minutes the little man's legs began to move in a semblance of walking. The Head Druid lessened his grip on the other man and Ogma started to stumble as if drunk.

"Good, good," said the old woman. "He's getting there. Best give him a rest for a moment; don't want him doing too much. You could use a pause yourself," she said to Taggart. "Then we'll get him outside, and I'll give him some of this." She held up a couple of capsules in the beam of light. "Didn't want to give it to him before, because it's strong stuff and might have done him damage, coming straight out of unconsciousness. Put him down in this chair and I'll prop him up for a few minutes."

Taggart found that he was only too glad to set Ogma onto the chair. Although he was a small man, the almost dead weight was a chore to carry around for any length of time. Jeremy helped place the gravedigger at the table, where he sat sprawling half-across it, while the old woman kept an eye on him in case he started to fall. Since there were only two chairs, Jeremy and Taggart looked around for places to sit and found a low wooden chest near one wall. They sat on it together, and from time to time Jeremy moved the light to check on the gravedigger. They rested like this, not saying much, until Ogma began to stir slightly. Taggart was just standing to go over to the table when he heard a noise outside.

"Shut off the light," he told Jeremy.

Taggart took his staff from the older Druid and moved cautiously across the room to stand by the open doorway. There were footsteps on the path, coming quickly toward the house. He gripped his staff tightly and stood to one side of the doorframe. Ogma started to move in his chair, but the old woman stood and put her hands on his shoulders. There was movement across the small yard and a figure appeared in the doorway, silhouetted by the moon. Jeremy turned his bright light on the person and Taggart moved swiftly in front of it, his staff raised. There was a small female scream.

"Brigid," said Taggart, putting down his staff.

"What . . . who were you expecting?" she stammered.

"'Tis only the lass," said Jeremy, and he turned the light back to the table, where the old woman was still holding Ogma.

"What's happened?" asked Brigid.

"Come and I'll tell you." The Head Druid took her outside and related all that had occurred. "That's as much as we know, at any rate. We have to find Rolf and do it quickly."

"I can't believe he'd do anything wrong," insisted Brigid.

"You have to believe it, now." The Head Druid took her hand in his. "Remember that before everything else, you're one of us, and you can't let your duty be put into danger by your feelings. Right now, all that is important is that he be found, so we can keep in control. Rolf is out on the land, and though I think I know where he's going, I must be sure. The beasts will have been on to him the second he stepped into the night, but we must also do our part. You must get the unicorn to lead you to him, and then come back and tell me."

"Shall I bring Rolf?"

"No. You're only to find him, not stop him."

"But if he can harm us as you say, he should—"

"Once he's found, we'll stop him ourselves—if it comes to the point where we have to." He stared forcefully into Brigid's eyes. "If we are to be able to trust him in the future, he must be given free rein for a chance to prove himself now. You, more than anyone else, must want that."

"I thought you didn't believe in him anymore." Brigid's voice was both surprised and hopeful.

"I'm still willing to give him the benefit of the doubt. He's done wrong, but he hasn't caused disaster—yet. But I'm not about to take chances, and I'm sure, feelings or no feelings, that neither are you. You're too much one with us."

Brigid was quiet for a moment, staring into the green eyes that were piercing her own. When she finally spoke, her voice was very low. "Feelings can't be made to go away, but if the choosing ever came between Rolf and what I do here—my bond to the unicorn and our traditions—you know there would be no choice."

She looked away. "But I hope—I hope so much—that Rolf will be able to join us."

"That will be up to him, Brigid; we've done as much as we can on our side." Taggart let go of her hand. "Find him quickly now."

"I'll be back shortly." Brigid turned and plunged into the woods, where Taggart saw a white shape already waiting for her. After a moment he went back into the house and once more grabbed Ogma under the arms.

"You said you wanted him outside."

"That's right," answered the old woman. "A bit of fresh air, and I'll be able to wake him quick."

Jeremy lit their way through the room, and soon Taggart had the small man on the path, clutching him as he stumbled about. The Head Druid walked back and forth in front of the house, and after a while Ogma needed less help; his eyes would occasionally open and he started to stagger about on his own.

"Hold him steady a moment," said the old woman, "and I'll stick one of these under his nose." She took a capsule from her pocket, and when Taggart had both arms around Ogma's chest, she crushed it between her fingers and held her palm beneath the gravedigger's nose. His breaths were shallow, so she pushed her hand up until it touched his nostrils and cupped her fingers. Ogma breathed in a couple of times, then snorted. He started to move his head back, but the old woman placed her other hand on his skull and shoved his nose back into her palm. He tried to shake his head free, but she held him firmly and he started to choke, his mouth opening in spasms and the air going into his lungs with ragged gasps. He started to shake his head from side to side, his eyes flickered open and shut, and the old woman finally took her hand away. "Get him walking some more," she said.

Taggart got the small man moving about the yard and soon was able to let go of him as he began walking on his own. Once Ogma started going into the trees, but the Head Druid grabbed him and aimed him back toward the house. In a minute or two the gravedigger was walking steadily by himself and came to stop by Jeremy, who had been following his movements with the beam of the light.

"What's it to ye, then?" asked Ogma, looking stupidly into the old Druid's face. "You with the light."

"Much better with his mouth closed," said Jeremy, glancing over toward Taggart. "We had our choice."

Ogma turned quickly to see who Jeremy was speaking to and almost fell. "Ach, my head's got a pick through it, for sure." He closed his eyes a moment, then slowly opened them. He saw the old woman glaring at him as she wiped her palm against her skirt. "It's the end of the world and I've gone to hell," he said, staring at her.

"It'll be hell wherever you are," she said. "Now get to walking, so we can have some sense out of you." She started to come toward him and he took a befuddled step backward, then straightened and started to walk some more. After a few turns around the yard, he went over and stood before Taggart.

"What happened?" he asked.

"Rolf got to you with some sleeping drug."

"Why, the young bastard."

"He stored it up," said Taggart. "He pretended that the pain kept him awake and that he needed it."

"Must have got you drinking tonight," said the old woman. "What'd you have?"

"He was wondering whether there was some whisky—the type that Ball-less Billy gave him. Real polite, just like the Germans; didn't want to put me to any trouble. Then said it was a bit strong, asked would I get him some water. That must be when he did it, all the while smiling at me with the grin of a corpse. And it's a corpse I'll be making him if I ever . . . " Ogma stopped speaking a moment, then looked away from the Head Druid's face. "I'm sorry, Taggart."

"I should have thought of it myself," said Taggart. "The lad was too smart for us."

"How long have I been out?"

"When'd he give you the powder?" asked the old woman.

"I'm not sure." Ogma looked from her face to the Head Druid's.

"My mind's still fuzzy, like Manannan's Mantle has settled over it." He paused once again, trying to concentrate. "It wasn't much after young Alice left—twenty minutes, a bit more."

"Then you've been under for three, three and a half hours." The old woman gave a laugh. "Do you feel rested from your wee sleep?"

"I've got a bloody headache splitting me in two."

"Aye," the old woman sounded pleased. "You'll be having that for quite a while yet."

"Pah." Ogma turned to the Head Druid and grunted because he moved too quickly. "What are we going to do about Jerry?"

Taggart began to answer but stopped as a dull roar started to filter through the trees from the road beyond. He looked at the others and then motioned them into the bushes as the noise turned toward them and started along the path.

"Jeremy," he yelled. "The torch."

The old Druid switched off the light seconds before a vehicle came crashing over the path and screeched to a halt in front of Ogma's house. Taggart stepped out of the brush to see a drab-colored army jeep before him, a light machine gun on a tripod where the rear seat should have been. Nigel was still clinging to the windscreen, while Mr. Stephenson smiled at him from behind the wheel.

"He wouldn't even put on the lights," gasped the young Druid.

"No need, I just followed his directions. I've been driving in the dark quite a long time—and not just in this war, either." He jumped from the jeep and looked up into Taggart's face. "You did it again. I just got back, ready to tell Nigel here to give you a call, when he gave me your message. I would have been on it faster, but some snafu expert held it for confirmation—confirmation!— that's what you have to put up with when dealing with locals. God knows how far across the old man is."

"I should have made myself clearer when I said I didn't want the army," commented the Head Druid as he eyed the machine gun. "What do you plan to do with this?"

"The jeep's the fastest thing I could get my hands on," explained Mr. Stephenson. "Especially when your boy told me we'd be going through the woods."

"Well, that you did, didn't you?" Mr. Stephenson turned in surprise as Ogma came out of the bushes. "That damn machine has made a mess of my path; you've done enough damage to let an elephant get through here without any trouble."

Stephenson kept staring as Jeremy and the old woman quickly followed the gravedigger, and then he looked back up at the Head Druid. "You certainly have a mixed crew, don't you?"

"Everyone serves his purpose," said Taggart. "But I don't like the looks of that gun." He glanced around as Nigel got out of the jeep. "Or that," he said, pointing to a slender blade held by the young Druid's belt.

"He wouldn't let me leave without some sort of weapon," said Nigel, as he freed the sword and held it in his hand. "He wanted me to take a rifle, or at least a revolver. It was hard to make him settle for this, but I wouldn't have anything to do with one of those dirty things."

"It's madness to come out into something like this without being armed," said Mr. Stephenson.

"I told you that we would take care of the situation ourselves," Taggart's voice was harsh and his eyes glowered. "Those damn things," he pointed to the machine gun, "are just going to cause trouble."

"And what do you think you can do with this group of—"

"Enough argument." The Head Druid's voice commanded with anger. "Our differences cannot get in the way now." He looked around him, trying to overcome his annoyance. "You can keep the sword with you, lad—maybe you can hack through some of the brush with it." He looked at the jeep. "Is that thing loaded?"

"Of course."

"We're not going to be facing an army."

"Well, you don't think the old bastard's going to be alone, do you?" Mr. Stephenson sounded exasperated. "He'll have the boatman and probably a guard. And then there'll be the son to deal with. I presume he has gone, as you suspected."

"Aye, he's gone," Ogma spoke painfully. "Put me out with some drug, he did. You won't be needing that gun; I'll squeeze the last drop of life out of him with my bare hands."

"Do you know where he is?" asked Mr. Stephenson.

"Not yet," answered the Head Druid. "But I will shortly; he's being searched out now."

"You've got your men after him, then?"

Taggart suppressed a smile. "He shall not elude us for long; my pursuers know every section of the Island."

"I'd still feel better off with some troops."

"They won't be necessary," the Head Druid assured him once again. "They'd just be making too much commotion, like that machine of yours." He pointed to the jeep. "Strangers racing about would just . . . " His sentence trailed off as he saw a bounding movement through the trees. A moment later Brigid appeared, looking cautiously around her.

"You've found him, then," said Taggart.

She came to Taggart, glancing curiously at Mr. Stephenson. She was about to speak but changed her mind and leaned toward the Head Druid on her toes, whispering into his ear.

"You saw him?"

"Yes," she answered, "He's sitting on the shingle, waiting."

"Does he have anything with him?"

"No—nothing."

"All right, Brigid, go back then. We'll come around the other way and be there shortly."

She turned to the woods and noticed the jeep for the first time. She walked closer, staring at the machine gun in fascination. She looked at the group of people. "You're not going to hurt him, are you?"

"No," said Taggart.

"Not unless we can't—" started Mr. Stephenson, but the Head Druid's voice cut in and smothered the other man. "Hurry back, Brigid, and keep a close watch on him." As she moved into the trees, Taggart turned quickly to the man beside him. "We won't be harming the lad at all. Your concern is that nothing falls into the hands of the Nazis—leave the rest to me."

"If you're sure—" began Mr. Stephenson.

"This is my place, I know what to do."

"Shouldn't we start moving?" asked Nigel.

Taggart turned to the young Druid and was disturbed by the look on his face. "Don't go getting over-anxious, lad. Most things can take care of themselves. But yes, we'll leave right now." He motioned Mr. Stephenson away from the others and spoke to him in a low voice. "You've got the lad quite agitated."

"Of course," answered the other man. "It's best to have them sharp and ready."

"In your work, maybe. But Nigel's no soldier; he's not used to this type of thing. An excited man can make mistakes."

"He won't do much with that sword."

"We Druids don't fear death, remember that." Taggart returned to the others, with Mr. Stephenson following him. "Brigid found the lad, but he's not where we expected him. He's moved quite a piece along the shore, not too far from where the Corkill cottage is." He looked at Mr. Stephenson. "They must have had an alternate plan in case things went wrong the first time round." He started down the path. " 'Tis only a few minutes in the motor. We can't go following Brigid through the trees, for various reasons. Nigel, you stay with Mr. Stephenson and follow the rest of us."

They walked quickly along the path, Ogma muttering about the destruction, and soon came to the place where Taggart had parked. As he opened the door, he spoke to Jeremy. "I have Nigel watching Mr. Stephenson, but the lad is so excited that you'd best keep an eye on him when we get there."

"All right, Taggart. I won't let him do anything foolish."

Ogma and the old woman settled into the back, and as soon as he heard the jeep behind them, Taggart started the engine. This time he did not switch the lights on but drove quickly along the narrow road, taking his chances with the moonlight. In a minute, he swung onto an even more unkept road, so seldom used that a grassy ridge ran along the middle of it. It twisted and turned unexpectedly, heading for the sea. Taggart was familiar with the treacherous lane—as he was with all the roads in the area—and did not slow for the numerous curves, causing the others with him to get jumbled about as he sped along. Above the engine noise and tire squeals, he could hear Ogma grumbling about his aching head. He looked over to see Jeremy grinning back at him.

Taggart had his door window rolled down, and when he heard the sound of the sea, he began to slow the car and indicated with his hand for the jeep to do the same. He drove on for another minute, then pulled abruptly into a small clearing and turned off the motor. The jeep came in beside them and the Head Druid got out of the car, quickly followed by the others.

"I didn't want to go any closer and have him hear us. It isn't that much of a walk; we're not far away."

"Where are all your people?" asked Mr. Stephenson, looking around him in surprise.

"The woods are full of eyes," said Taggart. "You don't have to worry about anything. Just keep behind me and do as I say and don't go wandering around on your own."

"Things I'm not supposed to see?"

"We all have secrets," answered Taggart. He led them along the road, his heavy staff gripped in his powerful hand. The road ended at the rough shingle that sloped to the sea, but before the Head Druid reached that far, he turned left off the track and went into the brush and wood. He walked cautiously for two or three minutes and then saw Brigid ahead, crouched behind a tree. He slowed even more to make certain she was alone, and by the time the others caught up to him, he felt it safe to walk up beside her. He peered over her head and saw Rolf a few yards away. Brigid looked up at the Head Druid and then back to the beach.

"He's hardly moved at all," she said, but the words were scarcely uttered when they saw him get to his feet and walk toward the waves. Then they heard the dull throb of an engine on the water.

"This must be it, then," whispered Mr. Stephenson. "We barely got here in time; they nearly escaped."

"Whether we were here or not, they never would have been able to get away," said Taggart.

"Your people in the woods?"

"As I told you before, they could not have crossed the beach."

"Then we're not really needed," said Mr. Stephenson.

"Of course we are," answered Taggart. "You want them alive, don't you?"

"If we weren't here . . . " he began.

"They'd never be seen again," the Head Druid replied.

"And you can believe that or not," added Ogma.

"But much more important to us," said Taggart, "is Rolf and what he does. That is what tonight is all about."

A thin beam of light bore in from the water, moved along the shore until it picked out Rolf, and immediately went off. The engine noise, which had been getting louder, was suddenly cut, and voices could be heard over the waves.

"We must make certain they don't try for the trees," said Taggart.

"But I don't see anyone," insisted Mr. Stephenson, looking hastily around him. "Where are your people?"

"Our ways," began the Head Druid, "the way we deal with trouble . . . " There was no time to explain. "You have never been more surrounded than you are right now." Taggart turned to the others. "Jeremy, you take Nigel and go along a bit further; we'll make sure none get by us." He touched the young Druid's arm as they went past. "Mind that you take care, lad; do nothing rash." He looked down at the small man. "Ogma, you stay here with Brigid—keep them on the beach."

"What will you be wanting with me, lad?" asked the old woman.

"I hope we won't need you for anything," answered Taggart. "But if something goes wrong, you'll have enough to do. It's best you go back in the trees a bit, out of the way. We can't have you getting hurt." As she moved away, he looked at Mr. Stephenson. "You and I will go along the other direction and make sure they don't try getting through there."

At the beach a rowboat appeared out of the dark waves, and a man jumped from the bow to help pull it up on the shingle.

"Guntar Kermode," spat Ogma. "So that's who they got to ferry them. The bastard would dig up his mother for the gold fillings."

When the boat was up on the shore, two other men got out. The older one carried a briefcase, while the beefy younger one held a machine gun. The older man stepped up to Rolf and apparently started asking about his shoulder.

"That must be his father," said Brigid.

"Aye, with the crown jewels. Too bad they're yammering in German; we can't tell which way Jerry will turn."

"Why, he'll be coming to us," she insisted.

"Don't be so sure." The short man turned to look at Brigid. "Pah, you're your mother's girl," he said, "being so silly in following your feelings." He reached up to touch his forehead. "I'll be glad to get my hands on him."

"He'll stay with us."

"Why should he?" Ogma looked back to the beach. "He's known you less than a week—his father and the Nazis have had him for years. He doesn't even think you trust him."

"What do you mean?" Her voice hissed in a whisper.

"When you were last with him, your yelling could be heard all over Man. And you didn't see him today."

"There wasn't time. After last night I had so much to do—you know about the beasts."

"Oh, I understand right enough. But Jerry was moping around the boneyard as if he wanted to join old Agnes what we was burying."

"If he does something foolish, it will be my fault," she said.

"Jerry's what he is," answered Ogma. "It doesn't matter what . . ."

"I have to help him." Brigid got to her feet.

"There's nothing for you—" Ogma looked up startled as Brigid went between the trees. "Don't go being a—" He made a grab for her as she stepped onto the beach but quickly ducked back so he wouldn't be seen.

"Rolf," she said, and all the men near the boat turned to look at her, the beefy guard raising his machine gun.

Jeremy gave a smothered curse and had to place a hand on the younger Druid's arm. "Hold to, lad, hold to."

Farther along the beach, Mr. Stephenson sputtered incredulously. "What in hell is she doing?"

"She wants to help him make the right decision," answered the Head Druid, his voice very low.

"She can get killed." Mr. Stephenson looked on in amazement.

"Yes, she can," agreed Taggart.

Rolf had turned from his father and started toward Brigid. "Go away," he said. "This is my job; go away, Brigit."

"You can't help them, Rolf," she said. "Come back with me."

Rolf's father started calling to him in German, but he was silenced by frightened shouts from Kermode, the boat captain.

"It's Crovan's daughter!" He turned wildly to the two Germans near the boat. "My God, what are we into—the Druids will be everywhere." They stared back at him blankly. "What do you dumb Krauts understand? We'll all be put away." He unsheathed a sharp fishing knife. "We've got to get rid of her." His eyes were wild with panic. "She's seen us; she's seen us." He started running along the beach, his knife glinting.

Rolf swung around to meet him but was roughly pushed down by the frenzied man's free hand.

"Get your pistol out!" bellowed Taggart into Mr. Stephenson's ear, but before the other man could act, a jumble of voices erupted from up the beach.

With a loud curse, Ogma burst out of the bushes and gave Brigid a forceful thrust that sent her sprawling toward the water. At the same instant, Nigel leaped from the trees, followed by Jeremy. He was brandishing his sword and rushing at the fisherman. The younger German turned his machine gun in their direction and started firing, while the fisherman turned toward Nigel. The machine gunner started running up toward the trees and hit Jeremy full in the chest. The old Druid was thrown backward without a sound, dead before he hit the rough beach. Nigel slashed with his sword and caught the fisherman in the stomach, before he himself was cut down by the bullets. The German kept running for the woods, firing at nothing until his gun was empty. Rolf's father moved quickly toward Brigid as she stood and grabbed her about the waist, pointing a revolver at her head.

"I can't get at him," said Mr. Stephenson, his own pistol now in his hand. "The girl's in the way."

"We'll wait, we'll wait," said Taggart. "Don't give us away."

Rolf slowly stood, moaning and holding his shoulder. Ogma also got to his feet, glowering at him and looking around for the young German. The German saw the gravedigger, threw his empty gun at him, and plunged into the woods. Ogma gently moved his throbbing head and started toward the water when the older German shouted at him.

"He says to stay where you are," explained Rolf, "or he will shoot Brigit."

Ogma kicked at the dying fisherman and swore. "Do you think you're worth it all?" he asked Rolf.

Rolf was about to reply but was silenced by a commotion in the woods. There was a low scream of terror mixed with disbelief and then a shriek of pain, going higher and higher until it was abruptly cut off. Then there was absolute quiet.

"One less Jerry to worry about," said Ogma.

"What . . . what happened?" Rolf managed to speak.

"Nothing you'd ever believe," said the small man.

Rolf's father had backed away in horror, dragging Brigid with him. His foot hit the briefcase he had dropped and he stooped to pick it up, clutching it in the hand he was holding against Brigid. Rolf started to walk toward them.

Mr. Stephenson kept watching the movement on the beach, the pistol in his hand. His voice was shaking as he spoke to the tall man beside him. "What in God's name happened to the other German?"

"He was taken care of."

"That he was, Taggart." He looked quickly at the Head Druid. "I've seen many men die—and in many different ways—but I've never heard anything like that and never want to again." Mr.

Stephenson looked back at the beach. "It was as if he were being torn apart." He turned with a start at some movement in the brush and saw the old woman coming toward them.

"I should go help them," she said.

"There won't be anything to do," said Mr. Stephenson. "Not after a machine gun at that close range."

"It's better Rolf's father doesn't see anyone else moving about," said Taggart. "There's no need to scare him worse than he is." He looked back as raised voices were carried to him on the sea breeze. "It would help to know what they're saying."

"I can help you there," said Mr. Stephenson. He gave a quick smile when Taggart looked surprised. "It's best to know the language when you're fighting them. Rolf is trying to get the old man to surrender, but he'll have nothing to do with it. See the way he's holding that briefcase? He's got the bomb all right."

"All this over a bomb?" asked the old woman.

"A bomb that you've never dreamed of," said Mr. Stephenson. "One that can turn Europe into ash."

"And more killing," muttered the old woman.

"We've got to end this," said Taggart.

"I can't get a shot."

"It doesn't look as if Rolf is having much success."

"No. The old bastard says he can use Brigid as a hostage to get across the Island. He says he thinks she's important."

"What's the lad saying?"

"He's pleading with him to give up—that he's in love with the girl. Shit, that's torn it."

"What?"

"The old man says he'll kill her if the boy doesn't help."

"Then we'll have to act." Taggart looked toward Ogma, then spoke to the old woman. "Keep out of sight, go down behind Ogma, and tell him not to do anything unless he's certain he has a clear chance."

As the old woman moved away, Mr. Stephenson nudged Taggart. "I'm going along a bit and see if I can get a better angle. I'll need a clear shot in this light."

Taggart was left alone, watching the scene on the beach. Rolf had moved closer to his father, arguing loudly, while the older man waved his gun and clutched Brigid ever more tightly. Rolf said something else, and his father turned more to face him. Taggart cursed, for this was just the shot Mr. Stephenson had needed. They were both yelling now, both distracted.

Taggart stood back and held out his staff. One quick throw and he could strike Rolf's father. He had hit things at a much greater distance and his powerful arm was capable of enormous strength. He was moving the staff between his fingers, searching for the center of balance, when a white body walked in front of him. The ivory horn glowed in the moonlight and touched his arm firmly. The Head Druid lowered his staff and nodded his head in understanding. This final decision had to be made by Rolf himself.

Taggart looked up quickly when the shouting on the beach became louder. Rolf's father was starting to move and Rolf was blocking his way. Brigid had started to struggle, and the gun moved alternately from pointing at her head to pointing at Rolf.

"Brigit, stop fighting or he will shoot," Rolf pleaded.

"I'm like the others," she gasped, "I've no fear of death."

She kept twisting against the man holding her and finally brought her head down and bit his wrist. With a growl he turned the gun back to her head and at that moment Rolf jumped at him. The older man swung his revolver to point at Rolf and fired. Brigid broke away and moved out of reach. The gun went off again, and Rolf staggered backward. His father started tugging frantically at the handle of his briefcase, and, as Rolf fell, Ogma reached down for Nigel's sword, grabbed it on the run, and went for Rolf's father. Brigid saw him coming and moved farther away. The German stopped pulling on the briefcase when he saw Ogma and fired a hasty shot. Ogma crouched and, when he was close enough, swung the blade in an upward arc. It caught the scientist directly below the Adam's apple and severed his head from the rest of his body.

The headless corpse toppled backward into the water, still clutching the briefcase. Brigid ran by it without a look and knelt beside Rolf. Ogma turned to see the old woman coming down the beach, and farther away the Head Druid and Mr. Stephenson appeared, walking quickly toward the spot where Rolf lay.

"How is he? How is he?" pleaded Brigid, as the old woman bent over the silent form.

"Let me have a look, girl. Get back out of my way."

"He chose me." Brigid turned to look at the Head Druid. "He chose our way of life, and not . . . " She looked over at the decapitated body, where Mr. Stephenson was retrieving the briefcase. "And not his."

"Yes, Brigid." He put an arm around the shaking girl's shoulders. "He's one of us." Taggart looked down at the old woman. "What can you tell us?" he asked.

"Lad's not so lucky this time. He's been shot in the same shoulder, and he's got one in the gut. We can't handle that—needs a doctor and an operation."

"He'll get them," said Taggart, turning to Mr. Stephenson. "And no questions asked."

"He'll get everything he needs and be back with you as soon as possible." The other man held on to the briefcase and looked around him. "But what will we do with the rest?"

"Never mind about that," said Ogma, wiping the sword on his pantleg. "I'll take care of it, you can believe that or not."

Taggart looked at the briefcase in the other man's hands. "What was he trying to do with that?" he asked, "when we saw him pulling at it?"

"Oh, it will be a special briefcase," said Mr. Stephenson. "For carrying secrets. If you don't want anyone else to get the things in it, you pull off the handle and it explodes. Not a big bang, but enough to burn what's inside. I've had them myself, though I've never had to use it."

"Then he must have had what you thought."

"More than that, I suspect." Mr. Stephenson looked at the briefcase. "He wouldn't be so desperate to destroy something we already have. There must be some of his own stuff in here—calculations, ideas, proofs. I bet we have ourselves a bomb."

The old woman interrupted them. "Ogma's got enough to do, and the girl's useless. Would you move Jerry up away from the water—damp won't do him good."

"Of course," said Mr. Stephenson. He laid the briefcase on the sand and helped the Head Druid gently pick up Rolf. As they started to carry the wounded man, he did not notice the old woman pick up the briefcase.

She clutched it to her and scurried across the beach and into the woods. She kept moving until she found a dense thicket of brush and, crouching out of sight, started to frantically pull on the handle. She cursed when nothing happened, and she tried even more forcefully, but her old arms lacked the strength. She paused a moment, then clasped the briefcase under her arm and tried again, sweat running down her face and pain digging at her chest. She gripped it under her other arm, tugging at the handle with a different hand, but her fingers were becoming weak. She gave one last frenzied attempt, but with loud swearing she threw the case on the ground in front of her when nothing happened.

She was swaying on her knees, gasping for breath, when a looming shadow enveloped her. She looked up, her mouth falling open in fear, as she saw the unicorn rearing high on its back legs and towering above her. She tried to move as the razor-sharp hoofs came closer and looked in amazement as they settled upon the briefcase. The fantastic creature gazed down, its blazing eyes glaring into her own. The beast's mouth opened, teeth glinting in the moonlight, and she could see each turn on its spiral horn when it moved its head. As the old woman looked at the powerful legs in front of her, her puzzlement and fear quickly turned to understanding and her lined face broke into a smile. She bent forward and grabbed the handle of the briefcase with both hands. Using all her strength, she pulled desperately a couple of times and with one final effort tugged so hard that she fell back in a cloud of smoke, the broken handle grasped in her fingers. She lay on her back coughing, then closed her eyes to rest. She went into a doze, jumbled ideas and shapes fleeting through her mind, and when she next looked up, she saw the Head Druid leaning over her.

"I thought we'd lost another one," he said.

"Nay, lad, not yet." She lay with a smile, not trying to get up. "I seen him," she said. "I never thought I would." She paused again. "He helped me," she said.

"With the briefcase?"

"Aye." The smile grew wider. "He stood on it when I hadn't the strength."

"Whatever made you . . . " he began.

"All those people, lad." She looked into his eyes. "All those people, dead."

Taggart glanced up at some noise in the trees and saw Mr. Stephenson come through the brush. The other man glanced at the smoldering briefcase, the trampled ground and strange hoof prints, and finally the old woman.

"Jesus, I wish I knew what was going on," he said.

Taggart helped the old woman to her feet. "We've got Rolf in the back of the motor. We'll take him into Douglas straight off and let the army doctors go at him. Brigid's with him right now."

"I'll go in with you," she said. As she brushed dirt from her skirt,

Mr. Stephenson came over to her, holding the blackened briefcase in his hands.

"Why did you do it?" he asked.

"I heard you and himself talking about some great bomb," she answered. "Such a thing is foul."

"But we would have it—not the Nazis."

"Burned people smell the same," she answered. She started to walk to the car.

"We'll get it eventually," he called.

"Aye, that you probably will," she said, not looking back. "But maybe with luck, I won't be here to see it." She did stop then and looked at him. "You shoot a man who's trying to shoot you, that's right and well. But you drop one of those bombs, you don't know who you're killing."

Mr. Stephenson watched the old woman walk away and then glanced at the Head Druid. "It's not that I don't agree with her," he said.

"You wouldn't have destroyed the papers," said Taggart.

"No."

"No," said Taggart.

Mr. Stephenson looked around the wood one last time. "I don't know whether I envy the boy or not, coming to a life like this." He paused, then moved away. "I'll get the jeep, and you can follow me to the hospital."

The Head Druid watched him, then went back to the beach. The bodies lay where they had fallen.

"Ogma's gone to get his cart," said the old woman.

Taggart knelt by Jeremy and touched his still body. The old woman watched him, then turned to hide the tears in her eyes.

"We've got the living to worry about," she said.

"A minute more," Taggart's voice broke. "I'll mourn a minute more."

XXII

It was again a bomber's moon, and Brigid's father glared up at it as he eased himself onto the doorsill.

"If you think I'm going to be jumping you like a hare, your mind's slipping as your leg's healin'. Move your carcass, Crovan."

"Aye, you'll be knowing what it's like to be a hare. That's what most witches turn into when they want a taste o' the clover." He looked up and carefully slid over to one side of the doorway. "I thought you'd be in there talking to Fenella for a while, as you usually do—telling her things I'm not supposed to hear."

"If you're not supposed to hear, then don't concern yourself." The old woman grunted as she squeezed past him. "I'm getting back fast because Alice went up north to visit the Jerry, and I want something on the stove for her when she returns."

"How is the lad?"

"Don't you hear enough about him from the girl?"

"Ach, Brigid goes on about how cute he'll be when the beard's more full and how she's teaching him some Manx and how he gets along so well with the Druid's children that the youngest calls him 'uncle.' That type of foolishness I hear more than twice and I stop asking. I don't prod her about his wounds, in case he's not doing so well."

"Jerry's doing good as can be expected." The old woman straightened her skirts and looked down at William. "The doctors said that he'll get little use out of that arm of his and I might be agreeing. The wound's getting better, but the muscles are way damaged. He'll be lucky to use the hand for holding and such." She shook her head slightly. "A hard thing for a young man to put up with."

"What about his gut?"

"Och, they were doing some fine stitching there. They let me in to watch—that Mr. Stephenson fellow had something to do with that. I hate messing around in there—so many things jumbled together it's a risk. I've never had to but once or twice."

"It's a long trip for young Alice to be making," said William, moving his leg back onto the doorsill. "I thought there was someone up there looking after the lad."

"Oh aye, that there is. Alice has gone just the once and I might be trying to do it next month. Just to check up on him, you know. But there's a good one keeping him fit and that's Teare of Andreas."

"Ah," William nodded his head. "A good man."

"That he is." The old woman smiled. "I met his great-granddad once, what was known as the Fairy Doctor." She nodded her head in memory. "That's being even before your time, old Billy. I was just a wee lass and my own grandma took me up to see him. That was a trip in those days, a real adventure." The old woman paused a moment, thinking. "I'm not one to be harking to the old days; we're better off now than then, when a loss of the herring was disaster—aye, and death for many who had nothing else. But there were some things—people meant more then; there were more friends and many neighbors. And you believed more, had a faith in things outside of yourself." She looked away from William's face and up to the moon. "It was a night like this, a big moon laughing in the sky. He took me into his back fields, way out to his farthest that went up the side of a hill. He held on to my hand—his was a big, strong meat of a hand, and yet so gentle on my own.

"We came to an old stone fence, barely up to his belt, but I couldn't see over it. He lifted me up so I was sitting on top, looking up the mountain glen, and, still holding my hand, he started to sing. I suppose it was an old man's voice, thin and breaking, but to me it was one of the most beautiful things I've ever heard. It was the fairy song, you see. He was calling the fairies to come give me a look."

William's voice was a whisper. "Well, what happened?"

"I was such a wee thing, and it's so long ago."

"You know I'll believe you." He reached up and held her hand. "You know that."

"They came, of course. He was the last man who's been able to call them. They came from down the mountain and gathered around in a tiny circle." She squeezed his hand in memory. "The Fairy Doctor lifted me off the stones that were just starting to get warm under me and put me in the circle. They was almost as tall as me, little faces and shining eyes." Her own eyes were closed and she swayed slightly, still holding tightly to his hand.

"Tell me?" he asked.

The old woman's face broke into a wide smile, and she opened her eyes to look at him. "I danced with them, lad." Her voice went on the wind. "I danced with the fairies."

WHY WASTE YOUR PRECIOUS PENNIES ON GAS OR YOUR VALUABLE TIME ON LINE AT THE BOOKSTORE?

We will send you, FREE, our 28 page catalogue, filled with a wide range of Ace Science Fiction paperback titles—we've got something for every reader's pleasure.

Here's your chance to add to your personal library, with all the convenience of shopping by mail. There's no need to be without a book to enjoy—request your *free* catalogue today.

ACE SCIENCE FICTION
P.O. Box 400, Kirkwood, N.Y. 13795

A-05

ALL TWELVE TITLES AVAILABLE FROM ACE
$2.25 EACH

- [ ] 11630 **CONAN, #1**
- [ ] 11631 **CONAN OF CIMMERIA, #2**
- [ ] 11632 **CONAN THE FREEBOOTER, #3**
- [ ] 11633 **CONAN THE WANDERER, #4**
- [ ] 11634 **CONAN THE ADVENTURER, #5**
- [ ] 11635 **CONAN THE BUCCANEER, #6**
- [ ] 11636 **CONAN THE WARRIOR, #7**
- [ ] 11637 **CONAN THE USURPER, #8**
- [ ] 11638 **CONAN THE CONQUEROR, #9**
- [ ] 11639 **CONAN THE AVENGER, #10**
- [ ] 11640 **CONAN OF AQUILONIA, #11**
- [ ] 11641 **CONAN OF THE ISLES, #12**

Available wherever paperbacks are sold or use this coupon.

 ACE SCIENCE FICTION
P.O. Box 400, Kirkwood, N.Y. 13795

Please send me the titles checked above. I enclose $_____.
Include $1.00 per copy for postage and handling. Send check or money order only. New York State residents please add sales tax.

NAME_____

ADDRESS_____

CITY_____ STATE_____ ZIP_____

A-04

WITCH WORLD SERIES

☐ 89705	**WITCH WORLD**	$1.95
☐ 87875	**WEB OF THE WITCH WORLD**	$1.95
☐ 80806	**THREE AGAINST THE WITCH WORLD**	$1.95
☐ 87323	**WARLOCK OF THE WITCH WORLD**	$2.25
☐ 77556	**SORCERESS OF THE WITCH WORLD**	$2.50
☐ 94255	**YEAR OF THE UNICORN**	$2.50
☐ 82349	**TREY OF SWORDS**	$2.25
☐ 95491	**ZARSTHOR'S BANE** (Illustrated)	$2.50

Available wherever paperbacks are sold or use this coupon.

ACE SCIENCE FICTION
P.O. Box 400, Kirkwood, N.Y. 13795

Please send me the titles checked above. I enclose $_____.
Include $1.00 per copy for postage and handling. Send check or money order only. New York State residents please add sales tax.

NAME_____

ADDRESS_____

CITY_____ STATE_____ ZIP_____

A-03

More Fiction Bestsellers From Ace Books!

☐ 14999	**THE DIVORCE** Robert P. Davis $3.25	
☐ 34231	**THE HOLLOW MEN** Sean Flannery $3.25	
☐ 55258	**THE MYRMIDON PROJECT** Chuck Scarborough & William Murray $3.25	
☐ 11128	**CLEANING HOUSE** Nancy Hayfield $2.50	
☐ 75418	**SCHOOL DAYS** Robert Hughes $3.25	
☐ 75018	**SATAN'S CHANCE** Alan Ross Shrader $3.25	
☐ 01027	**AGENT OUT OF PLACE** Irving Greenfield $3.25	
☐ 33835	**HIT AND RUN** Dave Klein $3.25	
☐ 88531	**WHISPER ON THE WATER** E. P. Murray $3.25	
☐ 80701	**TICKETS** Richard Brickner $3.25	
☐ 82419	**TRIANGLE** Teri White $3.25	

Available wherever paperbacks are sold or use this coupon.

ACE BOOKS
P.O. Box 400, Kirkwood, N.Y. 13795

Please send me the titles checked above. I enclose $_____
Include $1.00 per copy for postage and handling. Send check or money order only. New York State residents please add sales tax.

NAME_____

ADDRESS_____

CITY_____ STATE_____ ZIP_____

A-02